The Arzulian Kingdoms
Prince of Fire

Zara Steen

Unicorn

ISBN-13: 978-0-9917830-3-8
ISBN-10: 0-9917-8303-4

THE ARZULIAN KINGDOMS: PRINCE OF FIRE

Copyright by Smarin Publishing © 2013. All rights reserved. Printed through Amazon Create Space. No part of this book may be used or reproduced in any manner whatsoever without written permission of the publisher, except in the case of brief quotations expressed in critical articles and reviews. For information address Smarin Publishing: stephaniemarin@gmail.com.

This is a work of fiction. Names, characters, places and incidents are either the product of the authors imagination and creativity and are used fictitiously. Any resemblance to persons, alive or dead, businesses, events or communities is entirely coincidental.

DEDICATION:

For my sister
Bianca
without you this book would never have been written
Thank you, so much.

Soph, Thank you for taking the time to read my greatest writing accomplishment (so far). I appreciate your support. Love, Z.

CONTENTS

Chapter 1	Page 1
Chapter 2	Page 11
Chapter 3	Page 18
Chapter 4	Page 24
Chapter 5	Page 30
Chapter 6	Page 40
Chapter 7	Page 45
Chapter 8	Page 53
Chapter 9	Page 61
Chapter 10	Page 68
Chapter 11	Page 81
Chapter 12	Page 90
Chapter 13	Page 105
Chapter 14	Page 116
Chapter 15	Page 128
Chapter 16	Page 133
Chapter 17	Page 147
Chapter 18	Page 167
Chapter 19	Page 178

Chapter 20	Page 188
Chapter 21	Page 203
Chapter 22	Page 219
Chapter 23	Page 227
Chapter 24	Page 238
Chapter 25	Page 244
Chapter 26	Page 249
Chapter 27	Page 256
Chapter 28	Page 272
Chapter 29	Page 279
Epilogue	Page 284

ACKNOWLEDGMENTS

I would like to thank my parents for their continuing encouragements and support of my creativity, no matter how imaginative it gets.

Also, I'd like to thank Rebecca MacFarlane for her encouragement and support during the whole writing process of this project. I'm so grateful for a wonderful and talented writing buddy.

For anyone who has ever told me they believe in me, thank you for your positivity. I would not be celebrating this moment without your kind words.

CHAPTER 1

"Be patient, Samira. You will find your home." She could hear the words lingering but did not recognize the voice, could not see a face for she was blindfolded. She opened her mouth to reply but nothing came out.

Frustrated by blindness her hand rose to meet the masking material and pulled down, freeing her eyes. She spun around to where the voice came from and as she turned could only see the moon. It was full and luminous against a dark sky, hanging precariously above a large body of water that reflected the light back up and outlined a mountainous, snow-capped background.

She was alone, in the stark dark of night.

Yet, she sensed someone else there, someone behind her. As she turned around to confront the plaguing voice, the voice whose words were gnawing deep into her soul, Sammie woke up. The coolness of the late summer air hung heavily about her, and her bones ached from the chill and her lack of sleep. She wondered if she had finally escaped her constant nightmare, to her dismay everything was the same. She was in her cell of a room.

For the past four months she awoke to a strange place, a place its denizens called Arzule. It was a world so unlike her own, creatures she could never have imagined and plants and wildlife so mystical and enchanting. Yet, despite the beauty of Arzule, its wonder was overshadowed by its dark minded inhabitants, obscured by the danger that seemed to pervade Sammie's every day.

She lay there covered in blackness thicker than a coating of tar, while her eyes were making sense of the dark. She coughed bitterly and thought about her life as it had been before. As time passed on, it tested the limits of her sanity. She questioned whether that life had been real at all, or if it was something she had concocted. A world she had elaborately imagined to cope with the everyday in Arzule.

The last thing she had recalled before this place was her life in Halifax. She had lived in Nova Scotia, not far from the waterfront. She and her sister, Salha, lived together in a small two bedroom apartment downtown above an old antique shop.

Was it real?

She questioned constantly. Yet she had memories of people, her mother, her friends, and her neighbours. Her life as she remembered was remiss. She had been working as a freelance photographer, while her sister was a student studying to become a pharmacy technician, that much she knew for certain.

The feel of a camera was ingrained in her hands. So was the bounce of the light flashing forward before she captured an image, it frozen in time. Those were things she could never forget.

Their lives had been ordinary. During the week she worked, and on the weekends Sammie made time for the things she loved, hiking, writing, reading, enjoying music, and crafting. She often frequented the market by the harbour front, and relished the smell of the ocean.

Whenever she and Salha craved a bit more excitement, they stole away from the city and drove along the coast stopping in beautiful places like Peggy's Cove to rejuvenate and rest. Every time she drove into the winding road of the cove, she felt delighted by the whimsicality of the fishing town. The novelty of the feeling never wore.

Sammie closed her eyes and brought herself back there, back to the large and smooth rocks on the beach, to the light coloured sand, and to the cool water, crisp and biting on her skin. She loved examining the seaweed coloured in deep greens and streaked with a yellow undertone. She would sit watching it dance with the waves and occasionally rub her fingers against the bubbled pockets of air smoothing out the otherwise rubbery texture. She felt the sun warm her, and the gulls in the distance, the Atlantic Ocean invading her senses with the deep seated happiness she felt right down to her bones. It was the peace there that made her happy. The memory soothed her.

The only other excitement in her life was Salha's need to change her hair colour. It had become habitual for Salha to dye her naturally black hair and Sammie recalled that the night before she woke up in Arzule, she had been dying her sister's hair fire engine red. She recalled massaging the sticky serum into her sisters scalp through gloved fingers, the noxious sent so strong that it was like spoiled cotton candy. It had been a memorable day, an enjoyable one where they were so relaxed with each other, so carefree.

She and Salha had been laughing as she rinsed the red out. They had been wondering what Sal's ex-boyfriend, Eric, would think of the hair colour. He never seemed put off by Salha's hair, in fact he relished the new looks she constantly donned. Sammie suspected it made him feel as if he was dating someone new each month, as if he enjoyed the novelty of getting to know Salha all over again each time she changed her appearance.

Unlike Salha, Sammie had always kept her locks plain. Her brown-black hair was much longer than her sisters and was always kept in tidy layers. She felt she was plain but prided herself in thinking her style was classic.

As they had laughed Sammie recalled the time Sal dyed her hair blue and she had witnessed Eric delicately running his hand through her blue curls before pulling her in for a steamy kiss. He had whispered, 'I love it,' to her. There was such passion between them that she witnessed. Passion she had forgotten existed.

The passion had ended though just as she knew it would. Their emotions burned so bright they fizzled out. Salha had grown tired of Eric's inability to commit to her. They had fought the week before their sudden transportation to Arzule. Sammie smirked to herself, Eric had been stupid. Making dinner plans with a former flame was a surefire way to incite the wrath of her sister. Salha had decided it wouldn't work out between the two of them, their relationship was too on and off for her liking. So she turned it off permanently.

Even with the dramatics of Salha's dating, Samira had felt a slight tug of envy at the sight of Eric and Salha together. Most of the time she felt sorry for her younger sister's love life, which was always tumultuous. She was still young enough to find someone. At twenty-seven she had time and knew she did not look her age. Even though she was three years older, people often mistook the Khan sisters for twins at first glance. Sammie was five inches taller. So, how they thought they were twins she would never understand, but it happened nonetheless.

Unlike her sister, who never seemed to be without a romantic interest, Sammie's last serious relationship had ended years ago when she was twenty-five. She had dated, but it had all seemed so dismal. Salha and her friends often teased Sammie that she would end up an old maid if she never gave anyone a chance, but the truth of the matter was that no one seemed to really interest her. The qualities in a man that she desired were elusive in a live flesh and blood male, so she stuck to books. She fell in love with characters easily and often. Samira was never afraid to approach a man she wanted to date; being shy was not the problem. The problem was that there was no one she wanted.

It did not matter now. She was a slave. Love was the last thing on her list of priorities. Her main concern was keeping Salha safe and finding a way to get them back home. There was no one in Arzule to rescue them, not that she had ever been the type of woman to wait for life to happen to her. She had to be strong and resourceful. No one even knew who they were and why they were there. She didn't know why they were there either, and based on what her master had told her, humans were almost extinct. The small population of humans remaining in Arzule, were slaves. Their kind was not welcomed among the other species, considered lowly and ignorant.

Sammie shifted her weight so she could lift herself up by her shackled hands. The bronze coloured cuffs bit into her skin and she winced as her wrist reddened from the abrasion.

Normally her keeper gave her a bit more chain as she slept so that she could at least lie comfortably on her cot, but he had been distracted as he shackled her the previous night. He had been fighting with his mate and shoved Sammie into her room roughly, chaining her to the wall and then leaving in a huff. She hated it when they fought as she always received the brunt of their anger. Lately it seemed worse as they began to fight more and more over their child.

Loward banged into her door loudly before entering, he nearly filled the small room, which could be no larger than a eight by eight cube and loomed over her.

"Get up human," he shouted, "time to work."

She had grown accustomed to his looks, he stood at seven and a half feet tall and would look something like a satyr if it were not for his human-like legs. He was an Anuya, muscular and strong, and his skin was tawny. Tufts of light blonde, almost white hair, decorated his chest, stomach, and head, and yellow tattoos traversed his arms and legs. He had deep blue eyes that were large and fierce and two moderate sized, dark blue horns peeking out from the top of his head.

She never spoke to him anymore. She had learned her lesson about what her voice rewarded her. Once, she had make the mistake of reading off the list Kalawyn, his wife, had written for her to buy at the market. Sammie had been surprised that the language was English, or what they called Brooy. Loward had gotten up from where he sat and smacked her across the face. She had been shocked by his abuse since she had done nothing to anger him. Irritated, she had questioned him.

"What did I do to deserve that?" Her palm rubbed against her reddened cheek.

"Shut up human!" He barked at her, "none of your kind can read, and if you know what is best for you, you never pretend again."

Each word was spat out more fiercely than the former. That time talking back had only earned her a smack. Her lip bloody and bruised, healed fairly quickly, but the next time he had beaten her to a pulp. His treatment was so much worse than the slave traders who had captured her and Salha.

Haloya, his child, had come home one day, about four weeks earlier, crying because another child had made fun of her lack of horns. Since she lived with a slave, her class had named her a traitor and began calling her *human*. It was a pity the child had been teased since she looked nothing like a human to Sammie. Haloya's eyes were doe-like and the blue depth of them shone unnaturally. Her long blonde hair was almost white, wispy and enchanting and her heart shaped face was ethereal and much paler than her father.

Kalawyn explained to Haloya, "Sometimes in Anuyans there are late bloomers my little one, some whose horns grow to be much more beautiful and stronger."

The child's eyes sparkled with hope as Kalawyn continued, "They grow in iridescent colours glorious and magical. They take longer Haloya, please be patient. I know your horns will make us proud." Kalawyn had cradled the child lovingly and rocked her in her arms until Loward returned.

Loward's eyes were always darkly, but even more so that night. He seemed embittered, enraged by Kalawyn's actions.

"What are you doing?" He asked her heavily, walking through the door.

Shocked by his presence Kalawyn stiffened, her eyes slowly icing over. Even Haloya had grown quiet, frozen in her mother's arms.

"Nothing," she spoke back her jaw slightly elevated, but her body betrayed her fear. She trembled.

The Anuyan were trained to never show fear or sadness especially in the presence of a human and so Loward had stared at Samira extendedly before looking back at Kalawyn.

He grabbed her arm and pulled her from where she sat. Haloya fell fumbling from her arms to the floor before quickly seeking refuge in the corner. Samira knew then it was a ritual for them. Haloya grew quiet and calm, her face turned to the wall.

"Leave us!" He shouted at Sammie, and she hesitated. He had pulled the whip from his belt and was slowly unravelling its length. Sammie could feel the panic rising in her. Surely he wouldn't whip his own wife. Her body moved back slowly but her eyes, horrified were open, waiting to see what he would do.

"Leave!" He repeated.

"Why are you hurting them?" She had asked, unable to remain quiet.

He had turned angrily to her and she instantly regretted the question. He charged over to her and grabbed her by the chin, mushing her lips together painfully. She expected him to snap her in half, but rather than lift her, he grabbed her arm and threw her like a child's doll. She hit the wall of the fireplace, breaking off a few stones with her body as sharp pain went ripping through her. She had lain crumpled and helpless on the floor. Tears stung her face while the coldness of death was setting into her bones.

Kalawyn had looked down at her expressionless, perhaps a thin veil of curiosity peering through her eyebrows. Sammie could still remember the jingle of her earrings as she bent over her.

"You fool," she said to Loward, "you've killed her."

Realizing she would die, he left angrily. She laid there her arm broken and chest crushed, gasping for air, wondering if that was how she would die when an Anuya doctor returned with Loward and began healing her with what seemed like magic. The doctor's hands were wrapped in some type of shiny metallic glove and hovered over her wounds emitting a pale blue light. She had passed out from the pain and was luckily left alone for two days to rest. When she had awoke, it was as if she had never been hurt, and she would almost believe it was a dream, were it not for the scars.

She had stayed silent ever since, concerned her temper, her curiosity might cause her death. She only spoke to her sister in the market or in the yard when the two of them had been sent out by their owners. The silence was constant. Her voice surprised her each time she spoke.

She had been blessed and cursed that her sister was sold to Loward's neighbour, Thussan. He was not as volatile as Loward, but held the same disregard for her kind. On the day when the slave traders had brought her and Salha to the city of Uri they were the only humans in the bunch. Thussan immediately outbid all of the other buyers for them. And when it came time to choose which one he would keep and which one he would give to his neighbour for the debt he owed him, he eyed them both carefully.

Sammie and Salha had held hands and although they were terrified they tried not to tremble.

"Stay calm," she had whispered to Salha. They had to be strong to survive. Their mother had always been a strong woman and had overcome many hardships in life. When Salha was discouraged, Sammie always tried to remind her of that fact. After she died, all they had was each other and together they would face whatever came.

Thussan had examined them both closely, measuring their hips with a brass ruler and looking at their teeth. It was a disturbing sensation to have him hold open Sammie's jaw, his fingers poking at her molars. At the time, Sammie had been much heavier. It had only been a few weeks since they found themselves in Arzule and she had always been the heavier of the two.

With that knowledge, he had seemed to settle upon her, but then asked the trader, "which is the youngest?"

She had not understood his reasoning, but when the trader pointed to Salha, he changed his mind and picked her instead, leaving her to Loward and his stare of hatred.

They had both been taken by the same wagon to their neighbouring homes. It was not until they arrived at the doorsteps with Loward's family waiting for them and Braedynn, Thussan's male slave, coming forward that she began to piece things together.

Her suspicions were confirmed when Salha had seen her the next day at the market and fearfully whispered, "I've been married."

Thussan had purchased her sister to consort with Braedynn in the hopes of breeding more slaves for their city. Salha's face was transfixed with fear as she was called by him to return to Loward's home. Samira had given him a warning look, strong enough to strike him dead should he ever think to hurt her sister. His response had been apologetic, his eyes softening immediately, a look in them sincere.

Luckily in the encounters to follow, Salha was able to tell Sammie that Braedynn had been courteous and respectful. He had confirmed with Thussan that the marriage was consummated and luckily Thussan was too disgusted by them to witness the truth. As the weeks passed, Braedynn was careful to protect Salha and treated her with kindness.

Sammie was relieved but she knew as time passed Thussan would realize her sister was not pregnant. Although she gathered that the Anuyan knew little about human reproduction, she still worried that they would be harmed for their deception. She needed to find a way for them to escape and soon.

CHAPTER 2

THE CLANG OF SWORDS meeting sounded tinny, but fierce as Arkson shielded himself from attack on all sides. His muscles were flexing with each slight movement. He ran across the courtyard and swiftly using the brick wall of the palace as leverage, flipped back over his stalkers. With the soldiers in hot pursuit, the move gained him the advantage over his opponents. They were cornered now, trapped between him and the palace wall. They stood awestruck for a few seconds before they turned back to him and moved forward again to strike.

Arkson kicked back the first assailant to advance. Holding his sword far too low, the soldier toppled backwards, while Arkson flicked away his weapon. He met with the other two who were gaining ground. He evaded them by ducking beneath the blade of the second, tripping the wielder in a fumble and then met the third who holding his sword far too high. Arkson hit into him and bringing his own sword down swiftly. The third soldier had stumbled down to the ground in shock from Arkson's quick and furious advance. The blade swooshed in the air as he brought it down, but Arkson stopped the blade just before it broke the flesh of the man's chest. His eyes looked shadowed, black, and menacing as he looked down to his opponent. The man kowtowed before him with fear. The other two assailants lay in pain on the grassy knoll.

It was then a crackle in the sky broke and lightning bolts flashed down to meet the earth, distracting Arkson from his focus. His green eyes flickered grey for a moment staring longingly. It was long enough for the first man to regain composure and with a somersault brutally pushed his sword into Arkson's side. Rather than yelling out, Arkson simply fell to his knees, his eyes still locked on the sky as the blood trickled down his side.

ARKSON DREW IN A deep breath as the healer singed together his newest wound. The red light from the healer's copper staff burned into his flesh, but as it had happened so many times before, only seemed a slight annoyance.

For a prince, his uncle, Veros, found him increasingly reckless and gave him a concerned look. Veros had been the Queen Nathilda's brother and was the base for much of Arkson's looks. Although Veros had now aged, and so his hair was streaked argent, the resemblance was still surprising. It was striking that Arkson's hair was so dark though, his own uncle had sandy blonde hair when younger.

As the healer hit a tender nerve, Arkson held back his urge to cry out, growing even quieter. A palace window nearby had been opened and he heard the rustle of the leaves from the forest. It was a sudden whoosh of wind he heard next, strong enough to even throw a few yellowed leaves into his chamber and onto the floor by his bedside. Strong winds brought change his aunt had always told him. Maybe it would bring her back?

He wanted to smile, but the healer, hitting another tender spot regained Arkson's focus. The prince stared at him with a vexed look, wondering how much longer he might take. The healer was young, possibly a new trainee, and seemed slower than the others. Then again Arkson knew he should not be vexed with the young curer, it was his own fault for being wounded.

Arkson had been sparring with his soldiers in the deep grey light of the early morning when he had become distracted by the changes in the sky. Luckily the solider had only cut Arkson's flesh and though the wound was deep, it could be easily repaired. It was unlike him to be so distracted and he could tell that his Uncle wondered what had happened. Veros patiently waited for the healer to finish and as soon as he had left his quizzed his nephew sternly.

"What were you thinking my prince? You could have been killed!" He examined his nephew's face.

Arkson remained cold, unchanged. His dark hair hung around his face, matted from the sweat of pain, and his hazel-green eyes flickered with gold as light entered the room. He sometimes prayed for death, but that would never come easily to him despite what his uncle claimed. He was from a long lineage of Akorian royal males, males whose lives were woven with the power of their people. The long marking of the Zain upon his neck was changing colour with the shadows entering and leaving the room. The green of them seeming to fade to blue and then to purple.

"The lightening returned," he responded after a few moments of silence, "I was looking for signs of her." Arkson did not let his face betray the emotion of his words.

Veros sighed heavily, "I do not think she will return prince. The princess has left us."

"It is unlike her to leave the way she did Uncle,"

Arkson countered.

"There was no sign of struggle in her note, nothing to indicate abduction or force." Veros remained rational, objective.

"I do not believe she would leave me, *us*," Arkson spoke more persistent.

"She already has my prince." And with that he turned to leave, unable argue with Arkson's hopes and saddened by their loss. Nikelda had left them.

If Arkson had his full powers, his wound would have healed itself in a matter of minutes, and he mulled over that thought with displeasure. He played with a lit candle wick in the darkness of the room that was slowly brightening with the early morning light. He resisted the pain from the flame. After all, he had been reborn of fire with his father's death. The fire should be welcoming.

He envied his soldiers ease of fighting, the grace of their powers that moved through them effortless while he worked so hard to maintain. He still remained the strongest, the fastest, but by skill alone. With his powers he could be so much more and the loss had left him embittered. Losing his powers had even stunted his growth and although he was still a good height at six feet tall, most of his guards were taller than him.

His uncle often worried for him and he knew it was out of love. Yet Arkson felt less and less as the years passed. He had closed himself off, knowing what some of the nobles thought of him. He was a disappointment by circumstance, something he had lived with for twenty-four years. At thirty-four he wondered if things would ever change.

Nonetheless, he had always been admired by his people, primarily for his reason and resolve. What his father lacked, Arkson made up for immensely. Since his childhood he was always calm, focused, and planning for what was to come. It had taken him years to rebuild much of what his people had lost.

The strength of his father's noble supporters had become complacent, soft and focused more on luxury. Parties and social gatherings had replaced their traditional clan meetings and politics, things hinged upon pleasure. Yet he was so far removed from that all. Arkson was an Akori of his people, not the nobles, but even they were distant to him.

He sat in his throne staring down at the ring upon his middle finger. The sun stone ring had been the last gift given to him by Nikelda on his birthday. The gold shimmering quality was meant to remind him of his best qualities. She had told him that at each angle, the beauty of the ring changed.

Nikelda knew that each year he aged without a mate had saddened him more and more. So she crafted it for him as she had many gifts before. She made him gifts each year so that he might have something to look forward to, despite the sadness in his life.

His heart ached as he looked at it now. Why had Nikelda left? Why would she leave him and his uncle and aunt alone in Zatian? His younger sister had always been more reckless than he had been.

He recalled the months that had passed since his birthday in the spring. In his mind he had gone over every moment and nothing had indicated her desire to leave the city. It had been many weeks since she had left, but it felt as though no time had passed.

The day had been just like any other and after supper they had retired for the night. When he awoke she was nowhere to be found. After inspecting her room, he could see the open window panes and shutters moving with the wind. On her table she had left a note.

I will return. This is for the good of us.

The floor was streaked with black burn marks. Parts

of the hardwood could be broken off and looked like coal and a breeze from the window had the ashy dust swirling in circles. He suspected the damage was from her gift of energy sourcing. He wondered if the lightning had struck her and pulled her elsewhere. Where had she gone?

His thoughts were interrupted by a knock at the throne room doors.

"Enter," he called out.

The large wooden doors opened with their usual creaking noise to reveal his guard Alvaren. He was focused as he entered, and his face, weight-full, showed there was trouble resting behind his rich honey brown eyes. He walked briskly until he kneeled before Arkson's throne and spoke.

"Prince Arkson," he began, "I have returned from the trip to Uri." He paused as the prince's cold stare remained unchanged.

"Continue." Arkson encouraged even though his heart began to beat faster at the hope for what Alvaren would say.

"I was able to intercept the slave traders, my prince, and the rumours are true. There were two humans brought to Uri a few months ago, both female. They were sold to an Anuya named Thussan. I was unable to bring them back Prince Arkson. I am sorry that I have failed you."

The guard looked fearful of the prince's reaction, one knee leaning on the floor he bowed his head expecting some sort of punishment. Alvaren's dirty blond hair hung down messily and his mouth twisted in disappointment.

Arkson could never harm him, would never, he was too loyal, was his closest friend and more like a brother. Although he hoped that Alvaren would have brought the humans back with him, it was an unreasonable request considering the sheer brutality and commanding force of the Anuyan. Fighting one would be difficult enough for any soldier, never mind several in the close communities they often dwelled. Uri itself was divided in multiple sectors and even though Alvaren knew which one to go to, it could quickly become a suicide mission.

"You have not failed me," he replied knowing that he must act quickly before news spread within the palace that Alvaren had returned. Arkson knew that not all of his subjects could be trusted with such important information.

"Prepare the horses, we ride out to Uri today."

CHAPTER 3

SALHA FELT LIKE THE morning coolness was unbearable. There was little light in the sky and the cold feeling clung to everything. She felt miserable. Thussan seemed increasingly demanding of her lately, stating that her domestic skills were seriously lacking for a female of her kind. She was used to Sammie preparing most of their meals. Salha was excellent at keeping things neat and tidy but she certainly did not think herself a gourmet chef, plus being in a strange land was difficult enough without trying to figure out what the foods were. Then, she had to decipher how they were to be kept and how to cook them.

The vegetables and fruits on the counter seemed peculiar, some of them looked like yams or potatoes, others almost deadly. One fruit that Thussan had called *pikara*, was his favourite and of course it looked like it had stingers jutting from its surface pricklier than a cactus. It smelled awful, like sweaty old gym socks. Luckily, Braedynn had shown her how to cut it open with a cleaver, but being thick skinned and waxy she had to be careful with how she swung at the fruit.

    The first time she had tried to cut it open on her own, the knife had gotten stuck and in an attempt shake it loose of the fruit, she had shook too hard and sent it barrelling out the window ledge. It landed very close to the feet of Thussan, who at the time had been conversing with Loward in the garden. Thussan had looked up at her glowering and had raced back into the house to punish her. Thankfully Braedynn had cut him off, and managed to quell his intentions. She had been more careful lately, exceedingly cautious really, something that did not come to her naturally.

    On mornings like this one though, she found herself wistfully looking out the window and daydreaming about the luxuries of the life in Halifax that she missed. More than anything she missed her computer. She craved the ability to keep up to date with blogs of interest and read online. She'd give anything to read some Manga and she especially missed her opportunity for gaming—online games, board games, video games, anything! Although she felt like she might be trapped in an alternate world, there were no extra lives or chances to reboot. It was peculiar that her escapist thoughts brought her back to her reality.

    What seemed even more peculiar to her was the man who was now her husband. He said very little to her unless she spoke to him first. Yet, was so fiercely protective of her, it was amusing and impressive all at once. Salha knew she never had any problems capturing the attention of men, but he was different, it was as if he wanted very little to do with her, but was compelled to take care of her all the same.

    What she did know about him was his name, Braedynn, and that his work ethic made her feel deplorable. Never in her life had she seen a man who worked so hard. He tended to all of Thussan's animals and fixed and built anything that was needed. He kept long hours. He always woke before Salha and returned long after she had gone to bed. She admired him, but respected his need for solitude. She supposed he was also adjusting to their marriage, a marriage she suspected he had not wanted.

That morning because Salha was yet to be pregnant and Thussan was eager for slaves, he had advised Braedynn to retire early from his work more regularly. In fact, he had even suggested allowing Braedynn and Salha half an hour to themselves on a daily basis during the day. His words had caught her by surprise and she had froze on the spot.

He had pushed Braedynn towards her stating, "take the time now if you want."

Salha had shuddered, but it was at the thought of being pregnant in this strange place, not because of the man standing before her. Braedynn had looked down at her examining the disgust on her face and thankfully he looked none too pleased at the suggestion either.

"I can return earlier this evening," he spoke, looking at Sal as though he had no intention of doing so. His back turned to Thussan, he rolled his eyes, and left the room quickly after that grabbing his jacket and swinging it over his broad shoulders while he walked across the field.

Thussan had stretched back in his chair. "What an ungrateful human," he muttered under his breath. "Bring me my food wench!" he yelled at Sal who jumping out of her trance had quickly given him his hard boiled eggs and bread.

Even though the day had just begun, Salha was anxious already, not knowing what it would bring.

BRAEDYNN FELT RESTLESS, and it was a feeling he disdained. Never in his life did he expect the outcome of the past few months. He stood there with his hands balled into fists, while Thussan stood before him.

"Understand me tal'ak?" Thussan asked, his green eyes gleaming. He used the Anuyan word for slave, only it was far more degrading in that form. It suggested the human was filth, stupid.

Braedynn had just begun fixing a fence when Thussan approached to inspect his progress. He suspected he would start commenting on the work that he was doing, but instead he just continued harassing him about the same thing he had that very morning –Salha.

Braedynn bit the inside of his cheek and stopped himself from responding, so Thussan continued, "You have been married for over one moon cycle dammit and though I know you are thankless bastard for the company I've provided you but you should be grateful for what companionship you have. If that woman is not pregnant soon, I'll not be pleased and both of you will suffer the consequences."

Braedynn stared back at Thussan coldly, but his stare did little to prevent his mouth from continuing. "Granted I know that wife of yours is inept at most things natural to a female. Yet for your species she does look like an attractive one, she has no unsightly blemishes. What man spends all day away from his mate?"

Braedynn simply shrugged not wanting to bait him more.

"Attraction is not necessary for reproduction. I meant what I said earlier slave, you retire from work early, the earlier the better." Thussan smacked Braedynn over the head.

His cheeks burned in anger. Thussan had a way of making love seem unappealing, even to someone like himself whose senses had more recently craved connection. Finding himself married one day in the middle of the afternoon played havoc on his emotions. He was in Uri on a mission, not visiting for pleasure. Not to mention the fact that Salha would have little-to-no say in the matter should Braedynn have been a lesser man and ravished her. In this land she was his wife, and that entitled him to her company, whether she wanted to give it or not.

It was peculiar of Thussan to say Salha was attractive. Braedynn suspected the Anuya was quite like his mother, who foremost was an anthropologist, inquiring about the unknown. Braedynn's mother was always studying something. He missed the excitement in her eyes when she discovered something new about Arzule.

Thussan had the same sort of quality. Braedynn had observed him countless times pacing back and forth muttering things to himself about the human species. Most Anuyan were not as loquacious as Thussan, and few of them understood humans as much as he did. It was as though humanity fascinated and disgusted Thussan all at once. Braedynn wondered if his master ever thought wistfully about what it would be like to be his kind.

Or at least he thought so until Thussan's countenance shifted darkly. "Answer me human!"

Braedynn's blue eyes glazed with anger. They narrowed on Thussan, but he still managed to nod accepting. He wondered how he had managed to last this long without killing the Anuya, wondered how much longer he could. If Braedynn had been careless about life, about respecting other beings he could have just killed the Anuya to begin. He would have sneaked in two months ago, found what he was looking for and left. Any confrontation would have ended with him as the victor and he could have returned to the people who needed him, but word of the two women being discovered had complicated his plans.

Salha and Samira's arrival had made him enter the city of Uri as a slave, hoping that he would intercept the traders and free them. He had been too early, the news of the women came before they had even come close to the city.

And now, he had to retire early from a day that had just begun to be with one of them. His thoughts centred on Salha, her small heart-shaped face, her delicate mouth, and her large bright eyes. What a cruel joke fate made by bringing him a wife. He had already lost one.

CHAPTER 4

NIKELDA AWOKE WITH a start. The summer light spilled in from the window in the downtown apartment and thankfully a breeze wafted in from the outside world. She gazed at the apartment around her, the walls were painted pumpkin and the large brick wall that spanned the length of the apartment made the space beautiful. Paintings were hung in black frames along the walls and wooden furniture and bookshelves filled the space. It was a warm and inviting place, kept clean and airy, much like her chamber in the palace.

Sleeping on the furniture in the living room had felt right to her since she did not want to disturb the things of the women who lived there. She knew the chances of them returning might be slight, but all the same felt she should respect them. She had been in this new place for too long. She wanted to return to Arzule, but she had not accomplished what she wanted and feared that an early return might thwart her plans for her brother's freedom.

Her new home was as pleasant a place to stay as the

palace. It was the world outside the walls which seemed peculiar to her. The city was unlike anything she had ever seen, the roads were paved differently, and the people dressed so unlike the Akori. In the time that she had been there, she made herself familiar enough with her surroundings to know where she could find food, to know what to do among the people.

The details Alexandros had told her in her childhood about this world greatly helped, and the many books that the women who lived in her place of stay helped as well. She could tell from the paintings, from the way that their apartment was kept that they were sisters. She wondered which one would be her brother's choice. They were both beautiful, but she felt herself secretly hoping it was the taller of the two. The one named Samira, who clearly had no man involved with her. It was evident from the many messages of the machine by the door, messages from a man named Eric, that he and Salha were involved, or at least had been before her unexpected departure.

She feared for the sisters, but prayed that things would be on their side. Arzule was so different than their world, harder to survive in. Her survival had been relatively easy so far in her new found place that she came to know was called Downtown Halifax. The place where she stayed had all that she needed, only once or twice did she need to venture out and once she had found out where to find food, it was easy. It was as if things were given to her.

A man had shown up not long after she arrived to pick up something he called photographs and found what he wanted on Samira's desk. He scribbled a note onto a piece of paper before he left, placing it on the desk. Reading it upside down, Nikelda realized what it said.

Great work Samira, you've outdone yourself. Give me a call when you get a chance. I'd like to negotiate a contract for you with the firm. Believe me, it pays well and you'd love the team. 902-555-1298

    She had been uneasy when he arrived, but he seemed more afraid of her than she of him, and so she had allowed him to enter her new home since he seemed desperate. He had not stayed long, thrusting the money into her hand and asking her to give Samira his thanks before he left.

    On her other excursions out among the people, she discovered that the men here were different, not as intimidating as in Arzule. She intimidated them. They looked at her in awe, as though her looks were unearthly. Only she knew that their perceptions were true. Sometimes if she felt wicked, she would give them a menacing look, a little snarl maybe.

    When she grew restless, feeling captive, she would sit on the balcony where the sisters had planted a small garden. Being there was beautiful, staring at the rooftops and the grid of the city. Parts of it reminded her of her world, the homes unique in their shape and style seemed alive, their windows like eyes against the bright coloured boxes and angular shapes. There were weird looking structures, like smaller palaces everywhere, which she imagined had as many rooms as in the palace.

    She thought about spending most of her day peacefully sitting on that balcony. She also wanted to change her appearance though. The clothes she had brought with her were good enough. A few dresses and some pants with simple tunics didn't make her stand out too much on the streets, but everything else about her was not human.

    She wanted to cut her hair. She had yet to see someone with hair waist length in Halifax, and felt her appearance called attention to her. A child had recently asked her if her tattoos had hurt. She had no idea what to answer, or what tattoos were, until they pointed to her neck and arm. She had simply shrugged and walked on.

    In the apartment, she had found several boxes of

liquids used to colour hair. She planned to use one later that evening, seeing that the same practice in Arzule was incredibly costly and required a healer of skill, one willing to use their magic for something so frivolous. Her hair would have been blonde naturally were it not for her father.

When she and Arkson were younger, after meeting Alexandros, his hair so much darker than the light brown or sandy blonde more common of the Akori. Her father had ordered for Arkson and Nikelda's hair colour to be changed permanently, so that they might be distinguished from the rest of their people. He had been so transfixed with the hue of Alexandros's hair. How peculiar and vain a request that would have been she mused to herself, now more than twenty years later. It seemed so unlike her people who proudly showed off their Akorian traditions. At least her eyes suited the regular luminescent eye colours in hazels, greens, and blues.

She knew that changing her hair would take some time and then she would have to begin to prepare herself for her return to Arzule. It would not be for several more weeks, but she knew that she would have to bring some of the things she had found with the merchant's store below. It had some very rare Akorian jewellery. There were only a few pieces, but the instant she saw them, she knew what they were and she had to have them for when she returned. How they had ended up in this place was strange, but she would bring them back to their rightful place.

She got up from bed and moved to the kitchen where she planned to make her breakfast. It was a peculiar thing making food for herself, the first time she had ever done so was as a child, but there had been only a few reoccurring instances since the first. Arkson too frequently took care of her, or arranged for her meals to be prepared by the palace chefs before she even needed to ask. She had only allowed him to spoil her.

 Arkson and her uncle were the only males whose company she kept. By now, she should have been married, but it was of no interest to her. Arkson had lectured her countless times on the gift of companionship, but she had declined any suitor. The guards of Arkson's order were too brutish for her, and the nobles of her kind were far too refined for her liking. Their breeding was perhaps a bit too important and it showed in their manner and in their looks. The noble Akorian males always wore their hair long, coiffed perfectly and sometimes evoking envy from the Akorian females. It was peculiar to attend functions when both were in the same room, since not much could catch the eye of a male.

 She thought about the time when she had used her energy sourcing to make it storm during one summer picnic for her birthday. Veros had gone through great lengths to arrange the party for her fifteenth birthday. He had even purchased her a beautiful pale yellow dress, more beautiful than any other that she had owned. Yet she had been upset to learn that he had not invited Arkson's guards, who were more often than not seen as the trouble makers in the city.

 Since her uncle had refused to cede to her wishes she had invited them anyway, and when one of the nobles Julian had made a rude comment about the prince and his unsavoury friends, she pulled lightning from the sky. She had only meant to scare them with a bit of lightening, but her powers outweighed her skills and the table had caught fire. She was lucky that Arkson had thought quickly and shooting a look to his guard Alvaren, who had managed to match her lightning with a downpour of rain.

 She was much better now with her craft. She only needed to make slight movements with her fingers for the power to catch. She knew that it was her power which helped her survive, especially in this world.

Unsure of what to do with the oven in Samira's apartment as there was no place for fire, she was at least able to charge the elements allowing her to cook when she could not figure out which buttons to press or move.

She began to make her way over to the oven, when a knock on the door disrupted her thoughts and stopped her in her tracks. She paused for a few seconds thinking the visitor would likely go away and that she might just ignore the noise, until it erupted into loud banging. She sighed, annoyed for the disruption when she had yet to get food in to her stomach.

CHAPTER 5

Loward unshackled Sammie's hands and pushed her out into the yard. He directed her to feed the *gohri*, which Sammie had come to discover were creatures a weird mix of a cow and goat. She fed them every morning and so Loward's directions always seemed peculiar to her. It was as if he thought her incapable of learning a routine.

Even though the darkness of the early morning had gone, the sky was still grey and sombre. As she scooped up the pail for the water, she stopped and gazed at the reflection before her. In two and a half months she had withered away. She hardly recognized herself. The clothes that had been snug on her first arrival were loose. She had assumed that the coarse fabric had stretched, instead she saw the truth.

In Halifax, she had joined the gym to lose weight and become healthy, but even though she intended well, her plans did not always work and she hardly went at all. If she could see herself now as she had then, she never would have wished herself skinnier. It seemed perverse now.

Daily she starved.

    She quickly gathered the water and grunted as she carried the large pail to the troughs which were erected halfway through the field. The *gohri* made soft neighing sounds as they moved closer to drink. As creatures they showed no prejudice towards her and often nestled with her, thankful for her care. Their large dark eyes were kind, adorable, despite their peculiar bodies. She sighed wishing that there was someone else in this world that might feel the same and treat her with kindness. She stopped for a minute to admire the beauty around her.

    In a tree near her ravens gathered, their beautiful black feathers fluttering in a gentle breeze. They looked at her knowingly, and it was as if they gathered near her each time she was outside. She felt as if her sadness drew them near. The land around her was dotted with black iron fences and stone homes in whites and light greys. The tall wheat coloured grass spread out the distance of the fields, of which some had been tilled and harvested, unearthing a deep rich brown of the soil. It reminded Samira of chocolate cake and she wished she had something, anything to eat.

    There were several streams running through Loward's property, as it was customary for Anuyan to build along water. The few times she was able to get away from her captors for a bit and care for herself. She had been enchanted by the bubbling of the water and the cool crispness of the wet upon her skin. It was far too cold now to entertain that idea, the late summer had set in, and she shuddered to think what the winters might be like in this place.

    There were beautiful fish that swam in the clear water and contrasted sharply against the stones of the bedrock. Most of the fish looked like a mix between large Betas and Koi, and had elegant wispy fins in beautiful blues and purples.

Her daydreams interrupted, she heard a large grunt from Loward behind her and afraid that he might be angered by her showing affection to his animals, she quickly backed away and turned around. What she saw frightened her even more. Loward and Thussan were locked in arms. They held large scimitars, which with each strike ignited glints of metal that came flying out orange and fiery. She was mystified watching their large tawny bodies move almost as if they danced.

"I have paid my debt to you Loward!" Thussan grunted as he manoeuvred away from Loward's grasp.

Loward growled at that. "That human you gave me may have been worth the debt, but the interest you owe is yet to be paid. I'll make a claim to your property if you don't pay in full Thussan" Loward let out another ferocious growl.

Thussan looked shocked and then his eyes narrowed. He ripped his shirt off and threw it to the ground.

"Then I call *Primora* you worthless bastard!" Thussan shouted back, his temper flaring.

If Loward won, he would absorb all of Thussan's property, there would be no witnesses but the slaves to what had taken place. Sammie had read the contract of her sale at the signing. It stated that in Loward's death she would be released from her master's custody provided that he had been killed by natural causes or *Primora*. She had not known what that meant at the time, but she now discovered it seemed to be a battle between two Anuyan.

This law was written into the papers of her sale and was indicated for all slaves. She had learned that previously there had been too many *Primora* taking place in Uri between Anuyan who were greedy to absorb another's property for more power. This had been explained to a new slave trader negotiating the sales at the time of hers to Loward. She had overheard the details and so prayed daily to herself for his death, even though she knew that his lifespan exceeded hers threefold. He was already one hundred and thirty eight.

Kalawyn walked through the gardens and entered the field. She watched transfixed as Loward and Thussan fought. If Loward died, she would become Thussan's wife by Anuyan rights, and her daughter could be killed if Thussan requested to make way for children of his own. She looked fearful. Her body tense and alert to each clang of the weapons. They weaved back and forth for what seemed like an eternity.

Loward jumped forward in a quick movement only to be matched by Thussan and kicked back. And as Thussan moved to strike, he was met by Loward's blade as he manoeuvred quickly upwards. They skirted around one another, blades clanging. Thussan's skill surprised Samira as her sister always described him as more scholarly than her master.

Loward's brute force was met blade to blade in each strike, and exasperated he grunted out loudly.

Thussan kept calm and moved quickly to make up for the force of Loward's hits.

Loward moved forward to kick Thussan down, but too hastily made his move, and Thussan anticipating his action sliced into his leg. He backed off quickly, limping a bit.

"It ends now." Thussan spoke, cold chills travelling over Samira's back.

He advanced quickly towards Loward, hitting the blade from the base of his hand. Thussan caught him as he moved back with his scimitar and sunk the metal forward piercing into his heart.

Kalawyn froze horrified by her husband's slow death. The colour from his eyes faded as his blue blood slowly trickled from his wound. She sunk to her knees shrieking with tears as Thussan moved towards her with hungry eyes.

He pulled her arm towards him. "You are mine."

She shook his arm off and looked away, sobbing and shouting to their gods. "How dare you! How could you kill him!"

"I defended my rights Kalawyn, and now I have right to you!" He reached for her again, and she pushed back fiercely. Struggling against him as he pulled her to her feet.

Remarkably, she turned back to Sammie as if suddenly aware that she was there.

"Run!" she yelled.

Thussan smacked her across the face. "No! She is mine!"

"Not by law!" Kalawyn growled and tried to pull him back as he moved toward Sammie.

Sammie shocked by what had just happened, hesitated then looked up to see Braedynn and Salha standing nearby in Thussan's yard. Braedynn was holding back her sister, who was desperately trying to run towards her, trying to break free.

"Run Samira," he mouthed to her and she felt off kilter, as if she were suddenly drunk. Her panic was setting in and she needed to calm down.

She stepped back and then turned to run. She had no idea where to go, as she ran through the field to the front of Loward's house, her heart and mind raced. Once she got to the cobblestone street, she feared that she would be stopped by the Anuyan thinking that she was running from her master.

As she reached the front of the house, she fiddled with the gate, panicking as she looked back to see Thussan closing the gap. His pace was no more than a stride, but his long legs travelled quickly and she could see the darkness in his eyes. If he could not keep her, would he kill her?

Almost breathless, she calmed herself enough to open the latch and ran out onto the cobblestone. There were a few Anuyan in the streets, but those that did see her paid little attention. Her side burned and as she looked back to see Thussan exiting the gate. Stupidly she tripped against a loose stone and fell. She cursed and looked up to see a black horse rearing. Its rider looked down upon her coldly with searing green eyes and she was quickly surrounded by many other riders on white steeds.

They encircled her until Thussan cried out loudly "That human is mine!".

The riders with horses drew back behind their leader and waited for him to approach. She examined them; they definitely weren't Anuyan. Sheathed in dark cloaks and gold armour embellished with dark blue and purple enamel. They were something else.

Sammie cursed, and tried to pull herself up. She turned to face Thussan, awaiting his forceful grab.

"No, he won't kill me," she muttered to herself. "He'll keep me to make more slaves."

He'll certainly beat me, she thought to herself, but hopefully not within an inch of her life. Under normal circumstances she would fight back, but here in Arzule, there was no telling what surprise Thussan might posses. She shifted her weight to the ankle she had not fallen on and winced.

Thussan shouted loudly a second time, pointing at her "That human is mine!"

Arkson looked down from his horse, at the human again. She was different than he had expected, and unlike his people she had hair darker than his own. It was braided in the front, which he suspected kept it from her eyes, the rest were black shiny strands flowing messily everywhere most likely from running. Her skin was a tanned brown like the Phaerra of the North and her eyes were darker than any he had ever seen, almost black. He had heard what she had muttered and wondered why she spoke to herself. If this was a common human trait, he found it a bit unnerving.

"How much for her?" he asked the Anuya who, covered in blood, looked as though he had just battled.

"She is freed!" Another Anuya approaching them shouted. It was a female, her long blonde hair swaying in the wind, her eyes and face reddened by her emotions. She had been crying. Thussan moved towards Kalawyn to hit her.

"Stop!" Arkson cried, and the beastly Anuya, annoyed growled, but didn't hit the female.

All the while the human stood still, he could sense her heart pounding, sensed her fear.

"She has been freed by *Primora*?" he asked. The female Anuya nodded her head, while the male hissed at her. Her husband must have been killed Arkson thought; this was her only way for vengeance. "Then she will come with me," he stated.

Thussan angled his sword towards Arkson and his steed. "Let her decide, prince!"

Arkson's eyes narrowed, his armour betrayed his status, "Put that sword away Anuya!"

Sammie looked back and forth between them, wondering where this prince had come from and what she should do. If she stayed she would be beaten for running, and if she went she wondered what on earth a prince would want with her. He looked human, but she could tell from the tattoo on his neck, similar to all the other riders that he was clearly something else. Their eyes were a different, had a sheen to them that seemed unnatural.

Kalawyn looked at her with red rimmed eyes. "If you stay here, I will kill you." Sammie's heart ached. Kalawyn would make good on her promise. If Sammie stayed she would be dead by nightfall. She feared leaving Salha behind, but if she stayed it would be no good to either one of them. Closing her eyes she steadied herself and her breathing. She had to be strong, and calm her thoughts. She was intelligent and resourceful. She would find a way back to Salha.

"I'll go" she said.

Arkson gave Alvaren a nod, and he scooped up Sammie up pulling her onto the saddle. She sat there silently praying she would be alright. She especially disliked having to hold onto a stranger riding next to this supposed prince. As the wind picked up her rider's face crinkled as though she smelled.

It was not the first time she had experienced this reaction in Arzule. The slave traders had looked at her and Salha with lust when they awoke in the middle of a field. Thinking back on it, at the first glance they must have looked peculiar in their satin pyjamas, shivering and watching the slave traders move their caravan along. All Samira could think was *they better not touch me and heaven help them if they touch Salha.* Yet as soon as the first slave trader approached, his hand covered his nose and he cursed.

"Ah human," he had whined. Instead they had been led by swords to the cages and locked up. Samira had wanted to fight, but the fear in her sister's eyes and the shake of her head when she shot her a conspiring look, stopped her from taking action.

She had been thankful they at least smelled different, and hoped that the same smell would protect her now as she was being carried to yet another place further away from her home.

ARKSON TRIED TO KEEP his gaze forward, but every now and then his eyes would wander to his new charge. Her eyes moved quickly over everything, she paid little attention to him unaware of his intense examination of her character. She seemed unrealistically calm for someone being taken from her master, but then he realized she must have had to be composed considering her enslavement and the harsh penalties the Anuya would have inflicted for disobedience.

Arkson wondered what her voice sounded like. She had spoken so little it was hard to tell, and the more he thought about her voice, the more he examined her lips. Her lips were round and well balanced, they looked soft, and he wanted to taste them. He felt unlike himself, no Akorian ever elicited such a response from him. He closed his eyes to try and remove himself from the waft of her scent, which to him resembled the spicy warmth of a hearth.

He had been smart to ask Alvaren to ride with her. Arkson had other things to consider now. He had to be more prepared for the time ahead. News would travel quickly after he returned with her to the palace. It would not be long before his enemies knew of her presence and he had already been planning so much for the protection of his people, which he did not want to be discovered before its time.

He was glad that he had the foresight to have met with the riders so frequently these past few months, the kinship he established with his soldiers was stronger than it ever had been. If not for Alvaren, all that he had hoped for would not be on the brink of coming true. Alvaren had scouted on and off for weeks after news of two humans swept across the cites of Arzule. The regions were divided and he had ventured into all of them on Arkson's behalf. He was grateful for such a loyal soldier, for such a true friend.

Arkson would show his appreciation for his efforts

upon returning to the palace. He would reward Alvaren with land in the hills and the honour of a Zatian sword. Few soldiers were ever blessed with such an honour. The prince would proudly give the gift to Alvaren, but his thoughts kept drifting from the necessities for the ceremony of honour to the female guarded by Alvaren's weight.

He did not have to tell the group what precious cargo they carried, but the sour weather and tense mood seemed to weigh on them all. If Arkson knew anything about either, he knew that these would be signs of the challenges to come.

CHAPTER 6

SALHA WEPT IN BRAEDYNN'S arms, her body shook uncontrollably. She had watched in terror as her sister had been taken by the riders from Thussan. She and Braedynn had returned to Thussan's home. She was afraid that if he saw them linger in the yard they would be rewarded with a beating for showing insolence to their master.

Braedynn had taken responsibility for them both and convinced Thussan to bestow any beatings Salha earned upon him instead. Salha did not want to be responsible for his death. She felt like a coward, Sammie had always been the brave one. She should have tried to stop them from taking Samira. Her sister would have fought for her. She felt sickened and panicked. If it was not for Braedynn standing beside her, she knew she would be crouched over heaving out her breakfast. She had to compose herself.

Braedynn wiped her tears away and gazed into her eyes. She felt his affection unexpected even though all he did was look out for her best interest. Braedynn's hard exterior softened looking at her. Over the past few days, as she had been separated from her sister for longer than usual, she had felt herself begin to crumble, but he had been there to support her. Now Samira was gone, and had been taken to who knew where. What would happen to Sammie? What would happen to her? How in the hell did they get themselves into this situation?

His dark blonde hair fell into his blue eyes as she returned his stare. She was still worried about her sister, but his arms made her feel as though it would be alright. She had just begun to feel as though she might survive the horror of her new life and that she and Samira would find a way home. After a few weeks of being carted around in a cage and the passing months in her new found life as a slave, her mind was coming to terms with it all.

Braedynn looked at her so intensely she had to look away. She felt foolish. He might be her husband, but they had spoken no more than twenty words in exchange. How could he be so calm? How could he be this strong? He was a slave but never seemed like one. She could not imagine comparing him to any man she knew. There were none like him, none so collected and assuring.

It was a few minutes before he said anything. "It will be okay," he began, "you have me Salha, I will protect you." She could hear the determination in his voice, but could not bring herself to look up. As each tear felt he wiped them aside.

"I promise you Salha, I will keep you safe. I'll bring Samira back."

She stiffened from shock, the shock of what he promised her. She could no longer resist, had to see his face to read his true intentions, and slowly looked up. His eyes bore into her, the deep blue of them clear and piercing, making her heart tremble. He moved so slowly, but she realized quickly what he was going to do. He lowered his lips to brush against hers so lightly, so quickly, that it felt like a whisper. He straightened a bit, as though he might be embarrassed he had kissed her and without thinking Salha brushed her fingertips over her mouth. He had kissed her. Braedynn had kissed her. She had stopped crying, but her mind still raced with turmoil.

Braedynn was grateful that Thussan had left him alone. He was over at Loward's inspecting the home that was now being added to his property. Kalawyn had calmed a bit when she learned that Thussan would not be killing her daughter, although she had begrudgingly allowed him into her home so he could take inventory of his new possessions. Anuyan deaths were not given mourning time and Kalawyn had no say in the matter now that Thussan would become her husband.

This was precious time that Braedynn needed to look through Thussan's human archive of information. Some of it he kept in this house in a room just off of the kitchen, but the majority of it was held in a stand alone structure adjacent to the barn where the animals were kept. It was like a workshop, with lanterns strung along a pulley that stretched the length of the room. Along either side of the walls were two long wooden tables covered with artifacts, maps, and images of humanity in Arzule. The gadgets and devices were interesting, but they were primarily old Anuyan junk, much of the human materials scattered about were clothes, farming equipment, and and a few pieces of jewellery.

He had to remain focused. Even though his mind at the moment was scolding him for kissing Salha. He needed to find the component to his device. The key that would unlock its power. The key his mother had always kept on a long bronze chain. It looked like a flattened jack, a children's toy that had small arms poking out from an octagonal core and had a brassy colour, which blended in with almost everything in Thussan's shed. Braedynn cursed under his breath.

The more he looked the more frustrated he became. He at least had the opportunity to examine the maps and documents from the human villages. Most of the paperwork had been marriage certificates, street planning charts, and birthing records. There was little information on the powers or magic in the human societies of Arzule, but from what he knew of them already he was not surprised. The humans of this world kept little records of shaman and healing traditions and any gifts or powers were looked down upon, seen as something fearful and uninvited in daily life. The human cities had been foolish, looking at the other species as animals, and it had caused their demise.

He looked out the window to watch for Thussan's return. The Anuya had seemed quite pleased with himself after the battle with Loward. In the past few weeks he had heard him conversing with other Anuyan males about the timing of marriage and his own desire for a wife. Now that he had seen his own slave married and his neighbours all happily coupled, he knew it would be time to also settle down. It seemed an advantageous circumstance to have found himself a bride, even though she had been someone else's first.

Salha had been so panicked by everything that he felt badly for leaving her. It was a necessity though. They were running out of time. Thussan's resources were growing and despite the fact Braedynn thought him deplorable, he recognized Thussan's intelligence. Now he would position himself politically in the community. He would expand his control in this sector of the city and start using other Anuyan as his resources.

Braedynn had to get himself and Salha out now, before guards and visitors came on a regular basis. Plus, he deigned the idea of being exhibited like a piece of property which he knew Thussan would be sure to do should Salha ever become pregnant. If only that key could jump out at him.

Come on idiot.

He scolded himself, but he knew it was not his effort waning, his focus had just shifted.

SALHA SAT RIGIDLY IN the chair by the kitchen window. Braedynn after some convincing, had finally agreed to leave her and return to his work. Not much would be expected of them with the twist in events for the day. She did not understand why he would return to work, but she figured it was probably the way he coped with things.

He had kissed her, and she could still taste him on her lips, could still smell him. The way he had held her, so intimately, while he brushed away her tears. She was unravelling, but he shouldered her together. It was such an unusual outcome. What would she do without Samira?

The moments that passed seemed elongated and surreal. Closing her eyes she willed herself to wake, but there was no way to nudge herself alive and happy back in Halifax. She opened them fiercely, angry that she could not change her fate.

She was stubborn though, and would try again. She closed her eyes a second time, but this time all she could see was Braedynn, and she sighed with the heaviest breath. Where was Samira now and why was Braedynn the only person her mind could picture?

CHAPTER 7

Sammie's body swayed back and forth on the horse. Her head ached. As the ride slowed she was thankful, her eyes had carefully examined everything for the last several hours. She tried to remember the path they took to the new place, committing to memory any landmarks she recalled. The terrain seemed rockier and they tread lightly as they entered the city of Zatian.

Many of the structures were wood and white stone and the roofs were tiled in black slate, overlapping like scales on a snake. It was a beautiful city. The walls guarding its people were tall and built of black stone. From a distance the wall had a sheen that was evident even when the sky was overcast. There were beautiful trees that looked like oaks and elms with yellowed and reddened leaves dotted across the land and the township bordered both a body of water and a forest creating the most beautiful landscape that Samira found awe inspiring.

She wished she had a camera with her to captures shots of the gorgeous architecture and scenery. And since the water from the ocean pooled in the exact spot near a dense forest it created a lush breeze throughout the city that she found wonderfully refreshing.

The gateway had been heavily guarded and as they entered the bustling heart of the city, they stopped before a second gate, which opened to the largest building Sammie had ever seen. It was obviously the palace. There were many stone buildings with signs outside them indicating their wares and the grid like organization of the paved streets was fascinating. The smells wafting from the market closer to the gate of the palace churned her deep seated hunger and made her mouth water. She was grateful when a merchant walked by with a large basket filled with colourful clothes and Samira was distracted long enough to wonder what they looked like.

The palace was breathtaking and somehow resembled a mixture of many architectural styles. It had several turrets and the large windows that were prominent on each level in gothic style shapes. The stone unlike the walls of the city was a creamy white. She watched her surroundings in awe shifting further back on the large horse as the rider dismounted.

"Human," her rider called. She looked down to see his arm extended to her. She frowned, and had the urge to kick him and pull back the reins on the horse so that she could race back to her sister, but as if sensing her thoughts, the prince came over and demanded her down. Instead of waiting, he grabbed her by the waist and pulled her from the horse and she cursed under her breath for not taking the chance she had missed. As he lifted her down, she suddenly realized just how tall they all were.

All of the men were like giants. The prince was the shortest but he still seemed to tower over her average frame. His green eyes locked onto her. He had lifted her with such ease that she wondered just how much weight she had lost. He was obviously one strong prince, his arms firm against her waist. The dust from her clothing covered his hands and he clapped them, annoyed by the filth. He turned to walk and the others followed.

She waited for them to chain her and drag her along as the Anuyan had. No one stepped forward to shackle her and she once again wondered if she could run. As if by cue, the prince turned around to her once again, looking very annoyed.

"No shackles?" She asked eyeing him suspiciously a glint of fire in her eyes.

He raised an eyebrow. "Where else is there for you to go? If you leave you will die out there, or are you familiar with Arzule human?" He asked as he scratched his eyebrow regally.

She glared at him and wanted to spit out that she had survived being a slave, she figured she could handle the woods. She knew those words would be a lie, had no idea what those woods could hold. He could sense her annoyance, looked at her coldly, even though he admired her perseverance of surviving the Anuyan and their notorious treatment of humans.

"You are not a prisoner," he added finally, calmly and cooly.

"Then what am I?" She asked again, indignant.

He sighed, as if he were tired by her already, and replied, "a guest." This was not the place for them to talk. He could not speak candidly with her when so many subjects were near.

By the look of his company, she did not know whether or not she should believe him. Some of them looked confused, others appalled, but she could not tell if it was his words or her presence that appalled them. It was true that he had yet to hurt her, but why go through the trouble of offering to pay for her. What was she doing there? What did the prince want?

She followed them slowly and as the horsemen scattered off to various parts of the palace, the prince ascended a large staircase leading to what seemed a throne room. As she followed she examined the walls, they were all cream coloured with wooden wainscoting, the windows were large and there was elaborate stained glass made of small and intricate pieces in purples, reds and blues at the tops of all of them. She admired the beauty of each stained pane, and the curving shapes and organic swirling patterns that seemed alive, enchanting.

Despite her admiration, she hated feeling like this, hopeless and uncertain. She could not decide if she felt more alarmed or relieved that she was now the only one following him. She resented being brought to another city where she sensed they would just look at her as a lowly human.

As the prince entered the throne room, he said something below her hearing threshold to a guard stationed at the entrance and he left immediately. Arkson sat in his throne and silently stared at her, glancing occasionally at the door behind her. It was not until that instant that she really had the opportunity to get a good look at him. Her mind had finally calmed enough that she could feel less overwhelmed by her surroundings.

His dark brown hair fell below his chin and gently framed a perfectly masculine face marked by a bit of stubble around his chin. His green eyes had shimmering flecks of gold and brown that intensified as he looked at her. His arms peeked out from the rolled sleeves of his shirt and were tattooed with the similar dark greens symbols as the green marks traversing the length of his neck. It made his appearance all the more fixating.

She tried to carefully examine him so as not to suggest she found him attractive, even though her heartbeat betrayed the truth. Slow thunderous beats crashed through her chest. He had removed the armour and navy cape he wore on the ride. Her eyes travelled over his broad shoulders, which tapered down to a body that was lean and muscular. His white shirt looked crisp against his warm golden complexion peaking out near his upper chest and as her eyes travelled down to his dark blue pants for a moment, she wondered what he might look like naked. His weight shifted and her eyes met his once again. She was praying that he had not caught her glance, instead she found herself surprised by the look in his eyes. He did not look at her with boredom any longer, but with a hint of longing.

Arkson had watched the human look over him, he could sense she was not angered anymore, but she was shielding her feelings about him carefully. Her dark hair and eyes were piercing, but the rags she wore made her look plain. It looked as though the Anuya who owned her had covered her in a brown sac, but had thankfully still allowed her time to groom, as her hair was well kept and appearance was neat and tidy.

Brunelda finally entered the room, smelling the air suspiciously as she approached the throne. "Yes my prince," she said as she bowed, "you have called for me?" She then cast a weary glance at Sammie, wondering what had taken place in the morn.

Sammie looked at the female before her, she was tall like the riders and guards, but was far more slender in physique and much fairer. She looked to be about fifty in human years and her dark blonde hair was twisted neatly in a plait. She wore a simple light blue pinafore, cinched at the waist by a gold and enamelled purple belt, all of which had been draped over top the same sort of white shirt as the prince. Her blue eyes were large and had a young sparkle to them, suggesting that she was full of life.

"Brunelda, take her to the baths and then the dining hall," he said as he pointed to Sammie, "and I'll arrange for some suitable clothing for her as well."

Sammie looked up at him in shock, he was going to clean, clothe, and feed her. Maybe he was not such an ass after all.

Brunelda looked at Sammie as if she were a challenge. "I'll do me best to get the smell off her."

"Just don't scrub her raw," he said with a smirk and wink. Sammie recanted, maybe he was a jerk, and her anger returned. She glared at him as Brunelda grabbed her by the hand and led her down the hall to the baths. Arkson thought he might laugh. Brunelda always lightened the mood, that was until he thought about the baths and the fact that the human would soon be naked.

While she had stood there before him, he had the urge to strip her naked and let his eyes wander over her. The thought was so barbaric and unlike him that he disdained his emotions and felt troubled. More than anything though, he wanted to comfort her, give her a sense of peace that she was safe now, and that he would care for her. Could she be the one to end his torment? He dared not start to hope. It had been so long since he had the company of a female.

As SAMMIE AND BRUNELDA entered the baths, she was suddenly fearful that there would be more of Brunelda's people there. It was now mid-day though and she was relieved to find that the room was empty and the ten baths were cordoned off in private cubicle like enclosures made of wooden lattices covered in cloth. Brunelda brought her to one of the baths in the back, which was larger than the others and seemed more private. She began cranking a water pump and Sammie was surprised as the water that poured out was hot. The tub filled quickly, as the spout was the size of a basketball and before she knew it, Brunelda was pushing her towards a mirror and urging her to remove her clothes.

Sammie was normally modest, but after months of no hot water, she figured she had nothing to hide and as she pulled off her potato sack top and drawstring pants, she was mesmerized by what she saw.

I'm a freaking mess.

She ran her hands gingerly over her messy hair trying to flatten some of the poof. Her body was still the shapely frame that she recognized with full shoulders and breasts and an ample buttocks but it needed care, nourishment.

"Whoa," she whispered to herself, tracing the scar just under her breast that Loward had given her.

Brunelda hearing her walked over and tsked at her scars. "Those Anuyan are a ruthless breed." She gently placed her hand on Sammie's shoulder. "Come love, the bath is cooled enough."

As she limped over, Brunelda helped her slip into the water. Sammie felt the tension in her body melt away. To her surprise, Brunelda did help scrub her with a sponge, primarily her back, but was quite gentle and almost motherly.

"There, that should be peaceful," she said as she removed the braids from Sammie's hair and opened the soapy oil for her to wash it with. Sammie almost felt like crying, no one had shown her kindness like this in months and then she had paid for it at a spa. She had forgotten sometimes that she was capable of feeling at ease, that there was kindness in others. As her eyes teared, she wiped them away quickly.

"You're very kind," she said to Brunelda. She had a natural way of making Sammie feel at ease, safe.

Brunelda smiled. "That's why the prince sends me," she said with a wink "he knows I have the true heart of the

Akori, not those nobles who look down their noses at your kind."

"This place is called Akori?" Sammie asked wondering if Akori was the name for city or for her species.

"Oh goodness no love, I am an Akori, true to heart, unlike those filthy Anuyan slave keepers, but, then again, who am I to judge." She sighed as she scrubbed Sammie's scalp, "No my dear, the city you're in is Zatian."

"Zai-ti-yan," Sammie repeated phonetically, and then feeling somewhat childish realized she was being bathed. "I can clean my hair Brunelda, you don't have to..."

Brunelda tsked again. "Oh don't you worry *whelan*, it is my pleasure. We have to have you looking your best and from those bruises on you it'll take a few hours to have you all sorted out"

"*Whelan*?" Sammie asked.

"Oh," Brunelda said, "young maiden I mean."

Sammie was truly touched, even though she did not consider herself particularly young, or the maiden type, the nomenclature was appreciated.

"Thank you Brunelda."

CHAPTER 8

THE TIME HAD COME, even with the crazed events of the day, Salha was alone with Braedynn. He had returned from his work much earlier than anticipated. By late afternoon he realized he could not longer focus on work, especially since he knew how distraught Salha was at her sister's departure with the Akori.

He knew where they would take Samira, even had an idea as to why she was being brought there. It looked as though the Prince of Zatian would finally get what he had long waited for, his freedom. That was none of his concern now though. His main concern was the woman who was his wife, the woman waiting for him on the other side of the door he now had his forehead resting against.

He should not have kissed her he thought to himself. Braedynn scorned his actions. He had meant to leave her be all this time, to help her gain her freedom and then let her choose how she might want to spend her days in Arzule. Yet, he felt for her. It would have helped if she was not so attractive to him, her large dark eyes were full of innocence and every time he looked into them, the brown irises engulfed him. She was a beauty, her small frame voluptuous and curvy.

Suddenly, she opened the door. She must have heard him there, leaning in the dark coolness of the night.

"You are back," she whispered.

"Yes," he replied, feeling foolish for answering the obvious.

For the first time in the past six weeks since their marriage, she smiled at him, and with that small gesture Braedynn knew he had lost. He would not be able to resist her. She gently took his hand, and urged him to sit on the small cot that was their bed. Elevated by a ledge built into the room like a daybed, it was much better than the ground. She handed him the meal she usually saved for him. It was not much, she was not a cook, but it was appreciated after a long day of fixing fences and tending to the new livestock.

There was silence between them for some time and she sat quietly as they usually did when they dined. Salha broke the silence first.

"Thank you Braedynn," she said, "for calming me this morning." She was blushing, which made her even more endearing.

He nodded, unsure of what to say. Braedynn ate quietly and the two of them sat there, until he realized the quiet became awkward. She sat next to him with her hands in her lap. She had not eaten much, probably since she was anxious about her sister. He paused from his eating.

"For what it is worth, the males who took Samira are from an honourable species. It is unlike their kind to be cruel. They do not keep human slaves in Zatian." Braedynn hoped his words would give her some peace.

Her eyes lit up. "Do you mean that? Will she be all right?"

"I cannot say for sure if she will be all right, but I meant what I said Salha, I will help you get her back. We won't need to stay here much longer." He wanted to bite his tongue for adding the last part. Her brow furrowed at his words.

"But how?" she asked. Braedynn felt as though he had already said too much. He did not want to reveal details before it was necessary.

"I will be leaving. I will bring you with me. You can decide what you want to do then." He had to tell her the truth. He would just leave out a large part of it, the details she did not need to know.

Sensing that he would not elaborate more, she simply said, "thank you," gently squeezing his hand and then releasing it before laying down to rest.

Braedynn's heart pounded. For the first time in a long time, he felt flustered, emotional. He glanced down at Salha as her eyes closed. He leaned down and kissed her cheek softly, the corners of her mouth quirked up in a smile.

She was exhausted from crying, drained emotionally from her loss. She needed the sleep to recuperate.

ARKSON GREW RESTLESS as he waited for the human to return. He wondered how long it would take for her to be ready and then realized that he was beginning to be hungry. He had signed off on the returning documents for negotiating the newest treaties with King Guedan. He was angered by the demands, which were increasingly callous, and had diverted his attention to the newest import of weaponry for his guards.

He suddenly felt anxious about being away from her, for too long. He decided that he would go to the dinner hall. When he arrived there to see that she was yet to dine, he decided to have the cooks prepare a small banquet that he could invite the riders who had helped him with the human that day and introduce his new guest to his uncle.

As the chefs appeared before him they asked graciously, "what would our majesty care to dine upon this afternoon?"

Arkson opened his mouth to speak and then realized he had no idea what his guest ate. His exposure to the human race in Arzule had been limited to his childhood, and some of that had been so long ago he could vaguely recall the details. "Prepare an assortment," he instructed the chefs.

A bit baffled by this uncustomary request they looked at one another and simply answered, "as you wish."

Arkson turned to see his uncle in the waiting.

"My son," he said as he bowed his head. Veros had wondered if the rumours were true, if his nephew had found a female human and brought her to the palace. The whole city seemed joyful, and hopeful that their curse would be lifted. While others in the royal court, some of the guards and a few of the statesmen were aghast by the prince's actions and began to wonder if this silly cure really could be true.

"What do we celebrate tonight?" He asked, Arkson eagerly awaiting his answer.

Arkson looked pensive at the question, a bit pained even though he could see hope in his uncle's eyes.

"Hope," he said simply, "tonight we celebrate hope, will you gather the guards who assisted today in the trip to Uri for the supper?"

"Yes, of course" Veros replied.

"Good," Arkson said before ensuring that he made it clear Veros was to attend this special supper as well. His uncle chuckled as he left, hoping that his nephew had not jumped too quickly into a celebration when there was much more to come.

As Sammie dried herself with a large, blue towel, big enough to wrap around herself twice, Brunelda unwrapped the garments which had been boxed for her to wear. As she unveiled the clothes, Sammie admired the beautiful colours of mauve and lavender with gold stitching and ivory lace and then grew concerned when she realized that the top was missing any fabric to cover the stomach. It looked more like a bra than a shirt.

"What is that?" She asked Brunelda, who catching the fear in her voice, chuckled softly and said, "it is what young beautiful women in Zatian wear."

"I'd rather be wearing what you're wearing," she replied, which made Brunelda laugh even more.

"Here." She gestured for Sammie to come closer. "I will help you put it on." The garment came in two parts, the top looked like something Xena Warrior Princess would wear, and made her nostalgic for the days when she would sit on her couch in sweats and watch back to back episodes of Lucy Lawless kicking ass.

It was basically two cups of a gold brassiere, ornately held together by crisscrossing gold straps and clasped in the front beneath a large purple jewel that she reasoned could not make her cleavage any more noticeable. Sammie was suddenly very aware of her breasts and felt embarrassed by the attention the top called to them. The skirt on the other hand was a bit better, there was far more fabric and the top part of it was a gold belt which sat comfortably between her hips and waist. Large strips of mauve and lavender fabric resembling chiffon fell from the waist band, and although there were high slits on either side of her legs, she at least felt like her bum would not fall out at any moment, although apparently the Akori went commando, so she had that to worry about too.

"I feel naked," she said aloud to Brunelda.

"Aah," Brunelda said, waving a finger in the air, "I forgot these." She pulled out an ornate set of amethyst and black pearls set in gold, the whole thing reminded Sammie of Bollywood jewellery and as Brunelda clasped the necklace around her neck and she finished placing the last earring in her ear, she wondered how on earth she had gotten to where she was standing. Last night she had been a slave and now, she looked almost human again, like a princess even.

Brunelda seeing the delight in her eyes smiled and said, "oh, but we aren't finished yet, we have to do your hair and eyes."

Sammie finally let a smile from her lips, which quickly faded as a rumble escaped from her stomach. She had forgotten how hungry she was and at least that was a blessing for a little while.

Brunelda looked at her apologetically. "Goodness, I forgot to give you this to keep you from fainting."

She handed Sammie a small red apple. Sammie bit into it eagerly biting off three chunks at a time, and relishing in the crisp slosh of the apple juices.

Brunelda had pulled out a small golden device which looked something like a large pair of tweezers and Sammie suddenly wondered if she was going to get plucked. To her surprise, Brunelda flicked a switch lighting up a glowing blue band on it and began running it through her hair. Sammie looked at it amazed realizing it was straightening her waved locks. Brunelda's eyes met hers once again and as if she had forgotten something else, she stopped and then asked, "what is your name?"

Sammie's heart almost stopped. It had been so long since she had said it she wondered if the word would sound foreign on her tongue. "Samira," she replied. She hesitated but continued, "you can call me Sammie though."

"Samira," Brunelda repeated, "that is a lovely name."

As she finished Sammie's hair, she pulled out a tin with black powder in it and applied the eyeliner to Sammie's eyes. When Brunelda had finished Sammie looked at herself in the mirror one last time, shocked, by what she saw, she realized, she actually looked like a woman.

SALHA WAS IN THE mountains. She had no idea where, or why, or how she had even found her way there but there were snow-capped boulders ejecting high into the sky before her and the sound of a stream trickling somewhere behind her a distance away. She was warm though, covered in a long woven blanket and standing in front of a fire. Where was Braedynn?

She looked around concerned. He was her protector, never seeming to be too far. She had not seen a place anything like this anywhere else in Arzule and although she had not seen much of the world, it reminded her of the type of cabin she would find in rural Nova Scotia. The rich wood looked almost lacquered and evergreens were planted around the yard. She would need to inspect it further. As she crept closer, she could hear a voice singing softly.

There was a woman leaning over a crib, and a man walking across the room towards her. The man gently ran a hand through her dark, long hair which curled loosely down her back. Salha was warmed by witnessing the moment. They were a family and clearly happy. The woman spoke something softly, muffled by the glass pane, but the voice seemed familiar, and striking a chord with her, Salha had a lurking feeling she knew her.

The man held the woman in an embrace both of their heads tilted towards the crib. His dark hair hung around his shoulders fell forward covering his eyes as his gaze met the woman, and as he tilted the woman's face upward Salha's mouth fell open in disbelief.

It was her! She was the woman! Her hair left natural

looked alien to her, and as the man leaned down to kiss her, Sal's heart hammered sickly. That wasn't Braedynn! Braedynn had blonde hair and was tanned and was her husband! Where was he?

Reviving herself, she finally broke from shock and hit an open palm against the glass in protest. Rattling the window she continued, this time with her fist banging against it loudly. The man looked up, displeased, and Salha was horrified. His face was darkened, there's wasn't enough light to make out any detail except for his pale blue eyes. They were all she could see as they pierced into her and fear seized her when she realized he was moving towards her, rapidly. The man was walking steadily across the room as though he might walk right through the wall. Her legs were like jelly and she was unable to move. Where was Braedynn? He would help her. He had to be somewhere nearby.

"Braedynn!" she screamed.

She felt warm hands pulling her up and her eyes opened. He was there, Braedynn, was here, with her, and she was in his arms. She had been asleep.

"You all right Salha?" he asked, hiding his entertainment that his name had escaped her lips mid-sleep. She nodded and he was about to make a remark but then he recognized her unease and grew more attentive.

"I couldn't find you," she whispered.

"I'm here," he said to her as she let him pull her against him in an embrace.

"I know," she replied, her heart pounding from the dream.

CHAPTER 9

Eric felt a little hopeless. He had called Salha for the past ten weeks straight to no avail.

Only once he had reached an unrecognizable female voice, and then it had answered the phone only to bark at him "There is no person by that name who lives here, do not call again."

He had been to Salha's apartment that very morning and pounded on the door for ten minutes straight before anyone answered. He could hear movement through the door, yelling at Salha that he knew she was there. At that point he had just wanted to see her face and storm off. Finally, when she opened up he was taken aback. It was not Salha or Sammie as he had suspected, but a tall woman with long dark hair and green tattoos on her neck and forearm. Her eyes were a piercing green and he felt shaken to the core, embarrassed that he had not only gone there, but was clearly gawking at the woman in the Khan sisters' apartment. All of their things were there, but they were clearly not.

"Where are Salha and Sammie?" he asked.

"Not here, obviously," she examined him closely, "they are gone," she continued softening a little.

"Where?" Eric asked again, concerned. It was not like them to just pick up and leave, especially not for three months.

"Beats me," Nikelda replied, recalling the expression Alexandros had used countless times.

"What do you mea–" he began to ask before she slammed the door in his face.

AND NOW EIGHT HOURS later sitting at the cafe trying to sober up after an afternoon of drinking with his buddies, he was nursing an extra large black coffee, which seemed to be cooling far more quickly than he would like. The pear tartlet he had ordered had hardly been touched and for a man with a sweet tooth that was rare.

It was the woman at the apartment that he could not get out of his mind. She was attractive. Far more attractive than he cared to admit, especially since he had been so adamant about getting back together with Salha after being apart for a month or two, and now suddenly that seemed so unnecessary. He could not remember why he had bothered calling her all this time. Sal had only been honest with him, had broken up with him for obvious reasons.

"I'm not the one for you," she had said, "you're not sure about me, and I am not waiting around to find out if you're going to settle. Sammie's right Eric, I should never settle for anything in my life, when I know what I want, when I am capable of more."

Of course Samira had been right, she was right about so many things, whether people listened to her or not was another story, but Sal's sister had an uncanny way of being predictive about these things. She knew things before they happened, but only because she paid attention, understood people. She understood Eric better than he knew himself and initially when they had met he had found her attractive.

It wasn't until Salha had pranced into the cafe that he realized what Samira meant when she said to him that they would make better friends. Yet her sister was captivating. Salha had the most adorable face he had ever seen, but she was only fun, someone fun to pass the time with, to go out and to go on adventures. He could not picture himself with her forever and ever. Felt nervous anytime she mentioned something serious between them. Eric felt like he was being an ass. He had been. Salha was great to him.

He was about to get up and leave when another patron walked in the door and he looked up. It was her. It was the woman from Salha's apartment, but she looked different now, she had the same green tattoos on her neck and arms but her long brown hair had been cut to her shoulder and was now a dark blonde. If it were possible, she looked even more striking. And she looked through him quickly before realizing he was staring straight at her.

He waved. It was stupid. It was impulsive, and he felt like a chump. Especially when she frowned and sighed before walking over.

"So you're Arik?" she said, pronouncing his name like she was European, her eyes narrowing on him.

"Yes," he replied, "and you are?" He motioned for her to sit with him and she did.

"No one of importance." One of the staff noticing her arrival, stopped by to take her order. He was a young man, probably in his early twenties, and the way he looked at her, Eric wanted to punch his lights out. The kid had long stringy black hair, and several parts of his face were pierced but rather than find that deterring it was almost as if she were more amused by him.

The kid flirted with her. "May I take your order?"

"What would you recommend?" She asked him her

eyes examining him thoughtfully.

"For someone as lovely as yourself," he said with a charming smile, "I would recommend the blueberry pie with our house blend of coffee."

"Thank you," she said and nodded in approval and he walked away slowly, looking back over his shoulder once, before ducking under the counter.

She smiled! She actually smiled and Eric felt suddenly flushed, his cheeks burned from her beauty. Her eyes returned to him and the smile faded quickly.

"You should stop bothering the one you call Salha," she said to him moving the position of the vase on the table so that it was out of their line of sight.

"Did she tell you to say that?" He asked.

"No," she replied honestly, "what happened between you?"

Eric hesitated, he didn't know what Sal had told her already and did not want to lie and say that he had broken up with her to save face. So instead he played the diplomat. "We ended our relationship."

Nikelda examined him a for a few seconds trying to decipher if he spoke the truth. "She ended it with you, you mean to say."

"She told you?" He asked somewhere between hurt and offended.

"No," she replied again, "but I can tell."

They were interrupted by the waiter returning, and if Eric had wanted to hit him before, now he wanted to strangle him. Rather than leaving the food and walking away, he started a conversation with the woman. A conversation that went on for several minutes before his co-worker called him to assist with something in the stock room.

Nikelda smiled mischievously, "he reminds me of my brother," she said a hint of sadness revealed through her tone.

Eric's jaw clenched. This was unbelievable. "You flirt with your brother?" He asked his eyes growing cold.

Nikelda's eyes shimmered for a moment amused. "Jealousy is not becoming of you."

"I'm not jealous." Eric spoke flatly.

Nikelda shrugged.

"Where are Salha and Sammie?" He asked more determined this time to find out their whereabouts.

"I told you already, they've left for a little while," she said pursing her lips.

"On a vacation you mean?" He asked her.

She looked confused. The fork in her hand paused mid-motion.

"Never mind," he said frustrated, "where are they? They wouldn't leave without telling me."

She sat there eating her pie for a few minutes, until angrily he cleared his throat and tilted his head forward looking at her expectedly.

"They've gone far far away," she said her mischievousness reappearing.

"Next you're going to tell me they're in a fairytale kingdom," he said annoyed with her mystery.

"Perhaps," she said and then put her fork down finished with her pie, "what do you want from Salha, Arik?"

"It's Er-ic," he replied rudely, "and I want to make sure she is okay. I want to speak with her."

"She is fine Air-rick," she said attempting to sound closer phonetically. Then she did something odd, she looked out of the window at the moon, "and she should be returning soon."

That is if she's not the one my brother chooses.

"If you want I'll be returning to far far away in several weeks, you may join me if you like, then you can see for yourself that they indeed went on a..." she paused recalling the word, "vacation." Her eyes were lovely as they looked at him, enchanting and for a second he thought she might be flirting with him.

"I...I..." he stammered.

She smiled again, men here were so interesting. Drinking the last bit of her coffee she placed the cup back on the table.

"Thank you for your company," she said getting up and leaving some money and a cute little bunny drawing for the waiter.

NIKELDA WALKED OUT OF the cafe feeling strangely elated. She had spent little time with humans since her arrival in Halifax, and despite her misgivings about the nature of Eric's character, she found him adorable. She could see why Salha had spent time with him.

He was handsome. His sandy brown hair was cut short and close to his head, and his eyes a deep grey were filled with expression and worry and compassion. His presence was emphasized by his shoulders and his muscular arms stood out against the dark blue of his short sleeved shirt, but muscles didn't appeal to her though, what she found most striking about him was the honesty to him. His hands had flittered around in frustration as he had spoke with her. They looked soft, not calloused and scarred, and his palms led to long refined fingers. Hands that she wanted to touch, to comfort, to calm.

He had been drinking, that much she could tell, but he was still composed, more morose than anything. She sensed his worry about the sisters and his need to ensure they were alright. He might seem an annoyance but his heart was truly in the right place. Then he had even flickered feelings of desire for her, something she had not expected. Something that hit her with an unexpected twinge of tenderness.

Like her brother, it had been a long time since she had companionship. She had more suitors than her fill, but no one she had wanted to be with since Farloom. Her last companion had been an Akori from the city of Sathan, a colony of King Guedan. He was a politician who was plotting against the despicable king, but he had been taken from her. After she had returned from one of their sojourns, she had learned he had been apprehended and held captive in Guedan's infamous Hall of Bridione. The king kept his prisoners there, made an example of the Akorians who stood against him. She had found out what happened to him, begged Arkson to help her infiltrate the city of Alpohalla to find him.

It was too late though, like so many others he had been tortured and killed, before she could mate with him, before their lives together had even started. It had been a little over two years since his death, but he had stayed in her thoughts. What she missed most was his sonorous laugh, a laugh that had always echoed richly on her skin leaving goosebumps.

Now she was alone. She missed Arkson's lectures on the importance of her choosing another Akori with which to mate. She was a princess, a leader of her people, and she needed to live her life fully. She wanted to, but how could she? How could she marry and have children knowing that her brother remained alone? It would just do further injury to him that she sensed he could not endure. He would adore nieces and nephews, but then crave children of his own. She was alone now, but she did not want to stay that way. She knew that soon, once Arkson had found his beloved, she too would find her own.

CHAPTER 10

Arkson glanced at the shadow clock, he had been waiting for *her* for three hours and twenty minutes. And his company who had arrived a few minutes before, were already restless and ready to eat. He was nervous even though he dared not show it; to everyone in the room he appeared his usual self, calm, collected, and emotionally detached. It was the way he always seemed to them, and the way he usually felt.

Yet, there was something about the human that made him wonder if she might change him, if he would finally be able to lift the burden he bore to lead his people to victory. It had been decades since he had been cursed. He held the burden since the day it had happened, and now there was a chance that he might find a mate, that he could marry like most of his guards and his uncle. He would be relieved of his outcast status.

For a male Akori, marriage was the ultimate symbol of prosperity and achievement, if you could be mated and find a wife, then you were among the successful males of your people. As a prince to have spent the last decade alone, to pass the prime age of marrying, it was a sin and a sad event that so few rarely had endured. It was the reason he was yet to be crowned king. And as he looked over to the shadow clock one more time to see how much more time had passed. The doors to the hall opened, and there she was, *his* human.

As the room quieted Sammie felt like a deer caught in headlights. The banquet hall was beautiful, its walls a warm spice colour and was divided by a long, large, dark, wooden table lined with candelabras, white china, gold rimmed stemware, and red and orange flower bouquets. The table was filled with the riders who had accompanied the prince on his journey today as well as a few other Akori that she did not recognize. Their eyes were all on her as they stood, waiting for her to be seated at the dinner table. Had they been waiting all this time? She felt even more anxious. She hated to keep people waiting.

Brunelda had helped her rub a minty ointment onto her twisted ankle after her bath, and within minutes it had healed. She was grateful she did not have to limp around anymore, but she had wished that Brunelda would have mentioned that over half a dozen males would be dining with her that evening. Especially since she had informed Sammie that she would be eating with the prince. Even more, she wished Brunelda had given her a scarf or a jacket so that she could wrap it over her chest and stomach. Thankfully Brunelda had at least whispered in her ear that she should sit directly across from the prince at the very end of the table, before she walked over, and whispered something to him and left the hall.

Sammie drew in a ragged breath as she approached the table and was grateful when an older guest she did not recognize, but who looked remarkably like an older version of the prince, save for the shorter, grey hair, pulled out her seat and motioned for her to sit down. As she sat, she stopped herself from looking afraid, instead she wore no expression, hoping that the guests would continue conversing, and luckily, they did.

Arkson felt mesmerized the moment she had entered the room, she was far more beautiful than he had imagined and she looked good enough to eat in the dress he had picked for her. With each step her hips sashayed against the fabric, drawing attention to the curve of her waist, and the look of the gold necklace lightly biting into her flesh made him envious of the object resting just above her breasts. Her legs looked smooth and glimmered in the light and he ached to remove her sandals and run his hands along the length of them to her thighs. Arkson was drawn to her dark eyes, mysterious and beautifully captivating. Her long black hair hung silken, neatly tucked to one side behind her ear with a decorative comb. He cursed himself for not arranging a dinner for them alone, but he knew there would be time for that still. He wanted time for them to speak and get to know one another. He wanted time to learn her heart. His desire frightened him a little more than he would let on. He wanted to control himself before he drove her away. She already seemed so resistant to him but he was hungry, and it wasn't only for food.

The cooks entered the room explaining the meal they had prepared for the party and then bowed before leaving as a procession of servants brought out dishes filled with lemon garnished fish, a multitude of cooked and mashed vegetables, roasted savoury poultry, spiced stews and curries, and fresh baked bread.

Samira's mouth watered looking at everything and though she was tempted to only stick to the things she recognized, she was so used to starving that she did not care what she ate. As the dishes were passed around she took a little of everything until the mashed potatoes were passed over to her she scooped up a pile gently placing it on her plate.

The guest next to her, who she came to learn was Veros, Arkson's uncle was about to remove the bowl when she broke her silence and said, "please wait."

She grabbed another huge spoonful covering whatever clear space there was on her plate. Arkson's eyes zoned in on her expressionless, yet she felt like a bug squirming beneath a microscope.

"I like potatoes," she said to Veros, grateful that the other company still conversed. He smiled at her. Two and a half hours later, after a variety of desserts, pastries, cookies, custards, and cakes were removed from her sight, she thought she might explode. At least none of the riders gawked at her from the amount she ate, although she was certain that she may have eaten more food than a few of them. If this were to be her last meal, she figured she would at least die sated and happy.

Sammie could feel the prince's green eyes return to her almost rhythmically throughout the night and as the last course finished she had not expected him to instruct her to stay as the other Akori left and bid him well. She sat waiting for another servant to enter the room and take her elsewhere so that he might be left alone.

It was only when he rose from the table and motioned for everyone else to leave, the servants gathering the chairs, that she felt she suddenly thought about why he had brought her there, and in fear, she contemplated what she might become — the prince's concubine.

"You must be tired Samira." He said as he leaned against the table, cleared of its chairs and dinnerware, it looked empty solemn. He looked at her wistfully, his dark hair falling forward into his eyes before he brushed it back.

Startled to hear her name she looked up at him and began to ask, "how do you..." before she remembered that

Brunelda had whispered something to him before they dined. It had to have been her name.

"I am tired," she said.

"Will you walk with me?" He asked. He looked at her commandingly even though he posed a question. She wondered where he might take her and suddenly felt panicked and sickened. She did not want to go anywhere with him alone. Sensing her emotions he held his hand out to her in a gesture he hoped would comfort her. She stared at it.

"No," she said coldly.

He frowned and withdrew his hand. It was not a word he was used to hearing. He did not understand why she would decline.

"What do you want?" She asked him.

He looked at her pensive, a little surprised. "What do you mean?"

"Why did you dress me in this?"

He looked insulted. "You do not like the dress?" He spoke slowly, each word enunciated in disbelief and gazed at her thinking to himself.

I thought she looked lovely.

"No I do not like," she said gesturing to her stomach, "where is the rest of it? " He did not comprehend her tone, was annoyed that she was so ungrateful for some of the finest clothing that could be found in the kingdom.

"*That* is customary for my people hu-*man*," His eyes narrowed.

"And *I* expect nothing of you." He turned to leave.

She felt furious and got up from where she sat, he could not just treat her like a subservient creature, she was tired of it, "then why go through the trouble of bringing me here, I might just be a lowly human to you, but I am supposed to be freed now. Why keep me here against my will?"

He shot her a look of pure contempt. She dared raise her voice at him.

"Did you ask your former master this many questions?" He asked, wondering what made her so belligerent. Sammie suddenly felt a tinge of fear, but she observed him, nothing about him suggested violence. She wondered if he might be the type to snap quickly. She was too afraid of being used though, too concerned with being treated like a possession. She never wanted to be a slave again.

"That question implies that you're now my master. I thought I was a guest," she spoke heatedly.

"You are a guest." He replied, "a very disrespectful one."

"Disrespectful because I won't blindly follow your instructions like a slave?" She threw back at him.

"Stop interpreting what you want out of this conversation." He replied angrily.

"I refuse to be your slave!" She shouted. "I would rather die!"

"That can be arranged." He said coldly. She visibly cringed a little and he regretted his verbal outburst. It was so unlike him to lose his temper.

"If you're polite," he said sternly "you might live." He held his hand out to her again, her body grew rigid.

"I refuse to be your concubine," she said lowly, the words spilling out despite reining her emotions inward.

His look sharpened, as if she had insulted him further.

"Concubine!?" He repeated loudly. He clenched his jaw, and his eyes looked afire. His body straightened, "I am a prince, not a sailor or mercenary moving from city to city pillaging what he wants. If I wanted you in my bed you would be there now, not sitting here ungratefully throwing a tantrum."

With that he walked out of the room and she sat there

a little stunned, her ears burning. Had she been ungrateful? Did she misread the way he looked at her? Maybe he wanted nothing to do with her at all, but then why suggest a walk? It did not matter, within a few minutes, Brunelda entered the room, and lead her to her chamber on the other side of the palace, far from where the prince himself spent the night in slumber.

Thank goodness for that.

Concubine!? Arkson thought as he returned to his cold chamber. His mind raced. What had he done to give her the impression that he merely wanted to bed her? He knew that he had glanced at her with a little desire in his eyes.

Yes!

But he took no action against her! He had merely asked her to walk with him on a stroll in the garden. He realized she would seem uneasy about the privacy between them, but what other way would he get to know her.

What prince would take advantage of his subject in such a manner and selfishly cede to his bodily hunger? He practised his swordsmanship repetitively to try and calm himself. He would never seduce her heartlessly! Or would he?

No!

He hadn't before, and wouldn't now. Yes, the way that she looked was enticing, and it had been a while since he last feasted on a female. She was tempting, but she was different, capable of giving him what he had always wanted. Even though he had wanted her, he would never force her to do what she didn't want. Could she sense the draw of his desperation perhaps? Was he desperate? The thought disgusted him.

He felt angered by her insolence and her brazen words. She would rather die, she had said to him. How could he win her over if she held such strong and negative feelings for him? Perhaps they were very different beings, he thought. After all it was clear she was not from Arzule. She did not act the way humans did there, she was more like Alexandros, his childhood friend, who had come to Zatian with his mother Kae.

He and Alexandros had been so close, but he could not remember how that came to be. Then again, they were children. Children are innocent; they play. How would he ever communicate to her clearly? He pondered what could be done to mend their argument, and as his anger subsided, he felt a little hopeless.

Arkson thought of his sister Nikelda, she would know exactly what to do in a situation such as this. She could have been an ambassador of sorts for Arkson. Had she been there, he knew that she would have befriended Samira, would have made this easier for him. He was not used to needing to be so strategic with females, usually if he wanted something he was respectful, but aggressive and found a way to make it his own.

With Samira he could tell he would have to try a different approach, controlling the situation would be harder, especially where she was so intelligent. He appreciated the challenge, her manner was admirable, but wanted it to be a little easier. He would have to approach her in a way that made her feel more his equal. He stopped with his jutting actions and finally calmed. He had to rest, tomorrow would be another day, and hopefully they could both put the past behind them.

Brunelda opened the large wooden door to the chamber, the room, which Sammie expected to be more like servants quarters, was far grander than she had ever seen. It was a large room that had the same beige stucco walls as the remainder of the palace.

The left wall had two large armoires with a vanity neatly tucked between them, and in the middle of the room was a large four poster bed with an ornate crimson bedspread and overhead cover that flowed down to curtains. It was all embroidered with the same blues and purples found elsewhere in the palace. There was a roaring fireplace on the far right wall of the room, and next to it a crimson chaise in front of a bookshelf lined with books. Past the bed there was a wall of glass windows with a door that looked like it lead to a balcony. Sammie sucked in her breath appreciatively.

Brunelda crossed the room to a wardrobe and pulled out a long white tunic for Sammie to wear to sleep. "Must have been some strong words between you and the prince for him to send you all the way over here," she said chuckling lightly.

"Is this the unwanted side of the palace?" Sammie asked ironically.

Brunelda puffed her chest out and in a masculine voice said "'Get that human out of my sight' he says to me," and she laughed, "I've never seem him so affected. It's unlike his nature really. He's the calm one in the royal sort, not like his father and sister."

Sammie was curious. "Really? So he is generally even tempered?" She wondered.

"Oh yesserie *whelan*, Arkson's the kindest prince yet. He's a cold little bugger to the nobles but he's always so even tempered. He's a proper Akori really, congenial with his company of guards. Yet, he's suffered enough from his blazing father. Oh that Akori had the fire in him, passed it on to his son too." She shook her head sadly.

"But it was him who got us in to our predicament, not Arkson." Brunelda froze as if she caught herself saying something she should not have.

"Predicament?" Sammie asked. Brunelda waived her

hand lightly.

"Oh never you mind Sammie," Brunelda said calling her by her nickname for the first time, "be off to sleep, you must be tired. I will return in the morning to fetch you for breakfast," and with that she left.

Yet Sammie was not ready to sleep, her body, anxious and overtired, could not relax. She missed her sister, was in a new and strange place, and her mind was overwhelmed. She tried to think of a plan, but nothing seemed to make sense. The words felt all jumbled and incoherent and she wondered if she had ate too much. She lay in bed restless until she nodded off to sleep.

A FEW HOURS LATER she awoke, and unable to sleep she got up out of bed and lit a candle. She walked over to the bookcase with it in hand and carefully read the spines of the covers. The coarse texture of the books were dry and crinkled and reminded her of the old fairy tale hardcovers in her apartment. She missed her apartment, it was cozy and filled with all the things she loved, her books, her music, her cameras. She sighed.

A glint of light through the glass caught her eye and she walked over to the door staring in awe at a beautiful shower of comets in the sky. She opened the door, wondering how cold it would be on the balcony and finding the weather like a warm summer night, walked out to get a better look.

Her eyes were captivated by the balls of fire falling from the sky streaking shades of blues, reds and purples in melding swirls. It reminded her of Van Gogh's *Starry Night*. The depth of colour soaked into her and warmed her heart with excitement. This was amazing, she'd never seen anything so vast.

"Beautiful," she whispered, not knowing why she was so quiet when no one else was around.

"Not as beautiful as you," she heard from behind her.

She turned startled to see Prince Arkson behind her, leaning in the door frame. She was surprised by his presence and took in a deep breath.

He looked like a god to Samira. He was so handsome, standing shirtless in a pair of black drawstring pants. They were pants that hung low across a deeply cut hipbone of pure muscular beauty. They were pants that hinted at the strength of his thighs since they clung there and then fell loosely further down the length of his legs.

Oh yum!

Samira took in another deep breath. Around his neck, he wore a black leather pendant. It dropped down over his incredible chest and highlighted the way his broad shoulders tapered to washboard abs. He stood, sexily accented by the light of the night sky. The changing colours highlighted the rugged beauty of his face. She stood there wondering what he was doing there and examined his face for gestures that would betray his thoughts. She was curious, nervous. He had just said she was beautiful.

His eyes intensified gazing at her rawly and they travelled over her body covered by the white button down tunic. Its material was sheer from the moonlight and revealed her curvaceous frame beneath. He relished the look of her chest as it rose and fell with each breath. Her long dark hair was scattered by the gentle breeze. She looked wild, was a challenge he wanted to captivate.

Samira wondered what he would do, suddenly anxious and roused by his sensual look. Her lips quivered and the movement drew his eyes there, made him crave a taste of her. He walked over to her stopping centimetres from her body. She looked up at him with dark eyes, widened ardently and searching his face for meaning. Arkson smiled.

Before Sammie could move, or say anything she

watched him brushed her hair back and cupped her face with his palm, pulling her into a deeply passionate kiss. His mouth met hers delicately despite the power of his actions in drawing her near. He was gentle as he wrapped his arm around her waist. So gentle that she melted into the hard steel of him returning the kiss, and garnered a deep moan from his throat.

They were sweet, successive kisses. Kisses that made her blush as she returned them. His lips grew more firm against hers, more demanding and filled with need.
Her knees grew weak when his tongue slid along the seam of her mouth. He was nibbling her bottom lip and waiting for her to open her mouth to him, so she did. He kissed her more intensely, his tongue delicately stroking her own, before he pulled her against him. The heat from his body warmed her body, her hands were almost scorching.

Oh my goodness.

His mouth was locked on hers while his tongue was making her inflamed with its searing exploration. Boy did he know how to kiss.

This is too good.

He stopped for a moment to look at her before he kissed her again firmly and as his arms wrapped around her body pulling her even closer to fit his body perfectly, she felt light headed and realized what she was doing. She pulled away from him turning her back to him and breathed deeply, trying to calm herself from the passion she had just felt. The fire in her lips, in her heart, left her burning and uncomfortable. Instead of turning her back around to face him, he enveloped her body with his own, wrapping his strong arms around her shoulders, while he nuzzled her neck.

"What do you want?" She asked him without looking at him.

He tilted her face sideways, up to his and said softly, "I

want you."

CHAPTER 11

SALHA NESTLED A BIT closer to Braedynn. She was still unable to sleep, had been too frightened from the weighted feeling in her dream. It was almost the middle of the night and she felt badly for keeping Braedynn awake when she knew he would work early the same as always the next morning. The cold seemed even more biting knowing that her sister was nowhere nearby. She knew she was not strong like Samira. She was a bit feisty, but in general was accustomed to being dependent on others. She had been sheltered by her family from the harshness outside of her little world, and for the first time she was starting to wish they hadn't.

Her eyes were heavy but her mind was unable to rest. He had asked her what she had dreamed and embarrassed she didn't elaborate. So instead they had both remained quiet for some time until at last he told her about his mother. As they lay in bed with his fingers entwined in her long curly hair, the red colour from it fading, he enjoyed her company and felt like telling her something about himself that would bridge the gap between them.

"She was beautiful," he said softly. "She had the most exciting energy to her, like she always craved excitement and adventure, and she took me everywhere with her. On every adventure, to each new place, we went together."

She smiled sweetly as he told her what their life was like before she died in his childhood. It sounded as though they had quite the nomadic life, travelling from city to city, uncovering rare treasures in locations and people.

She felt safe with him, was comforted by the companionship he offered her that came without a price. He did not seem to expect anything from her, as other men often had. He opened up to her freely, held her like a friend might. Not once had he taken advantage of her trust when she slept beside him. Not even during their conversing that night did he try to seduce her, despite that he had kissed her that very day.

He told her about living in the city of Kalapan, it was a few days journey from Uri. He explained that he had moved there after his mother had passed. When he was a teenager he had wanted to explore the world on his own and so he had left the place of their home.

He elaborated about how he had been a blacksmith in Kalapan and had been lucky to be taken in through apprenticeship and adopted to a family. His people were doing well for themselves when the storm riders from the southern deserts had come through the village.

"What happened?" She asked him looking up at him.

"The day seemed like any other," he began, "we could hear the sounds of the riders coming from over the hills, the rocks on the ground trembled, and we knew in the village that something awful was coming, that there would be too many of them." His face was lined with pain.

"But how could your village have known what would have happened," she asked.

"There were rumours of war. There were always rumours of skirmishes with travellers," he answered, "but we suspected it would be a legitimate battle, not a raid to use us as resources. Especially since we were a settlement, a town full of people. When the rumbling came we sent the younger men, and as many women and children we could to the mountains in hiding. The rest hid in the church, in the caves built beneath for protection."

"You stayed behind," she said, touching his chest lightly.

He looked up at the ceiling as he spoke, detached, remembering the fight. There were hundreds of men who were killed on the plain before the city. The grass was stained red, the soil clumped from blood. "Most of the surviving men had been rounded up like cattle and sold to slave traders, but the traders who were a mix of Anuyan and Batchi, another ruthless species in Arzule, did not realize how fragile humans were in comparison and killed too many of their captives through beatings."

"I'm so sorry Braedynn." Her face pinched in pain for him. "All of your people."

"I tried to free those that I could," he said to her, leaving out the part that he had used his powers, fought alone against hundreds while some of his men were slain. He had managed to save as many people as were now populating the mountains.

Yet, during the fight he had been overpowered, knocked unconscious and dragged to a Batchi township, away from the other slaves. When he awoke in the night, he went on a rampage and killed his captors, burning fires in the night and causing havoc for the Batchi while he escaped to the mountains outside of the Kalapan.

"Then you were brought here," she said.

He could not bring himself to lie to her, so he did not answer.

"You need rest Salha." He pulled her closer and brushed her forehead rhythmically to ease her, but she felt as though she should be comforting him. They had both experienced loss.

Since their village had been taken so easily the Batchi scouts they set out for the other human villages and within five years the human population on Arzule had gone from hundreds of thousands to just hundreds. Their numbers were rapidly decreasing by the day.

Even though Braedynn despised Thussan, his collection of human artifacts was at least one comforting reminder that there was something to show for his kind in Arzule. He hoped that one day the human population would be able to rebuild. He knew that humans needed time to rebuild, and Thussan's ideas of reviving their numbers would help, Braedynn just did not want them to be a society of slaves.

He had allowed himself to be taken by Thussan for motives his own and though he trusted Salha, he was not yet ready to reveal the truth to her. In the meantime, he tolerated Thussan who seemed to look at them as though they were an experiment. He disliked how Thussan constantly made notations on their behaviours, but he supposed his ignorance would have to remain overlooked.

Braedynn never feared Thussan and Salha did not understand the source of his courage. Salha had been thankful that Thussan never yelled at them and hit them so easily as Loward. She had seen so many bruises on her sister that it broke her heart. She wondered where Sammie was now and what was happening to her. She prayed her sister was alive. Her mind had imagined too many horrible things morbidly, and she shook each away terrified that her thoughts might make them true.

Half an hour later, when she finally fell asleep it was in Braedynn's arms. He had helped her calm down, had soothed her.

Braedynn was finishing up the last touches on the map he was drawing for Salha. He had awoke early despite the late night talking with her and decided to get working even though he would rather have stayed sleeping by Salha's side.

Thussan had left them for the day while he took Kalawyn and Haloya to the temple to consecrate their joining, the ceremony was long, twelve hours of chanting, spiritual exchange and then celebrating. For a species who were so quick and dirty about everything else, Braedynn found their marriage rites peculiar.

It would be the perfect opportunity for he and Salha to leave were it not for the fact he had yet to find what he needed. Thussan had only hired two Anuyan guards to watch over his property and it would only take Braedynn a few minutes to take them out. He was frustrated his search the day before had turned up nothing.

He had begun making plans to escape from Thussan the week before, but Sammie's departure had thrown his previous plans off course. He would have needed her help for it to be successful. Every time he looked at Salha now, Braedynn knew she was filled with despair. Samira had always taken care of her, she was all Salha had until her marriage to Braedynn, but there was nothing he could do, not until he found the key to the amulet that Thussan had taken from his people.

So far his searches had turned up nothing, he had uncovered a few other scriptures from the Batchi which might be of use to him in the future. He suspected that Thussan either wore the amulet key on him or kept it somewhere in his bedroom, nothing indicated that it might be kept elsewhere.

Braedynn had wanted to tell Salha about his past

during their talking the night before, all of it. He wanted to let her know about his powers, his mother, his life before Uri, but he felt like the time was not right. He did not even know how to tell her that he was from earth too, that like her he had found himself in Arzule unexpectedly when he was a child.

He and his mother were brought there abruptly. He had been eight when he had arrived. On earth it was 1962, and from what few things Salha described about it now, it was clear things had changed drastically from when he was still there. Life for a human was not the greatest in Arzule, but it was all that he knew, he could not imagine himself going back, even if there was a way.

He felt as though it was a gift that she had been brought to him, no other human in Arzule had understood his sentiments as well as her, his intelligence surpassed them. They did not know how to read or write. It was discouraging that he had tried to educate his people and had been thwarted by the slave traders. He swore to himself that he would never let anything happen to her. And now it was even more important that he protect her, he was all she had.

The morning sky was still dark grey but he took his candle with him and ventured towards the threshold of Thussan's room, luckily it was too dark for the Anuyan guards outside to make out his figure there. So now would be the only way he would know for sure if Thussan kept the key on him or if it was locked away in some hiding place in his room.

The guards could enter the house any time to wake he and Sal up to start their morning work, so he prayed they were still distracted. He had peered out and saw them smoking pipes sitting on the back steps of the house.

Today would not be a good day to die, and he hated the idea of killing them since it would be so unexpected.

They looked like they had families, if they stayed outside then they would surely return to them.

The room was not much, he had actually expected a lot more of Thussan. Except for a bed and a wardrobe and mirror, there was nothing else in the room. The wardrobe looked old though, probably from the early period about seven hundred years past. It was still in one piece, and incredibly ornate. He had seen a few of these before, there was an elaborate locking mechanism with a system of pulls which had to be moved correctly before it opened. If Thussan had anything of value he did not want them to find, it would be hidden here.

Yet Braedynn didn't have time to sit there and fiddle with it, he probably had only a few more minutes. He would have to use his powers and hope that no sage nearby sensed anything. If they did, Thussan might have unexpected visitors and it would make more trouble for he and Salha. Anuyan sages preyed on necromancy since their population had so few with the gift. Like *Primora*, the power could be killed for, and often was.

He closed his eyes placing his hand on the main clasp of the door and envisioned the correct path unlocking the door. Instantly a low click took place and he quickly pulled the door ajar.

There were three boxes on the middle shelf and without having to look through them all, Braedynn knew which one might contain the key. It was his mother's box, lined with mother of pearl and carved of teak. His hand moved over its surface savouring the nostalgic feeling it brought to him. He was tempted to take the whole thing, but if he did it would surely raise Thussan's alarms. He would have to leave it behind, for now.

As he opened it gingerly, the key slid forward, dangling from the brass coloured chain. He let out a sigh of relief. He had found what he had come there for; he had the key.

"What are you doing in here?" A hoarse voice croaked.

He turned ready to strike. Had the body pinned quickly against the door frame before he realized that the body was smaller than his own, that it was soft and feminine. His eyes adjusted in the dark.

"Salha?" he whispered.

She whimpered. Her heart was pounding, shocked by how quickly he had moved. She was trembling.

"I'm sorry," he whispered quietly, smoothing out her hair, "I thought you were a guard"

"We shouldn't be in here," she said quickly rediscovering her voice. She was still waking up. She had dressed quickly in her clothes and apron and gone searching for him when she noticed the bed empty.

Braedynn closed the wardrobe door and grabbed her hand leading her out into the hallway. The guards noticed them coming from an unexpected direction as they left Thussan's room, their eyes met before looking at them suspiciously.

"What were you doing down that hallway slaves?" The taller of the two spoke.

Braedynn's eyes grew dark as navy and he looked at Salha motioning for her to move aside. She spoke before he could hit, placing her hand on his arm.

"Well, I was cleaning Thussan's mirror on that end since he told me to do it while he was away, when my husband... distracted me," she said averting their eyes and making herself blush.

She's brilliant.

Braedynn wanted to kiss her then and there for being so clever, but would the guards believe her? He relaxed his body purposely and shrugged at them. One of the guards broke out into a cackling laugh. The other slapping his knee, keeling over with laughter from her explanation. Braedynn guided her towards the kitchen.

"Well at least they didn't think it was disgusting," she said turning back to look at them, one wiping tears from his eyes.

"Thank you for that," he said to her earnestly.

"I really should be thanking you," she replied with a smile. Salha still had no idea what Braedynn had been doing, but she didn't care. She trusted him, it had to have been something important.

CHAPTER 12

SAMMIE AWOKE HEART pounding. She looked around the room trying to recall where she was, and then remembered the night before. She rubbed her head thinking about her dream, it had not been real, but she could not help noticing that her lips felt a little swollen from Arkson's lavished kisses. She lightly tapped her fingers over them, wondering what would have possessed her mind to make her dream of such things, especially about an Akori who thought himself so clearly above her.

Brunelda knocked at the door before entering with a large smile.

"Good morning Sammie, good to see you rise early. We will beat the crowd," she said cheerfully. Brunelda helped her make the bed and the two of them walked to the second set of baths on her side of the palace. It was busier than the day before but luckily there were only few Akori there and Brunelda had reserved the largest one in the back again for Sammie.

This time when she withdrew her clothing from the

box she was relieved to see it was a one piece dress with three quarter length sleeves. It was as ornately detailed as the garment she wore the night before but in rich forest green and embroidered with silver stitching and pearls. Its sweetheart neckline was still a little low cut, but the body enclosed her stomach and the fabric was not flopping flimsily from the thigh high slits. As she walked out from her bath area, the other females whispered and giggled about her.

She looked at Brunelda a bit confused by the sudden reaction to her. Brunelda simply said, "ignore them."

Sammie assumed they sniggered because she was a human, until a louder girl near the front baths said to her friend, "looks like the human is older than we thought, she wears the robes of an old Akori."

Her friend covered her own mouth trying to stop her laughter and then added, "I would never be caught dead wearing that before the prince. Brunelda should have told her how to win an Akori over. She was a beauty in her day."

Brunelda hearing them gave them a curt look and curled her hand to a fist before she shook it at them. Samira was surprised by Brunelda's action and when the girl moved forward as if to open her mouth again, Brunelda stepped forward waving her hand for the girl to keep her mouth shut.

Sammie was shocked. So the prince had not dressed her to be paraded around like an object. As she walked out of the baths she saw the females lined up outside the baths, the younger ones wore outfits similar to what she had the night before, some with pants others skirts, while the few older Akorians in the bunch donned dresses like hers. Nothing seemed as ornate as any of the clothing she had been given but they were still beautiful. Sammie wondered where they had all been the day before, she did not recall seeing any female but Brunelda and that was only after

Prince Arkson has summoned her.

"Brunelda, where were all the females yesterday?" she asked.

Brunelda smiled, "It was a day of rest for them, each month there are a few days where the females of Zatian may stay home and rest, there are days for the males too, it gives our families time to come together."

"What about you?" Sammie asked, "you're a female?"

Brunelda smiled more brightly. "I am in the prince's service, I may take leave whenever I choose."

"What about myself," she began to ask Brunelda, "I do not work, but am capable. There must be something I could do in the palace."

Brunelda looked at Sammie a little surprised and then shook her head. "Prince Arkson might not like it, he wants you to rest, you have been a slave Sammie."

"He doesn't have to know," Sammie replied, hoping she might be able to convince Brunelda to help her fend for herself.

"I will see what I can do," Brunelda replied with a glint in her eye that suggested she was impressed with Sammie's behaviour.

ARKSON ATE HIS BREAKFAST in the dining hall, but he could think of nothing but the dream. Samira had felt amazing in his arms, her lips had tasted like honey, her body was firm but supple and he wished he had taken the opportunity to decorate her delicious neck with a tantalizing series of kisses.

As she entered the dining hall behind Brunelda, he still found her beautiful, even though she wore the garb of an older female that covered her prudishly. Her dark hair had been pulled off of her face and braided in a long plait, and the colours he had chosen suited her. Her legs still looked ravishing at they poked out from beneath the slits and he sat there imagining himself sweeping her into his arms, lifting her skirt and burying himself deep within her while his hands could feverishly trace the outline of her chest.

Her glance up to him broke his thoughts and he tried to place his mind elsewhere to calm the ticking throb in his lap. He was glad he broke decorum and did not rise as she entered the room. He tried to change the wanton thoughts filling his head but the dream he had the previous night seemed to have led him further into fantasy. Oh the things he wanted to do to her. He let out a deep breath.

His uncle entered a few minutes later and afraid he might still be at part, grabbed the papers in front of him as if reading them, holding them as he began to rise. His uncle stopped him immediately. "Cease, my son, propriety always becomes you."

He was thankful that his Uncle had always been so carefree and never demanded he follow tradition. He sat in the middle of the table to be polite. Veros was not one to huddle too close to the prince whenever they had guests, closeness always bred secrecy and rumours, two things he often avoided.

"When will you return to Uri to meet the traders?" Veros asked him as he buttered a large piece of bread and gathered some grapes from the middle of the table.

Arkson wanted to wince but stopped himself, instead he looked to see Samira's response. She had heard Veros say Uri and had looked up at him.

He frowned and responded to his uncle "In three days time."

Veros smiled and laughed graciously. "Aah plenty of time to enjoy your new company before departing again." And he looked over to Sammie. She ducked her head down and returned to her porridge, embarrassed.

The prince remained silent for the rest of their dining, only glancing at Sammie once more before finishing. As he got up to leave, she, Brunelda and Veros all stood up to obeisance. She was learning the customs of the Akori by observing. Veros left not long after bidding her a well wishing for the day and kissing Brunelda's hand gently. As she sat there with Brunelda, the only thing she could think about was going back to Uri to see her sister.

"Brunelda, do you think the prince would take me with him to Uri if I asked?" Sammie asked.

She pursed her lips unsure. "He still seems a bit angered *whelan*. Give him a day and then ask."

Sammie's heart sank, she missed her sister terribly, even though they had only been parted for a day, the fact that she was a three hour journey from where she was made her more cognisant of the distance it would take to get back to her. She had contemplated escaping the palace, but then what would she do. She was resourceful, but Arzule was such a strange land, and she feared being captured as a slave and taken further from where she was now.

She spent the rest of the morning wandering around the palace aimlessly looking at the tapestries and examining the artwork, and then she returned to her room reading the books on her shelf. She had finished reading the first three books and had moved on to the fourth when Brunelda entered the room, summoning her for lunch with the prince. Sammie was surprised. She wondered why he kept dining with her if she had angered him.

Brunelda spotted the books piled on the bed and smirked.

"A little light reading," she began sarcastically, "let me see lass, *The Akori People*, *The History of the Akori, Volume I* and *Volume II*?"

Sammie chuckled lightly before placing Volume III down carefully make sure her place was still kept.

ARKSON HAD SPENT THE morning finalizing his plans to return to Uri with Veros. He had planned the trip for some time. He was meeting with a dignitary there to discuss a weapons trade with a western tribe. As they rolled the maps for the journey and finished their tea, Veros looked at Arkson with a mischievous look on his face.

"You like her," he said to Arkson.

Arkson held back, even though he and his uncle were close, even his feelings for Samira he would keep from him.

"I have nothing to say." Arkson said to him, pulling at the corner of a map they had left on the table, and looking more brooding than he had in the past month.

Veros chuckled. "You do not need to, only a female would make you seem more sullen than usual."

Arkson hated when Veros was right about his mood. He has wished Veros did not mention their trip to Uri since he could clearly see Sammie's interest in returning to the city. He did not want her to leave. If he took her with him, he feared she might leave him or get hurt. There were Anuyan who might take her as a slave again and he might not be able to protect her there from their laws. He was a prince but there were limits to what his royal lineage could procure elsewhere, and without his powers he was lessened to the skill of his blade.

"What do you think of her?" He asked his uncle.

Veros arched a brow surprised. "Of the human?" He stroked his chin playfully feigning thoughtfulness.

Arkson rolled his eyes. "Forget that I asked, dear uncle."

Veros laughed. "I think, dear nephew, that she is a beauty, but more importantly, more precious than a gem. Her personality is rare. She is quiet and intelligent, pleasant and polite, but strong willed, very much like yourself." He patted Arkson on the back.

Arkson's stomach rumbled and even though it felt as if

it had only been a few hours since he last ate, he knew it was near the time when he would dine again. Veros could sense his nephew's mind in turmoil, but it was not his hunger.

"Time to dine already is it?" He was uncanny sometimes.

Arkson sighed. "How do you do that Uncle?"

"I just read your mind," he said with a wink.

"You do not have that power Veros, " Arkson said to him knowing that the Akori powers were more along the lines of empathy, energy sourcing, and levitation.

"Says you, my prince." Veros teased.

As they left the throne room and returned to the dining hall, Veros could see that Brunelda and Sammie were already there, patiently waiting for Arkson and him to return, and standing near the glass doors leading to the gardens. He felt as though he had not seen Brunelda all morning and so as Sammie looked out at the flowers and topiaries he motioned for her to come to him.

She smiled sweetly and walked over to his side, bowing lightly to the prince while passing and motioning with her eyes for him to move in Sammie's direction. Arkson frowned and instead went to meet the chef, to see what was being prepared.

Sammie felt cozy staring out at the gardens and felt as though she could drift off into a deep slumber. Even though the sky was dark, it had rained earlier and everything was richly steeped in wet colour.

After convincing Brunelda to approach Arkson about discussing employment with some part of the palace, Sammie had read that morning, but the day, which seemed drearier than the previous had a draining effect on her mood. She was glad she had kept herself busy by reading and had found the books very informative about the Akori. She learned a little more about their culture and their customs.

As she looked over to Brunelda with Veros, she noticed something that she had not seen before. She had come to learn that the tattoos on the Akori necks matched their mates. When two people married, as if by magic, the tattoos, called the Zain, would meld and reshape to markings that represented a combination of the two. Brunelda and Veros's markings appeared to match and she tilted her head as she examined them until the prince returned from the chef's room and caught her furtive glance. He looked at her suspiciously, and then invited them all to be seated.

Brunelda and Veros sat close to one another too absorbed in their conversation. So Sammie sat next to the prince since they would share condiments across the large wooden table more easily that way. He said nothing to her, but when she needed some butter from his side of the table he grabbed it for her handing it over. As their fingers brushed she felt the hairs on the back of her neck stand up, as though his touch had electrified her.

"Thank you," she said. She had always been dutifully polite, even when she did not want to be. He responded with a nod, which she figured was better than a scowl and so they sat there for the remainder of the meal quietly eating.

After they all ate, Veros and Brunelda still absorbed in their conversation ended up leaving Sammie and the prince alone. Samira had watched Brunelda laugh loudly as Veros was gesticulating ferociously. When they were alone, Arkson finally seemed to soften, "What did you do this morning?" he asked her.

"I read," she said simply, not knowing what else to add.

"You like books?" He asked her.

She nodded.

His brow crinkled as though he was impressed. "What did you read?"

She listed off the titles from her bookshelf and he seemed further impressed with her.

"Prince Arkson," she began, so unsure of whether or not she should ask the question that burned on her tongue. He might be angry with her, but it was too late, she had spoken. So she asked another. "Where is your sister? Brunelda mentioned her to me and I have yet to meet her."

He thought about lying to her but he couldn't. He kept his answers terse. "She left. I don't know why. Her note said she would return."

"She didn't say goodbye?" Sammie asked seeing the pain flutter quickly beneath the surface of his coolness.

"No."

She looked at him, sorry for him. She knew how much she missed Salha and how he must feel the same. "I'm sorry. You must miss her."

"It is no fault of yours. I do miss her. Thank you for your concern." He said it so matter of fact, but beneath the surface his heart rumbled. Did she care about him, truly? Her words held such sincerity, such kindness. She had been so angry before, but now she was serene, examining him.

He did not smile as he got up but he held his hand out to her and said, "come with me."

Sammie still felt a bit nervous, but after their previous night she thought it best to give him the chance. As she placed her hand in his she was not expecting him to hold it so freely, his fingers intertwined with hers, as he led her from the dining hall down a long corridor, which ended in front of two large brass doors.

She stared at them praying there would be piles upon piles of books inside and not a king size bed. He did not disappoint her, the library was far larger than she would have thought, its doors were misleading. He let go of her hand and watched the wonder fill her face as she stared at the shelves, which decorated three floors lined with titles. He walked over to a shelf and picked a book from the middle and then brought it back to her. As he handed it to her, he said nothing, but when she read the title her cheeks burned with embarrassment. Luckily her complexion would never betray her emotions. He had handed her *Akori Etiquette*.

He sensed her discomfort and said softly, "maybe we will understand one another better." His words made her feel better and she did notice his eyes scan across her hotly. Maybe he did not think so poorly of her? He turned to leave.

"Prince Arkson," she said hesitantly. He stopped, the hairs on the back of his neck tingling. Every time she spoke his name it made his blood rush. What would she say to him, probably just a thank you.

"Thank you, and..." She was nervous. "I apologize for last night."

He softened, she had humbled herself. "My apologies as well Samira." He felt relieved, this was a start. He turned to go, but she stopped him again.

"I wanted to ask you something," she said.

He dreaded the words that he knew she would say. He turned back to her slowly, his dark hair falling into his eyes.

"When you return to Uri, may I come?" She looked at him hopefully.

His looks hardened. "No, you must stay here."

"Why?" she asked him earnestly.

Why must she always question me?

He was irritated, but felt more curious about her reasoning. Would she try to flee from him if he brought her back? She'd be safer with him than with any Anuyan.

"No," he repeated, "you cannot accompany me." And this time he left, feeling too incensed by her touch, by her beauty, to speak rationally.

Samira felt sick. She had to find a way to get back to her sister, but he had been right, she knew nothing of their world. She gazed at the books around her, hopefully one of them had the answers.

She read for hours until, at last Brunelda returned to her and invited her for supper. As she entered the library she whistled, gazing at the amount of books that Sammie had spread out along a desk. She had read an additional six books to the four she had in the morning and was working on a seventh.

Firstly, she had finished the book on Akori Etiquette and had moved on from books solely on Akorian history and culture to Arzule's history. It was interesting to learn that in the tenth century of Akorian history, as a peoples they decided to abandon common use of their traditional native tongue and adopted more practical use of the Brooy, which was seen as a common language among the different species in Arzule.

She read about the many other types of species in Arzule, some which were near extinction and the multiple cultures and practices of ones still very much thriving such as the Anuyan. They were depicted as intelligent, brute force creatures capable of great strength and cunning, but that she did not need to read in a book. She had learned that first hand.

The world of Arzule was strange with many dangers, filled with things she did not fully understand. She had examined the many weapons of the people, aside from swords, spears, and cannons there were magical contraptions, things which had been enchanted for more powerful destruction.

She read of one which was incredibly terrifying, a

triuny, a rare type of spear which was bound with electricity and huge surges of light. The Akorian people had not seen a *triuny* in centuries. Its electrical pulse sent painful vibrations through an Akorian's Zain markings, which could be targeted to a specific clan. The longer it stayed activated the more power it consumed, spreading its effect. Whole armies in the third century of Akorian history had been levelled by such weapons.

Samira was starting to realize why the prince might not want to leave her alone to her own devices. Yet he still had not told her why he had sought her out and why she was there, which made her curious about his motives, in her eyes kindness had its limits. He clearly had not meant to make her his mistress, she realized that now, even though his looks of desire were evident, she was baffled.

His hand had been intertwined with hers lightly when he brought her to the library. It was as if he was simply assisting her. Her fingers had tingled after, and she could still recall the warmth from his hand. The sensation was peculiar, had been like a whisper against the neck, pleasant and soothing.

As she and Brunelda walked to the dining hall, she was determined to make her own fate. She had been given the chance to live and she need to start devising her plan of action. She could find her way back to Salha, but she would need help. Arkson would be able to take her, but first she had to convince him.

"Brunelda," she began, as they sauntered to the dining hall. "Do you think I could choose my own clothes for tomorrow? I'd like something different."

She smiled at her. "Of course *whelan*, why not? I shall advise the prince tonight so that we can visit the palace tailor after we dine."

WHEN SHE WALKED INTO the dining hall Arkson was

seated already, his uncle was at his side. She looked at him hoping there was a way she could get through to him, but it was no use. He kept his hardened exterior in tact.

He had been so distracted by the feel of her hand. So enticed by the warmth of her skin that he withdrew from her now. Arkson and Veros stood for their entrance, but his eyes would not meet hers.

Even after they finished their meal when Brunelda left with Veros, promising to return to her for their expedition, he remained resolute. This prince *was* a cold bugger.

Sammie broke the silence, "are all the females in this world expected to be docile creatures?"

Arkson was surprised by the frustration in her voice. "Obviously it is a trait you have yet to learn Samira."

"Is that what you want of me?" she asked, "to be servile and quiet, and do as you please?"

Arkson's jaw clenched. It was not what he wanted of her, he liked the fire in her. "It would make things easier if you listened to me Samira."

Samira felt that she clearly could not get through to him. She stood, angered further, but was collected, as cold as Arkson.

"That would be one sided prince. How do you expect to understand one another, to understand me, if you only speak at me?" She placed her hands down on the table for emphasis, leaning against it to brace her temper from flying.

"Samira," he began, but she cut him off.

"Don't Samira me Arkson! Let me finish what I have to say." His eyes looked at her, enchanted, not angered. She said his name, with no title, stood above him as she spoke. She was remarkable. No fear in her as she faced him. What a woman! She made him erupt with heat.

"You are wrong," she continued, "things would be easier if you spoke *with* me."

He grew silent, then a smile crept up from the corner of his mouth.

"You are right Samira," he began, "but you are hard to speak with when angry."

Her eyes widened from his admission and she straightened.

Did he just say I am right? Of course you are! Yeah.... but he just said it. He just said it!

Hearing it from his mouth was sweeter than she would have ever thought, he was so full of surprises. Was he trying to charm her?

He tilted his head softening. "And...well, you are *so* very angry." Arkson remained composed, collected and the sheen of his green eyes looked sexy as he gazed at her. When she had bent forward at the table, all he wanted to do was pull her across it and towards him. He wanted to pull her into his lap, to feel her hot breath against his lips.

She wondered what he was thinking, and when his finger brushed against his lips, her cheeks flushed with heat. Arkson could feel the sudden wave of emotion being clearly emitted in his direction. He could feel her pang of desire and he wondered if she always controlled her temper.

What would she be like truly angry?

Even the words of the previous night were tame compared to what roared inside her now. There was fear then, but that was gone, all that remained was her fire and it warmed him.

As chance would have it Brunelda returned for her that very second.

"Alright *whelan* let's..." she stopped herself from continuing, noting that Samira and Arkson had been drawn closer. Like a mischievous cat, Brunelda smiled to break the awkwardness of the moment and Samira left with her quickly.

Samira sighed deeply as she walked. She finally got him to admit he was wrong, but she was not going to stop there. Oh no, she was going to get what she wanted. Arkson had no choice in the matter now.

CHAPTER 13

BRUNELDA OPENED THE DOORS leading out of the palace and the night sky was beautifully filled with stars. Sammie was enchanted by the moons. There were two of them in the sky, one blue and one red. It was breathtaking the way they lit up the path from the palace walls and off into the corridors of the city, leading directly into the market quarter. She felt the exciting energy she always felt when refreshed by the cooler night air and admired the lanterns dotting the horizon. As they approached the tailor's shop she could see beautiful dresses on wooden mannequins, fine scarves of silk and ornate coats and suits.

Inside the shop there was an Akori who looked to be a little older than Brunelda, his face was handsome and covered in a thick salt and pepper moustache. His hair was kept short, like some of the soldiers in the castle and his spectacles were gold rimmed and circular in shape. He beckoned them forth with a friendly wave and a smile that made his eyes crinkle with delight.

As Sammie looked at the beautiful *skiori*, the two piece

dresses and *apathi* the one piece garments, she had discovered their names in her afternoon reading, she was incredibly impressed with the beautiful detail and designs. She tried not to be distracted by all of the things that looked elegant and would be beautiful to try on. She was there with a purpose.

"This must be the lovely *whelan* you mentioned to me Brunie." He held his palm forward to take Sammie's hand and knelt down doting a kiss on the back of her hand. He then patted it softly, and took her arm in his own.

"Well my dear what dresses can I delight you with?" He waved in the direction of the more modest dresses similar to the one she wore, with a wink in the direction of Brunelda. Instead, Sammie motioned towards a blue ensemble, something like the purple dress she had wore on her first night with the prince, but it was not nearly as ornate as she wanted.

"I would like something like this," she said. His eyes brightened and looked pleased.

"Except," she continued, "I would like it in red." He walked around her, his mouth pursed in consideration. Sammie figured he was probably gauging what her measurements were.

Brunelda gave her a mischievous look, and the shopkeeper raised his finger as if it were a eureka moment.

"I have just the thing!" He shouted running to a wardrobe behind his work desk, pulling it out very delicately. He brought back a stunning red sequined brassiere with gold thick crisscrossing straps that looped down beneath the cups of the top and was decorated with a large amber brooch on the front clasp surrounded by small rubies. Folded beneath it was the matching skirt. It had a gold waistband and was made up of three layers of crimson chiffon silk with the same thigh high slits as her other skirts. The shopkeeper had read her mind.

"I'll take it," Sammie said, hoping her plan would work.

As they walked back to the palace, Brunelda was giddy. "That dress is the most beautiful thing I have ever seen, the prince will be stunned when he sees you in it." She smiled back at Brunelda, that was the plan. She still struggled internally with her choice. Her smile broke a bit as her lips quivered with her nerves.

"How would I get a private audience with him?" She asked biting it to suppress the movement.

Brunelda looked at her impressed. "That can be easily arranged *whelan*, you just let me know when."

"Tomorrow morning," Sammie replied, "before breakfast."

Brunelda nodded her head and grabbed her hand, skipping with their bags up the stairs of the palace and over to Sammie's room joyfully.

After Brunelda left, Sammie prepared for bed, she was tired from her day of reading, the knowledge was still all being processed in her head, and as she slipped into her white tunic, she let her mind wander to her dream from the night before. Devilishly, she grinned to herself at what had taken place. This morning she had still been a bit angered by the prince's actions, confused by the dream. Now she felt as though it was her minds way of telling her to give the prince a chance.

She still had her misgivings, but at least now she was determined to get what she wanted, she was ready to make a deal. She would just have to channel her inner *femme fatale*. She could definitely use a Mae West film to give her the edge she needed right about now.

Why doesn't Arzule have television?
She sighed.

ARKSON AWOKE WITH A START. A loud bang upon his

chamber door rattled him. He grabbed his sword from beneath his pillow and stood ready to fight before he realized an attacker would not knock. He sheathed his blade and shouted "You may enter!"

Veros walked in full force ahead. He was smiling. "Be ready in half an hour, Samira calls for a private audience with you." Then he turned on his heels and pulled the doors closed with a loud thud.

Arkson stood there annoyed from being awoken, and then he realized what his uncle had said. He sighed heavily, usually he was given some forewarning for a private audience for approval. Veros knew him too well. He probably would have declined if he had been given the time to contemplate consent. He drew a bath, quickly washed and dressed, even though he could make her wait if necessary, he felt it would be unkind to keep her sitting in the passage. She wanted to speak to him. What would she have to say? His heart began to thud.

THE MORNING SEEMED to come quickly, she awoke before Brunelda arrived and had gone to the baths to bathe. They had been empty while she was there and just as she returned to her room she met with Brunelda.

"You look beautiful in your dress Sammie," she said to her placing her hand delicately beneath Sammie's chin to admire her face. "Your audience with the prince is in an hour, I was expecting to help you get bathed and ready but it looks like you are almost complete."

Brunelda stayed and helped show her how to do her hair and watched as Sammie used the make-up given to her on her first night. When she was done, she looked at herself in awe, she had half an hour to wait, and her nerves were making her anxious. She read the proper etiquette over again for an audience with the prince. You were not allowed to touch him, and had to wait until you were spoken with before speaking. She memorized the other necessary gestures and then she left following Brunelda to the other side of the castle. They reasoned that by the time they got there it would be a few minutes before her meeting.

"Once you reach the first room, stop there Sammie, Prince Arkson will come to meet you." Brunelda squeezed her hand as if for luck and then left her. As Sammie walked into the passage leading to the Arkson's room she examined her surroundings. Cordoned off from the rest of the palace, the prince's room had its own separate entry way with a long hallway leading into a room that looked like a waiting room. The walls of the passage unlike the rest of the creamy coloured palace were a medium stained wood with small circular windows.

In the waiting chamber was a chaise and fireplace like her own room, with several large paintings and tapestries decorating the walls. There were a few copper and metal statues of things that looked like inventions and she found them intriguing. Normally her curiosity would have her examining them carefully, but at that moment she didn't feel like herself, she felt bold.

She knew that Arkson would meet her there for their conversation, it was customary for the Akorian royalty to keep their bedrooms very private. There was only one window in the room, and since the sky was changing colours as the morning light came Sammie walked over to it and waited there, her back facing the prince's wooden bedroom door. She prayed he would come out to meet her.

Arkson took a deep breath as he stood before the door. He had glanced at himself in the mirror and felt that his attire was suitable, rather than wear a formal suit of a traditional private audience, he wore a white shirt and his regular dark green pants. As he opened the door, he expected her to be seated at the chaise. She was not. He looked up to see her standing before the window, her back to him he could see she was dressed in a red *skiori*. He gulped. She looked incredible as she turned to him. Her chocolate brown eyes were darkly kohled and pierced into him, his whole body was suddenly on fire and before he knew what he was doing he gestured for her to enter his room.

Sammie was relieved he invited her to his room, for what she was planning on doing it put her mind at ease that no one else would be able to walk in on them and she felt it a good sign he broke with tradition and invited her into his place of privacy.

She had been curious about what the room might be like and had wondered if it would be as cold as he seemed. She was surprised to find that it was quite warm and rather inviting. The room was not much larger than her own, there was enough extra space for more bookshelves and a bath, which was surrounded by a lattice enclosure.

Arkson turned after closing the door and watched her as she knelt in the traditional audience stance, one knee on the ground the other bent, foot resting on the hardwood floor and her right arm raised waiting for him to give her permission. The sight of it took his breath away and made his heart ache. She had read the book he had given her. The way she bent forward slightly, revealed even more of her chest and his mouth watered for a taste of her. He wanted to draw his fingers along her neck. He swallowed hard and tried to keep cool, even though he knew she could tell he had left himself vulnerable.

As she knelt, Sammie's heart raced, he seemed so softened to her, so unguarded. He moved forward and gently caressed her open palm with his own, sending shivers over her. He had accepted her request to speak.

"Go ahead Samira," he said "ask me what you came for, but know that if you are asking me for what you did yesterday, the answer is still no."

She looked up at him with pain on her face, he had hurt her. He took a deep breath feeling guilty, looking into those dark eyes that captivated him.

"Why?" she asked, "aside from the fact that you do not want me to leave here."

His jaw clenched, she knew the right thing to say to make her point. "It is dangerous," he said.

"You'll protect me," she replied flatly.

He would protect her, with his life if necessary. How did she know that though, had his emotions betrayed him more than he wanted? There were other dangers outside of the ones she thought. He shook his head.

She kept her resolve. "Please..."

He did not know why she wanted to go back there. He had given her everything she might need, there had to be something else. His mind raced, she must have left something behind.

"Why Samira?" Now was his time to ask.

She looked up hopeful. "I left something there and I need it back."

He had been right. He ran his hand through his hair, suddenly feeling a little panicked. Samira observed that he was considering, then he turned his back to her and hardened. "Tell me what it is, I will get it for you."

Damn.

He had picked up on her omission. She was afraid he would say that to her.

"Only I can get it," she said to him.

If I tell him I have a sister, who knows what will happen.

He shook his head.

Why is she so persistent?

"If I give you something you might want, will you give me what I want?" She asked him. She examined him closely, watching his body language. He stiffened, his ears perked.

"You have nothing I want," he lied. He wanted her company, he wanted her to fall in love with him.

She crept up behind him so close that he could smell her, but she did not touch him, she followed the rules.

"Arkson please..." The need in her voice, it was driving him wild, he needed to calm himself before he turned around and pulled her closer to him. She did it again, spoke his name with no title. It was —intimate. He turned around to face her, she had walked up behind him gaining the strength she needed and when he looked at her with soft sleepy eyes, she knew she had to try.

With his eyes locked on hers she unclasped her shirt slowly pulling away at the fabric until she held it in her hand, she lightly tossed the top onto the chaise and then unclasped the skirt slowly sliding out of it and then casting it in the same direction. She tried to be seductive, but her heart practically hammered in her ears when she looked up at him.

His own heart pounded as his eyes travelled over her naked flesh. He wanted to lift her up and carry her to his bed, to kiss every inch of her and caress her until she cried out in pleasure, in his arms. He wanted to spread her legs feverishly and slide himself into her body, stroking her sensuously until she was breathless and sated.

Yet, as he looked into her eyes he suddenly felt ashamed at what he had done, he had made her desperate. He wanted her, but not like this, he wanted her of her own free will, not as part of a bargain.

He quickly stepped over to the chaise grabbing her clothing and the blanket beneath them, wrapping it around her and pulling her into him. She examined him closely, he was not going to agree to the deal. Instead he held her close. She leaned further into him comforted by him in her despair even though he was the cause. She admired him for his strength, she could feel him throbbing against her stomach, had witnessed the carnal look on his face. After a few seconds of silence, he broke.

"You may come with me Samira," He said leaning his cheek against the top of her head, "but you must promise me something."

She looked up at him relieved. "Yes," she said to him. She hardly knew him and he held her so intimately, so carefully.

He cupped her face with his palm and gently traced his finger against her lips sending more shivers down her spine. "You must return with me."

Her lips tingled, ached for his own lips. Intoxicated by the look in his eyes and feeling like it was worth the compromise, she nodded.

"You must say it," he said huskily, praying that she would keep her word.

"I will return with you from Uri." She answered attentively, hoping the details would put him at ease.

Suddenly Samira realized something, she was in Arkson's arms and his face was not wrinkled from her scent. In the palace there were still some who covered their noses when she was near, and others who more extremely heaved as if she smelled like something wretched.

"Do I smell to you?" She asked him, leaning back a little, her eyes examining his face.

"To me..." He said looking at her eyes through her long lashes. "You smell like fire."

He did not tell her that it was a sign of mating that your partner often smelled like your favourite scent. He stared at her a moment too long, as though he was in deep thought.

She thought he might lean in and kiss her. Instead, he caressed her cheek with his thumb. He turned to leave, to let her dress. Before he walked out she stopped him. "Will you promise me something?"

He wondered what it might be and nodded hesitantly.

"Will you promise me when we return that you will teach me how to defend myself?" She looked at him with hope and with resolve. Her request was unusual.

Arkson was relieved, she did not ask to be able to leave again, she wanted to learn something for her survival.

"Yes Samira, I will." He left her there to re-dress and as he pulled the door behind him, he leaned against it feeling some of the tension fall away. She would come back to Zatian. He still had more time.

Sammie had a peculiar feeling as he left her. All this time she had resisted him, and in a few minutes alone that him, she had agreed to more than she wanted. There was something about him which drew her to him that she could not comprehend. She did not know whether it was just her heart aching to quell the loneliness that she had sometimes felt in the past three years, or if it was something more.

She pinched herself lightly, wondering if she would wake, but she was still not dreaming, this was all too real. She wondered if Arkson knew she was not from Arzule, she suspected he did, yet he obviously knew little of the full truth.

Now she had a chance to see her sister again though, which was the most important thing. Although she knew Braedynn would protect Salha, could see the feverish look of love in his face every time he gazed upon her, she wondered just how much a slave could do to protect his wife. She was determined to find a way to get them back home, they could even bring Braedynn with them if Salha wanted. She had often thought about the chance of the situation, if Thussan had picked her instead of Salha she would be the one married right now. She had wondered if Braedynn would have loved her so effusively, wondered now if the prince would have looked at Salha with the same lust in his eyes.

The day had just begun, but she felt emotionally exhausted. Meeting Brunelda outside the prince's door she felt her cheeks blush lightly, thankfully she knew her complexion usually showed little of the change and Brunelda made no comment. Brunelda's appearance was eerily calm, she looked almost pious.

Brunelda came forward and held her hand as they walked towards the dining hall. "Did you get your wish love?" She asked.

"Yes I did," Sammie replied, still a little breathless from the overwhelming confrontation with Arkson.

"Thank goodness," Brunelda spoke, "maybe things will finally start to go smoother around here. I will help you prepare."

CHAPTER 14

In Alpohalla, King Guedan cursed loudly before his soldiers. His grey eyes were cold and unwavering as his messenger had brought him news he disdained. He ran a hand over his close cut blonde hair in frustration. The Prince of Zatian had found a female human and brought her to his lowly princedom.

Guedan had been working with the Anuyan and the Batchi to reduce the human female population in Arzule, and they had met with much success. The remaining women were somewhere in the hundreds, many already being owned and the others hiding in the reclusive and sheltered lands of Brinn that no creature in Arzule could travel upon, but the disgusting human race. The enchantment of its grounds were notorious, deadly.

Since his mother had cursed Arkson's father decades ago, he had promised her he would fulfill the duty of exterminating his distant cousin's lineage and right to an Akorian throne. He knew that Arkson and Nikelda had been weakened for some time and with Nikelda's disappearance there was only Arkson left to deal with, before he could absorb their lands and expand his kingdom properly.

The news did not bode well for him. If Arkson married the human, he would ascend as King to the throne of Zatian and his full powers would be restored. He had to stop him while he was ahead, and called for a *Jahrbringer*. He prepared to mobilize his troops. He was going to squash Arkson before he had the chance to succeed.

Guedan walked to his balcony and admired his kingdom, the beauty of the city was renowned, it's structures were tall glass with metal enclosures, well organized and well maintained. In the past ten years, he had expanded the kingdom greatly and had been funnelling most of his resources into the expansion of his necromancy. There had been little reward thus far but he knew he was on the brink of something large, something that would enable him a much swifter victory over any remaining independents.

Guedan was studying the historical passages of the Akori to find out more about the portal shifting between the realms. He knew Arkson's human was not from their world, there was no other explanation for her sudden appearance and spies had explained her traits were unlike others here. If he could harness power from other worlds he would be invincible.

He only hoped that the prince's will to live was still weakened by his sister's disappearance. Despite Arkson's lack of powers, Guedan had found his last encounter with him at the Akorian Games harrowing. The weakling he had coerced into submission had grown into a young warrior. A warrior who had spent all of him time brawling with himself. Guedan knew that Arkson was his own worst enemy, but he feared that the human would open his eyes to this, that her restoration of his powers would be the key

Arkson needed.

Humans were stupid though. They knew little of magic, were fearful of everything. They never seemed to understand what they were told. Even if Arkson had one in his midst, it would no doubt take some time before anything were accomplished and even at that, their seal would have to match before it could be completed. She would have to accept him.

At that meeting of the clans, it was clear that Arkson had become braver than any other Akorian, stronger and faster too. Arkson was relentless and he needed to be put down. Guedan had succeeded in capturing so many Akorian cities so far, and none had been foolish enough to unite against him, but the time was coming when he knew Arkson would act. Guedan would kill him before he could.

The last Akorian games they both attended had been ten years ago. Arkson had surprised all of the clans showing up for the traditional challenges for the first time. Each competition existed of several tasks to complete, and the males who excelled in these qualities would represent their region. When he and his company had arrived, they looked young, unpolished, and a bit too eager. In Guedan's eyes they were clearly not refined Akori, and appeared to have an innocence to them.

He should not have underestimated them. The challenge of swordsmanship had whittled down many of the other clans until only two were remaining, Arkson and himself. He had witnessed the young prince in action. He was cold with wielding the sword, calculated and exact in his methods, always using his opponents weakness to his advantage. When he had stood before Guedan, the king had expected the prince to be more timid, but he showed no change in demeanour.

They stood before one another on the grassy strip for what seemed like hours before Guedan, tired of Arkson's game charged at him quickly. It had not taken more than a few minutes but Arkson had broke Guedan's charge and in one swift motion flipped him onto his back, sword tip pressed against Guedan's vocal chords. Guedan had cursed loudly, but even though the prince had that victory, it was short lived and would lead to retribution.

He had even warned the foolish prince by message from his general to back off in their fight. Kitan had used Guedan's expressed exact words.

"If you know what is good for your people Arkson, you will lose this fight. Guedan will make life miserable for the Akori of the Zatian annex if you win. His attention will be diverted from defeating the city of Crium and its King Dallus, to enslaving you, you and your precious city."

Arkson had only nodded to the words, said nothing to indicate compliance. Kitan had later reported his suspicion to his King that the Prince Arkson would not waiver from the threat.

Guedan had followed through as promised, drafting harsher limitations on Zatian, using their resources more steadily to feed his army of Akorians. If it had not been for the fact that he had already found his mate in the tribute paid from the city of Opamut, he would have requested the hand of the lovely Princess Nikelda, as well to bring further injury to the bastard prince.

He had wanted to hold her captive in the tower of Bridione, his jail, so that he could visit her whenever the desire came, but his advisors had coaxed him out of the action. They were right in telling him that the colonies might disapprove to the point of revolt. It was too bad though, Nikelda would make an excellent concubine. Well, after he had beaten her into submission.

King Guedan returned to his throne, looking cooly at the *Jahrbringer* that had been brought to him. For an assassin he looked young. His eyes were pale grey and his hair so blonde is was almost white, was pulled back into a low ponytail. He had come highly recommended by his guards and the scars on his arm suggested he had his fair share of battles.

What Guedan wanted was a battle, but not for the task at hand. It required more skill and cunning, he needed someone capable of scaling the castle walls undetected. Hakeem was gifted with levitation, like some of the males in Arkson's guards he could use his powers to keep his body elevated from the ground for longer periods of time. Guedan had only witnessed levitation in a few of his subjects and most of them could simply bounce off of things more effortlessly for longer periods of time, it was not like flying, more like prolonged stasis in the air.

Hakeem was something else, far more powerful and destructive and clearly looking forward to the challenge. He had been one of the most successful soldiers in Guedan's army when they were at war with the city of Boja, his strongest threat in the Akorian clans and after the war,. He had used his skills to become a highly valued assassin. He would take pleasure in bringing down the lowly Prince Arkson.

"I am here by your command my King and master, how may I serve you?" Hakeem's voice was sly, shadowed as he bowed before Guedan.

Guedan's jaw grew slack with boredom, "Speak when spoken to vile servant."

Hakeem nodded, his eye flittering a moment before they closed in a lower bow.

"I entrust a task to you that is most important. Do not fail me or it will be your death." Guedan motioned for the attendants to leave as Hakeem's head shot up to him, not out of fear but with eagerness.

"I will not fail you, my King." Hakeem answered..

"Good." Guedan replied. "There is a woman in the

palace of Zatian, a human."

Hakeem's eye's returned to Guedan, filled with surprise.

"I want her dead." Guedan pronounced with finality.

"A human dead, not the prince, my King?" Hakeem could not contain his curiosity, he had hoped he would be assassinating the Prince Arkson.

"No, the prince is for me to destroy, but this blow will be a greater damage to Zatian. Leave immediately as it will take a week to get there. I have already sent some scouts, but knowing Arkson they might not succeed in harming her. I am sending you to complete the task should they fail."

Guedan looked back at Hakeem to see his response. Sending spies on a suicide mission was callous, but the assassin did not falter and in that instant he knew he had chosen well.

Hakeem arose from his stance. "I will not disappoint you my King."

ARKSON KNEW THERE was a spy in his kingdom. He could feel the betrayal in his bones, lurking in the corners of the palace. What he knew for certain was that it was not any of his guards. He would have sensed it sooner. He would have caught a glimmer of it in their emotions, no matter how much his company tried to hide their fear from him, he knew how many of them were intimidated by his strength. It was the fact that he had sheer strength alone that made them fear him. He knew it was what Guedan feared most about him too, and it would lead to the king's downfall.

Arkson was never one for torture, but the fact that he was getting closer to Samira now, made him want to protect her at all costs. He would torture to find the spy, but that was unnecessary, he was far too intelligent to be brutish. Arkson knew that if he had all of his company in close quarters long enough, he would learn the information necessary to find out the traitor. After an extended period of time that person would reveal themselves to him. He just needed to make sure he prepared the right plan, and bring Alvaren in the loop.

When Alvaren arrived he had no idea if Arkson calling him was in an official capacity or not. It was rare for him to be called into the passage. Arkson had more often called their meetings in the throne room, so for a request with such privacy needed, he knew it must be important.

He nodded entering the passage and knelt before the prince. Arkson met him quickly shaking his hand as he pulled him to his feet and patted him lightly on the back.

"Let us sit then," he said to Alvaren.

He nodded in agreement taking a chair across from the prince, so that they might speak candidly. Alvaren leaned forward bracing his elbows on his knees, his chin resting on his intertwined hands.

"This is important." He stated and asked Arkson at the same time.

Arkson leaned back in the chair crossing his leg gallantly. "We have a spy," he pronounced.

"I suspected as much," Alvaren replied, "who do we think it is?"

"I'm not sure yet," Arkson replied rubbing his fingers over the scruffiness already growing in after this morning's shave. "We're going to find out though."

Alvaren smiled. "All right, what's the plan Ark?" He was one of the few soldiers who Arkson permitted to call him by nickname. After all they had been raised together like brothers. Alvaren's parents had died when he was a child, and orphaned, Brunelda and Veros raised him like a son.

"First we have to fish them out, then we'll turn them

loose on Guedan, and then the real planning begins. This is not going to be a fair fight. Guedan will stop at nothing to subjugate the city."

"He is a dirty bastard," Alvaren quipped.

Alvaren knew that Arkson worried, but he had faith in him as a leader. He had yet to steer his people wrong, and all that they had accomplished this far was thanks to his unwavering belief that he should not take more than his people.

"I'll need your help, and we need Elastor to play a part."

"The part of the spy," Alvaren replied, already knowing what Arkson planned.

"Yes, but I fear it will be hard to make it believable."

"What of Elastor?" Alvaren asked a little amused since their friend was enthusiastic about everything.

"Can he be trusted to play it properly?" Arkson countered his mouth twisting.

"I'm not certain," Alvaren spoke honestly, "Shall I play the ungrateful and jealous one?"

Arkson laughed. "Can you even act?"

Alvaren chuckled as he recounted their make believe as children, he never seemed all that convincing.

"No," he said laughing.

"The spies would know better," Arkson said with a smile. "We'll call the company to the Hall of Haldero."

"Maybe we just should omit the truth from Elastor then?" Alvaren said.

"Perhaps..." Arkson laughed.

ELASTOR'S SANDY BLONDE curls cascaded down into his eyes. His face was stone as Alvaren declared the accusation. "You've been found guilty of treason against our city. What have you to say of these charges?"

"I have nothing to say of these charges." His teal blue

coloured eyes glared at Alvaren.

"So you did not advise King Guedan of our plans for attack?" Alvaren tilted his head, his dirty blonde hair shifting.

"I did no such thing." Elastor purposely tensed his jaw, Arkson watched as it ticked.

"You made no message to Guedan of our attack plans in a fortnight. You did not advise him that we would travel by sea to attack the city of Alpohalla?" Alvaren's face remained cold, resolute.

The group of soldiers and nobles had been assembled in the Hall of Haldero around the table of justice for two hours now. As Alvaren had questioned Elastor of his duty to Arkson, had interrogated him on his lineage and legitimacy of his previous honours, the soldiers were starting to weaken. Their emotions raw and drifting to the surface after such prolonged observation of the interrogation. It was harder for them to hide their feelings. Most of what surfaced was boredom or outrage at the accusations, as Elastor was well-liked in the court.

Alvaren slammed his fist against the desk which Elastor sat behind stoically. "Answer me Elastor!" The words heated and dragged out, echoing in the room. Arkson remained solid his face like steel betraying no emotions.

It was then that Arkson could feel it, the slightest twinge in emotion from Caron, a wave of guilt quickly layered beneath fear. His face struck with pallor and his hands moving nervously. Arkson's eyes connected with Alvaren's quickly and looked in Caron's direction. The words not needing to be said he knew immediately what Arkson suggested. Alvaren's eyes followed and realizing that he had become the subject of their observation Caron arose from his seat, and with full speed was running out of the hall.

Arkson growled getting up to follow while Alvaren grabbed two swords from the table. Weapons were never worn during trials because of their heated nature and although necessary, Alvaren cursed fumbling with the second weapon. As they ran in pursuit Alvaren threw forward a hilt. Arkson caught it as he rounded the corner hard nearly bashing two noble *whelans* returning from the market. He nodded politely quickly diverting the blade from their bodies.

"Move!" Alvaren cried as he repeated the same action.

Caron cursed as he ran down the stairs through the courtyard. If he could only get through the baths and into the kitchen, the terrace there led off to the canal. It had been days since he had received contact from Guedan, he had no way out of Zatian except to steal a boat or horse and the former was a far better idea. He knew that there was no way to make excuse for his emotions in the room. Now that they had surfaced, he could not take them back. He had fed information to Guedan, that was simply the truth. Guedan's offers were too tempting to refuse, being a noble in his kingdom was far more promising than being the same in Zatian as an inferior annex to Alpohalla.

Arkson jumped down the first flight of stairs trying to make up ground between him and Caron. He knew where the traitor was headed. Alvaren was not far from him either, cutting through garden rather than the grounds to try and head him off from the right, but Caron's levitation gave him an advantage. His body was graceful and panther-like as he glided over the ground and objects in his way.

He opened the front door to the baths, just as Arkson rounded the left corner of the hall off the courtyard, and Alvaren reached the base of the right side stairs. Arkson ran quickly down the hall, charging through the female baths as Akori screamed and grabbed their towels. Their whispering about the rakish prince burned his ears.

Alvaren followed with a charmingly courteous,"Ladies," before entering the south hall. He looked ahead to see Arkson charge through the swinging doors of the kitchen, and followed onward, smirking to himself, and ignoring the calls of the females for him to return to them.

"Left!" Arkson called as everyone cleared to the right side of the room. Caron had weaved through them all a few seconds before becoming caught up in the vegetable cart and jumping over it quickly to move forward.

He had reached the end of the upper level kitchen and was teetering on the railing of the terrace, suddenly realizing the height was more than he had anticipated. It was a long fall and his powers would probably fail him. Had there been some other structure off which he could bounce, he might make it, but if he jumped now he would break both his legs in several places and he couldn't heal himself quickly like some other Akorians.

Arkson pushed through the doors to the terrace, slowing as he watched Caron turn on the precarious railing to face him. His graceful shift revealed pain on his face, his strawberry blonde hair, hung low on his neck in a tie but whipped around his face from the wind. His pale blue eyes were uncertain.

"Why?" Arkson asked, raising a hand to stop Alvaren from charging forward as he burst out onto the terrace.

"What can you offer me Prince Arkson? What have you done for my family?" Caron's voice was cold despite his fear. Arkson's eyes directed Alvaren to the water not far from the ground beneath them.

"What about the land given to your family in the lower Zatian plain, what about the schooling for your children, the money you're given for your wife and her family?" Arkson had done for him what he had for all the noble families after the take over by Guedan. Since they weren't a colony like successive cities being too far away from Alpohalla, they were compensated from the King Mactyllo's on pocket. Their own properties had been used as resources for Guedan and he could not allow them to go without.

"You're a fool prince, we'll never be free of King Guedan." Caron's eye's looked saddened, hopeless before he stepped back free falling.

Alvaren stepped forward his hand stretched out as a surge of water rising up from the canal enveloped Caron's body. He kicked and screamed swallowing too much water and nearly drowned from his foolishness. The wave dissipated leaving Caron caked in mud and passed out on the ground be low them. Few others than Arkson had seen the sheer power that Alvaren was capable. He reached forward patting Alvaren's back in thanks.

As Alvaren turned the kitchen staff were wide eyed giving him a large berth. Arkson ordered one of them to watch Caron from above while they gathered him. He would be knocked out for some time and when he awoke he would be questioned and jailed.

Luckily, Elastor had known better than to follow them in case any additional spies remained in the room. The seed had been planted though and they could pass on the false information that Alvaren had mentioned during the interrogation. He and Arkson would rendezvous with him later, and he would be absolved of the charges publicly. They needed Elastor too much now to keep him in hiding.

"What a day." He sighed to himself, happy to have prevented Caron's death. The sky was beginning to darken as the evening set in, after a power surge like that, tonight he would surely rest.

CHAPTER 15

Salha had finished preparing the meal for Thussan, Kalawyn and Haloya for when they returned. The wedding had overlapped into the next day and too tired to return from the temple Thussan, had arranged for him and his new family to stay in the Bilu gardens, a sacred place for travellers. The morning had been quiet between the two of them, Salha had completed her household duties while Braedynn had finished his yard work. The guards had said little to them except that Thussan had sent message he would return that evening.

Braedynn, knowing it would be best if he looked as though he had retired from work early, returned to their room to clean himself up. Salha had been there sitting patiently waiting for him. She usually left him alone or was too busy in the kitchen preparing supper, so it was nice to have her company.

"What a day," he said sighing.

Salha had sat there for the past hour thinking about how it felt to be in Braedynn's arms. About the man who was her husband, who was more of a man than any other she had ever known. Braedynn had done little to win her over in terms of romantic gestures. He simply was himself and it was devastating to her already penchant heart. The man had won her over, and every time she saw him, she melted a little more. Was she too much of a sopping mess to think straight? Maybe. She had spent the day questioning herself over and over about the strength of her feelings, until she realized they kept reoccurring because of the power in them.

"Let me help you," she said moving towards him to help remove his shirt. She lovingly wiped his chest with a cool, damp cloth. He luxuriated in the touch of her hands gently caressing his sore muscles. He kissed her chastely, compelled to thank her for her kindness. And as he moved to pull away respectfully, as he had many times previously, she pulled him closer, kissed him more deeply. He felt incensed by her tongue gently, and provocatively exploring his mouth. He wanted to warn her that if she continued, he might not be able to stop himself from pulling her clothes off and making love to her. He wanted her.

"Salha," he began in between kisses, "if you keep—"

She placed her fingertips over his mouth to stop him. "Braedynn I want to be comforted, to comfort you."

Braedynn was speechless. She had pulled away and began to unbutton her dress. As she let the dress slowly fall to the floor, he wondered what to do. Salha did not know why she had not made love to him sooner, the look of him was enough to get any woman aroused. His chiseled face was the most beautiful she had ever seen, and his body was taut and tanned from all the work he did daily.

There had been times when she wanted to reach out and touch him so badly, to wrap her fingers around the muscles in his arms and pull him over her, but the time always seemed inappropriate, and they had just started to truly know one another. After their marriage she had been so fearful of him, until she began to realize his true nature. He had proved himself to her so many times, and she had realized, with him comforting her after Sammie's departure, just how much she cared for him. She was falling for him.

She pulled her hair out of its ties and let it fall. She hoped he wanted her. He had made little advances to her aside from the kiss on the day when Samira was taken. He was respectful and traditional, but they were married and she needed his love, realized that she truly wanted him. When he was close to her, she felt at peace, as though what he promised her had to come true because he could never lie.

As her hair fell, his mouth twisted wantonly with a deep breath, she returned to him brushing his dark blonde ear length hair from his blue eyes. As her fingers brushed over his full lips, she wanted to kiss them until they were bruised. Braedynn's hands wrapped around Salha's waist and he let his fingers wander over her back to her thighs. Lifting her body against his, she was ecstatic while he kissed her lips, cheeks, and neck with fervour. She could feel him harden against her, and she excitedly realized that he did want her just as much as she wanted him.

"Are you sure that you want this?" He asked her, returning her to the ground. His eyes were filled with desire. His heart beating rapidly as he awaited an answer.

She kissed him again.

"Salha, please answer me," he began, holding her by her shoulders away from his body. "I need to know if *you* want me? If *you* want me to make love with me?"

She looked at him and smiled coyly. "I want to make love with *you* very badly," she managed to whisper to him.

The tension in his body fell away and was replaced with tenderness as his mouth met hers.

She pulled away from him long enough to crouch down and remove his pants, slowly, seductively, as she moved back up to meet his lips with her own, she brushed the length of her body against his. He skillfully pushed her onto the bed and heatedly held her with his strength.

"Spread your legs," he whispered into her ear as he pushed her curls to one side. She felt a little overwhelmed by his body heat wafting over her while she was pinned against the mattress. The broad shoulders enclosing hers were hot and the way his body tapered into a delectable v-shape, enticed her as she ran her fingers all over his chest. His hands and mouth caressed her all over, and even though his words were powerful, filled with need, it was with love that he took Salha.

Each simmering motion was more potent than the one before, until they both exploded in release and tired by their day, by their expression of intimacy, they curled up and fell asleep, the night drawing in closer.

BRAEDYNN AWOKE AS THE night set in, and momentarily he was unsure of his surroundings, had forgotten where he was. Then he remembered the soft taste of Salha's lips, and pulled her warmth closer to him. He admired her while she slept and wondered what part of himself allowed him to be so possessed by her. She had come from another world unannounced and had obstructed his clear and concise vision of things as they were to come. The other parts of himself were at war. He only wished he could have done more to help Samira, but to reveal his powers now, reveal himself to Arkson it would be too soon.

He had the key now though, things would be righted. It was nearing the time of their departure when things could start to change, but they had to wait for the right moment. He knew that in a few days Thussan would be leaving them with guards again. He was taking Haloya and

Kalawyn to his parents house in a neighbouring sector for the day. That would be when they made their move to leave, it would be the perfect opportunity and another one might not arise for some time after.

His men would be waiting for him in Brinn, eager to know if they were closer to uncovering a way to prevent the Anuya and Batchi from further success in enslaving their kind. The village in the mountains was growing slowly, but surely. There were a few shops in the heart of the settlement, a market-style grocer and an apothecary were the most prominent. The men had even been resurrecting a temple and school, under the camp leader's instruction, when he had left for his mission. It had so much potential. He recalled the small log houses that were scattered along the green, filled with new families and humans brought together by their despair.

It was heartwarming watching the small community as they toiled away in the garden to feed their children, as they worked together to build a future. He hoped that there would be a future for he and Salha there. He would have to make it work, somehow.

CHAPTER 16

FOR THE WHOLE DAY, Sammie and Brunelda had prepared for her journey to Uri. Brunelda took her to the palace market where they purchased the items Sammie felt she would need. Suddenly Sammie had a thought, she had purchased a dress yesterday and now she was buying things in the market with money she did not have.

"Brunelda, are you paying for these items for me?" She asked curious, and feeling a bit sheepish at her spending habits. She had yet to be paid for what little work she did in the palace. She had no idea what gross she may have even earned considering her lodging, food, and clothing had all been given to her.

Brunelda chuckled. "I would gladly buy these things for you Sammie, but Arkson refuses. I was informed to get you whatever you may need."

Her words struck a chord with Sammie. She had truly misjudged the prince. So far he had asked nothing from her but to stay in Zatian, and she felt as though she had done little for him in return for all the gifts he had given her. It was peculiar that his generosity did not make her feel guilty. She knew he would have it no other way, but still he asked nothing from her and the previous morning he had even declined the offer of her body. Her fears of being a concubine had been negated yet she knew he must want her for something.

As if Brunelda read her mind, her discomfort, she had placed her hand in Sammie's. Sammie wished that she had some means to make her own money regularly, but so far nothing had presented itself as an option. She had managed to convince the cooks to let her assist with preparation of their dinner. And she had gone to the palace infirmary and assisted the healers with organizing their tools. She had even organized Arkson's library, or at least the parts of it which needed it, and yet her conversations with Brunelda about working always ended with Brunelda telling her she did not need to worry.

So, she mostly kept herself busy reading and looking for little things to do around the palace. Sometimes she would sit on the palace roof garden and write. She had yet to leave the palace walls and venture down to the coast, but she had admired it wistfully.

"No feelings of guilt are necessary, Samira, he gives to you freely." Brunelda always used Sammie's full name in moments of seriousness. It made her realize the sincerity of her words.

THE DAY HAD PASSED quickly and before she knew it, night had fallen and she had retired to her room for sleep. She had changed into her tunic, when a knock at her door made her curious. Brunelda had left half an hour before and mumbled something about surprising Veros. Sammie had laughed finally gathering that Brunelda *was* married to Veros, she *was* Arkson's aunt as she had suspected.

Sammie opening the door with a chuckle said,

"Brunelda I thought Veros would have—" she stopped short, it was not Brunelda standing in her doorway. It was Arkson.

He rubbed his neck and looked a bit sheepish when he glanced down at her legs peeping out from her tunic. She wondered why he looked that way when he had since her naked less than forty eight hours ago. She opened the door for him to come in her eyes falling over his frame with heat. She admired his sinfully silken dark hair, his amazing green eyes and his delectable broad shoulders that she desperately wanted to lean against. *What am I doing?*

"Brunelda is with Veros," he said as he entered the room, "So I came to tell you myself, I will send for you before sunrise tomorrow morning."

"Oh okay," she said with a smile, which suddenly made him feel as if he might melt. He had yet to see her truly smile, and he found her completely charming. She wondered why he came to tell her, he could have sent someone else. It did not matter though, she felt happy to see him. He looked incredible to her in the firelight, his hazel-green eyes flickering wildly.

He stood there quiet for a few seconds and then pointed towards some of the things she had purchased at the market. "I see you have found all that you needed."

"Yes," she replied, "Brunelda took me earlier." She suddenly felt very appreciative for him, she wanted to let him know she was thankful for all that he had done for her. He nodded and turned towards the door, he was about to leave so she spoke his name, "Prince Arkson," she began. As he turned around, she walked forward and hugged him, her face ended up being buried in his chest. She could hear his heart pound, and looked up at him.

"Thank you for your kindness, for taking me to Uri with you," she spoke to him so sweetly that he melted as he wrapped his arms around her. He smelled delicious to her, and she did not want to let go. Sammie slipped her finger into the breast pocket of his shirt, pulling the fabric taut and looked deeply into his eyes. She suddenly wanted him to kiss her, she wanted to see what he would taste like, if it would be as luscious as in her dream.

He planted a soft kiss on her forehead and hoped that it would placate her desire, even though he knew she wanted more, even though he wanted more of her himself. He dared not kiss her lips, she was not ready. To his surprise, she did not let go, could not. Arkson felt powerless. If she held onto him he could not resist her. Sammie felt outside of herself, compelled to hold onto him.

He hesitated before his hand brushed her jawline and he lifted her chin allowing him to see the flesh of her neck. She felt a bit vulnerable as he kissed her feverishly in a soft trail from her earlobe to the heart of her neck. The smooth skin of his face was surprising and warm. She sighed with pleasure, her hands gently massaging his back.

He could feel her heart race, sense her desire and his lust intensified tenfold. Arkson pulled her body up quickly and to his delight she happily wrapped her legs around his waist, while his hands caressed her thighs. He continued to kiss her neck and cheeks and forehead. Samira kissed his neck back nestling her nose against him as his fingers smoothed over her breasts caressing her hardening nipples, she gasped running her fingers through his hair and pulling him closer. He sighed with delight at her touch, her need equal to his own. Their bodies grazed against one another with such passion.

Arkson wanted her body bare. He leaned her back against the door, gently pinning her arms above her head with one hand as he kissed her neck and unbuttoned her shirt with his other hand. His touch electrified her, Samira felt wanton, he was strong enough to carry her weight so effortlessly it made her wonder what else he would do to her.

As her shirt fell open she rubbed herself against his throbbing below the waist, she suddenly felt grateful the Akori wore no undergarments, wishing he would pull off his pants and enter her. Instead he used both hands to pin her arms against the door, she willingly complied, surrendered herself to him as he returned her thrusts with his own. Their faces were inches apart, lips almost touching.

His hands trailed over her arms as he braced her weight until he lightly massaged her breasts, slowly rubbing at her peaking nipples. She felt lightheaded as a thin layer of cotton was all that kept them from joining. His pulsating against her was torture. She trailed her fingers over his chest before she delved into his pants delicate massaging him. He was throbbing so much!

Before she could pull him out, he gasped. "Stop Samira!"

He grabbed her hand and gently raised it to his lips, kissing her wrist and palm successively. They both panted as he leaned his forehead against hers. She was more passionate than he had imagined and he wanted her so badly. Yet despite their mutual arousal he knew she had felt differently the morning before, he wondered what had changed. He gently cupped her face and then placed her two feet back on the ground. He backed away slowly while she stood there curious, her body blocked the door. His eyes were still focused on her naked flesh.

"You don't want me?" She asked a bit confused, breathing heavily.

"I want you more than anything," he let escape from his lips before he could stop himself. She rubbed her arm.

"Was I too forceful Arkson?" she asked, a little embarrassed.

He laughed, "no Samira, not at all." He moved backed

to her and hugged her closely sensing she felt guilty that she had done something wrong.

"I just want to wait." He looked deeply into her eyes. "We should not rush" he said. Sammie took in a deep breath. He was right, they had known each other for two days, and she was ready to go to bed with him!

She let it sink in. She was never one to sleep with anyone quickly, even though she could be spontaneous and impatient. She never was with men. This was so unlike her, so brazen!

What was it about him that got her so thrilled? He could see she was lost in thought removing herself from him. He tickled her neck and she came back to him.

"I'm sorry," she said, and he smiled at her with a gorgeous smile, making her legs feel weak.

"Me too," he said and kissed her nose.

He buttoned her back up, and then whispered, "Until tomorrow.."

After he left, Sammie stood there, his scent lingered upon her leaving her senses stimulated. What was happening to her?

IN THE MORNING SAMMIE had gotten up early and with Brunelda had prepared herself. Brunelda had neatly braided her hair in a french braid. She wore navy blue velvet pants tucked into black boots with her white tunic and a coordinating velvet vest and waist coat. The gold buttons on the coat were beautiful and she hoped that she would be warm. The weather had changed in the past few days and seemed much cooler.

When she arrived in the throne room with the other riders a few of them eyed her. She wondered what they were thinking and if they knew why she was coming with them. Arkson arrived and stared at her intensely for a moment before directing his guards to their horses, they left and he walked over to her.

Her breath caught as he moved closer and she saw him more clearly, the darkness of the morning was fading and the light in the sky made him look so alive, his eyes were so vivid and his frame was warmed by the golden hour making him incredibly attractive.

"You will be riding with me Samira." He looked at her playfully, and she tried to contain her smile while following him.

"Is that bad for the horse?" She asked wondering how the first horse, on which she had ridden to Zatian, managed the extra weight of her body.

He admired her consideration for the animal. "My horses are much stronger than the others," he said, "we will be bringing a second anyway in case we need to switch."

She nodded her head in acceptance of that and watched as he mounted the large black horse and then assisted her on as well. She wrapped her arms around his waist, and let his scent invade her. She tried to focus her thoughts on the trip, not on Arkson's muscular body beneath her fingers. As they rode out to the others, she realized he was right, the horse they rode was almost twice the size of the other riders.

"What is your horse's name?" She wanted to distract herself from the feel of Arkson, from his magnetism and presence.

His head tilted back to her slightly, but his eyes never left the land in front of him. "Thunder, my sister named him when we were children."

They set out and she observed the surroundings, wondering if her memory had served her well in recalling the landmarks and the way back to Uri. For the most part it had, although she realized she may have taken a little longer to recall it all.

About halfway through the ride Arkson needed to stop

for a rest. All he could smell was Samira and for the past hour he had become increasingly aroused. He sensed she was feeling the same too, which made it worse for him. He had been right in bringing her to Zatian, no one had ever affect him so. He found her so irresistible.

After she had offered herself to him it had not taken long before he had been drawn to her late at night. He had paced the palace halls resisting as much as he could until he could not control himself and went over to her room. He could have sent someone else, but he was compelled to see her. It was their touch that previous morning that had drawn her to him the next night.

As his guard's horses stopped by the stream to drink, he pulled his up a little further so he and Samira could have a bit of privacy. After Arkson had led the horse to the water, and gently stroked his mane, whispering thanks for his hard work, he walked to where Samira stood near the edge of the woods, she was looking at some flowers bent down over them so that her shapely bottom was all the more evident.

He looked to see if his guards could see them, and reassured they were out of view, as he approached her, he gently cupped her bum cheek with his hand. She jumped up startled and he pulled her into a hug lifting her up by her waist while they both laughed. As Arkson put her back down, her body slowly brushed against his, leaving them both electrified. Sammie wanted to kiss him so badly, but she knew he would pull away. He was holding back, and hiding something from her.

"Those are forget-me-not, aren't they?" She said to him as their laughter lulled.

He looked back at them quickly. "Yes," he replied amused, "are you thinking of becoming a botanist?"

She smiled. "I read about them in your massive library, since I have little else to do with my time."

"There are other ways you could pass the time," he replied, and the tone in his voice gave her a seductive shiver as though he wanted to pass the time with her.

"Oh?" she said, not wanting to add the how.

"I could think of a few things" he said. A pang of heat curled up between her legs.

Her mouth grew dry, "like what my prince?"

He held his hand out to her and she took it as they walked over the rocks returning to the horse. He looked at her a moment before his expression seemed to change.

"Do you feel captive in the palace Samira?" he asked, hoping it was not the case.

"Sometimes, yes." She looked at him wondering if her words would cause him pain.

"I don't want that for you. I want you to feel as though the palace is your home. You may go where you like Samira, I can always arrange a guard for you." He looked at her intensely awaiting her response.

"Is that necessary though?" She wondered why he always wanted her protected and safe.

"More so than you realize," he replied.

"I can care for myself Arkson." Her eyes gleamed with strength.

"I do not doubt that Samira, but this world is different than yours." His eyes grew dark, "there are very serious threats to your life."

She wanted to ask him what kind of threats, but she wondered more what he knew of her world. "How is it that you know I am not from here?" She asked.

"No human from this world is like you," he replied and left it at that. "We must be going now to arrive on time."

She wanted to ask more, but was eager to see Salha and her questions would only delay them from leaving. They continued on their way.

When they arrived in Uri, she expected Arkson to follow her to her destination and then bring her directly back with him while he attended to his business. Instead, he had told her that he needed to attend to the meeting but that he would send his soldier Alvaren with her for protection, that she need not fear him because he would protect her with his life. Sammie felt a little uneasy about being separated from Arkson, a feeling she never expected to have.

As she walked with the guard trailing her, she found her way to the Uri market hoping that she was not too late to catch her sister. Thussan had sent Salha and Braedynn to the market daily to get the things he required for the supper she made. Sammie did not know how, but Braedynn had convinced Thussan to allow him to always accompany Salha on these trips as he worried about her mistreatment by an Anuya. When she saw Braedynn her eyes lit up, and out of the corner of her eye, she saw the disapproval on the soldier's face.

Alvaren placed his hand upon his sword, wondering if she would try to signal Braedynn to distract him while she made off somewhere. She looked near Braedynn, if he was there her sister was not far. At the next stall over she was looking at the apples.

Sammie looked at Alvaren. "Stay here, I'll be right back."

Alvaren did not smile. "I am not letting you out of my sight." He said plainly.

She nodded and made her way over to Salha, her heart pounded.

As Salha turned, her face grew excited with joy at seeing her sister. She thrust her basket of wares to Braedynn arms as she ran to Samira with open arms. They hugged warmly smiling, as Samira brushed her sister's hair from her face. Tears stained their cheeks.

"I worried you were dead!" Salha cried.

"No Sal," Sammie said, "I am still alive and kicking." They both smiled again.

"I am so relieved." Salha chuckled feeling euphoric.

"I have to get us out of here Salha." She cut to the chase since she had little time, "I'm going to find a way to get us home."

"How?"

Sammie shook her head frustrated. "I don't know yet. I'll think of something Sal."

Yet instead of responding with the nod that Sammie had expected Salha's looks changed. "I don't want to go back Sammie. There is no way back."

Samira was confused. "What do you mean?"

Salha cringed, afraid she had hurt her sister. "I'm not going back."

"Is it because of Braedynn? We could bring him with us?"

"Braedynn is going to get me out of here, I won't be in Uri much longer, there's nothing left for us in Halifax, Mom and Dad are gone. I never did anything right there anyway. I have a fresh start Sammie. I have a chance for a new life here." She looked at Samira sadly.

Samira was bewildered. "As a slave?" Her eyebrows narrowed. "What about Eric?" She had really wanted to say, what about me?

Salha looked distressed, she hated fighting with Samira, loved her sister dearly, but finally felt like she was in the right place at the right time. "I won't be a slave for much longer, Eric is in the past, I am married now Sammie, I am going to start a family."

"You're pregnant!?"

Salha looked at her. Her stubborn streak beginning to show. "Not yet, but soon. Braedynn and I have plans for when we get to Brinn, he has a house there for us."

"Soon!" Samira exclaimed. How could her sister have a child here?

Samira was deeply hurt, Salha had moved on, made plans without her.

Sal could sense Samira's pain. She hugged her again.

"Please, come with us." She pulled out a small map, and gave it to Samira. "We have to get out of here first, but when we do we'll come free you."

"I am free," Sammie said, detached, distant as she realized she had made plans for she and her sister for so long, and now Sal wanted no part in them.

"You can leave the man who took you away at any time?" Salha asked, looking back at the guard behind Sammie.

"He's an Akori actually, and yes." Sammie said lying, she sometimes felt as though she was held captive by Arkson. She gestured to Alvaren, "he's just for protection."

"Well what type of man is he that you need to be protected?" Salha said sounding like their mother.

Sammie's face lightened a bit, but her insides were still wrapped into themselves. "He's a good guy Sal, a prince. Don't worry about me, I will find my way to you." She took the map and folded it into the satchel that she and Brunelda had bought for the journey. "Please, be safe," she kissed Sal's forehead and squeezed her tightly knowing that she would have to make it back to Thussan soon, her outings were always timed.

Braedynn stepped forward and unexpectedly hugged them both, he towered over them, "I will keep her safe Sammie, I promise, and then I'll be coming for you."

Samira smiled weakly at Braedynn. Salha piped up. "She can leave when she wants, she will come meet us."

As she left them standing there hugging one another close, Sammie felt alone. She knew her sister had not meant to hurt her, but she suddenly felt like she had been hit in the stomach. She was ready to topple over and when she reached the soldier and looked up, she was surprised to see that it was not Alvaren, but Arkson standing there.

He could sense her pain. Had watched as she hugged a woman who looked just like her, felt a pang of jealousy as a tall man had hugged them both, which quickly faded when he realized the man only had eyes for her friend, who must be her sister. They looked so similar it was a natural assumption. This must have been her secret, but he did not understand why he would keep it from him.

She looked distant. "What about your meeting?" she asked, wondering why Arkson was there when he had business he had to attend.

"It did not take long and the second partner did not show, could only send a messenger for cancellation today." He examined her face, knew there was something wrong, "Did you find the thing you were missing?"

"Yes," she said, not looking him in the eye.

"She is your sister?" He asked.

She looked up at him, he must have seen them. She wondered how much he witnessed, what he saw. Did he see Sal give her the map she wondered. She should be worried about that, but she was not, instead she only felt comforted by his presence. It was as if he had known she needed him.

"Yes, she is my sister," she replied.

"You could have told me," he said apologetically, "I could arrange for her purchase, I can find a way to free her." She felt touched by his kindness. She thought about it for a moment and then felt against it since she did not know what Sal and Braedynn had planned.

She did not want to interfere and put them at greater risk. Plus, she knew if Arkson approached Thussan with another offer, he would tighten the reins on them, monitor Salha and Braedynn more closely fearing their desertion.

"She and her husband have plans," she replied, "I just

pray that they are safe."

Arkson could feel the same pain that overwhelmed Samira, he wanted to pull her close and comfort her, but it was neither the time nor the place, drawing attention to them would not be ideal.

"Samira," he said, hoping he could reach her, but she was somewhere else, lost in thought, his empathy sensed her change and withdrawal.

"Take me back Arkson– to Zatian." He held his hand out for her and gently squeezed it as she took it then proceeded to lead her through the throng. Feeling lifeless she followed.

CHAPTER 17

WHEN THEY RETURNED to Zatian, Arkson was troubled, he could see that Samira was affected, and did not know how to reach her. She spent the rest of the day alone, not even asking Brunelda to keep her company. The following day she ate with him and Brunelda and Veros and then returned to her room to read. He could find no way to bring a smile to her face at any of their meals.

He was afraid of losing her, but he also worried that keeping her against her will would do more harm than good. He had to be honest with her and make time to tell her why he had so desperately wanted her to stay. He wanted to explain to her how he felt about her, how long he had waited for her arrival. He planned to let her rest the night and then go to her the following morning, but he was still worried.

Samira had felt hopeless, frustrated for the day. She sat ruminating about the past. Her body clenched together willing everything to work out for the better, until at last she cried out of frustration, the tears pouring out almost as quickly as they stopped.

    Her sister was so stubborn. Once she had something set to her mind, she would follow through with it and there was no changing her mind. They could both be stubborn, but Samira was afraid her sister's decision would be the end of her life. Thussan clearly was not as brutal a master, but how were she and Braedynn to escape?

    She wished she still had her mother for guidance. She thought about growing up with her sister and mother, the day trips they made to the zoo, the times they had adventures by the harbour. Samira's mother always had such a zest for life. Even on her deathbed she was filled with laughter. Samira took in several deep breaths to calm down and then she did what she always did when she couldn't find a way to let go.

    It was a silly thing, but it made her feel better and reminded her that there were things out of her control that she would have to let flow. She closed her eyes and spoke to her mother, "I need your help Mom, I don't know what to do. Please give me some guidance, a sign."

    She fell asleep, tired from the tears, drifting awake a few hours later when a memory winked at her. She recalled what her mother had said to her and Salha after one terrifying incident that took them all to the hospital.

    Salha had said to their mother, "When can you come home mom?"

    And at that Sammie had instantly shot her a look to back off, but Sal had protested. "We really miss you mom, we need you."

    Samira had felt guilty Salha put such pressure on their ailing mother, but at the same time she knew it would push her, encourage her to heal. Even then her sister was stubborn.

    "I'll be home soon my little ones," she had begun, but then something potent moved through her and she became serious. "I will always be there with you in spirit, but someday I will leave you both and you will have to learn to fly on your own."

Her mother's words resonated with her. Her constant battle with illness made Samira and Salha appreciate life so much more in their teen years, sometimes they had been reckless. Salha was still reckless, until Arzule.

After her mother's death she and Sal had felt alone. It had changed her, Samira became cautious even though she still remained independent and confident. Taking risks were not her forte, even though she craved more meaningful adventure in her life. She scolded herself for ever thinking such thoughts, look what it had rewarded her.

Her mother's encouraging words, that she was capable of anything remained ingrained, yet Salha had seemed lost and that was why Samira always felt like she needed to lead the both of them through life. Now, she realized that her decisions were her own, she could not make them for she and Sal any longer. She had learned a long time ago Salha listened to no one but herself. She had protected her sister for as long as she could and now it was time for her to move on.

She had come back to Zatian because of promises, one that she had made to Arkson and one that he had made to her. She made a new promise to herself as the night drew near. She had to start living for herself and the most important part to that was learning self-defence. If she did ever leave this palace, she had to be damn sure she knew what she was doing.

THAT NIGHT SHE FOUND herself drawn back to Arkson's library. It was starting to feel like her secret hideout. Pulling a few books from the shelves, she sat at a table in a comfy wing back chair reading into a peaceful state of oblivion.

Arkson had been too worried about her during the day that he wanted to see her before retiring to bed and entered the chamber observing her as she read. He watched her silently for a few minutes before he spoke, "you're quiet Samira."

She jumped a little, surprised by his appearance. He walked slowly towards her, each movement of his body seemed laden with erotic strength, his muscular frame tensed as he approached her, apprehensive despite the inherent pride. His hair had fallen into his eyes and she wanted to reach up and push it aside.

"I'm reading," she replied, "would you rather me read aloud with no audience?" She arched a brow at him quizzically.

"No," he replied, "smart ass."

Her eyes widened, suddenly wondering how he knew that expression.

"It is not only now," he continued, "you are often quiet. It makes me wonder."

"Wonder what?" She asked aloud meaning to only ask herself the question. He sat next to her, leaning over the table.

"You're quite the mystery Samira," he said wiping a stray lock from her face, her breath caught as he looked into her eyes. "What goes on in there?" He asked tilting his head slightly and gesturing towards her head.

The look on his face was intense, but she could not help herself, nervously she laughed, breaking the tension. And he looked at her surprised.

"I could say the same about you." She replied biting her lower lip.

His gaze rested on that lip, he wanted to bite it too.

A sweet smile broke on his lips. "I suppose," he answered, "you can talk with me Samira, when things are bothering you. I want to be your friend."

"I thought I already was your friend." She replied, suddenly wanting more from him than friendship. He looked pleased with her remark.

"You are," he replied, "I guess I just want you to be able to open up to me about what matters to you most. I'll share with you too."

"What will you share?" She asked curious.

He was quiet for a several seconds, as if he was choosing the right thing to say.

"Everything," he spoke, his voice rich and evocative.

To Samira, that sounded like a lot more than just friendship. And then he got up from the table, needing to leave before he touched her inappropriately. Now was not the time for lust, not with Samira feeling so distressed.

"Training tomorrow?" she asked, before he left her side.

He nodded, and then clasping his hands behind his back sauntered out of the room.

IN THE MORNING WHEN Arkson came to get her, she was prepared for her day of training. As she opened the door, he could sense that she felt better and when he saw her she took his breath away. She was dressed in a traditional female warrior's outfit, she wore a black mock neck shirt, which was laced in the back like a corset, it had the same enamelled gold piece as he and the other riders and hugged decadent curves he wanted to caress. With it she wore a simple pair of black tights rather than the thicker pants with protective panels the female Akori usually wore. She had to start off small and would build up to them for now she needed to make her movements easier. Around her hips hung a belt and scabbard, her long black hair was left loose, but was brushed back from her face.

He entered her room waiting by the door. She quickly

returned an open book to the shelf and as she approached him, he could see the determination in her eyes.

She smiled at him. "I am ready Yoda."

He looked at her a bit confused. "Yoda?"

"Ummm, teacher, I meant," she corrected herself, suddenly amused that he missed out on her clever reference.

He wrapped an arm around her waist and with a wink said, "I guess I could teach you a thing or two." It was as if he hinted at something more. She glanced at the bed a bit hopeful, wondering what compelled her to such thoughts. Instead he lead her out the door and down into the palace sparring green.

When they reached the area, she saw four soldiers standing in wait, on the corners of an outlined patch of field. One of the soldiers goaded Arkson playfully and he whispered in Samira's ear, "please indulge me a moment."

He hopped into the middle of the square and stood relaxed while the others prepared themselves in fighting stance. In one flash of movement they all moved towards him and she watched amazed by his quick movements and skillful hand. He flicked his sword gracefully, effectively and with power, bringing each opponent to their knees or laid out on the grass. He was a magnificent fighter and amazed her, aroused her with his agility and speed. She wanted to be capable of the same skill, the same sheer force. He walked away from them and returned to her.

"I am impressed, Prince Arkson." He half-smiled and then shrugged modestly, bringing her over to another patch of grass while she showed her how to properly hold the sword, and the correct stance. Even though his body was incredibly close to her and his masculine scent drove her senses wild, Samira paid close attention to his instructions, practising dutifully as he spoke. She was there to learn, it was a necessity.

He had only eyes for her as he began, some of the soldiers walked by making comments. He ignored each one and focused intensely upon her form and direction. She listened well and learned quickly, making her an easy student. He examined her face as she moved, there was such elegance and beauty to her, but something raw and powerful beneath that, she had a wildness he had never expected since she was so quiet. He caught glimpses of it when she was angered, but she shielded it so well.

By the time their usual breakfast hour drew near, he could tell she was ready to try a couple of light hand to hand combat movements, but as he motioned for her to strike towards him she hesitated. She could sense the nearby soldiers watching them and felt shy. He looked at them, made a small motion with his hand and they left.

Samira prepared herself mentally for what would ensue. She took a deep breath, and moved forward to strike. He prevented her from hitting him directly, but she kept trying. She manoeuvred this way and that, and she felt she was doing alright until he knocked the sword from her hand, twirled her away from him wrapping his arm around her chest pulling her body into his.

Their hearts raced in unison, he had been so focused on instructing her, but was now distracted by the feel of her body. He could feel her breasts hardened from his touch beneath his arm. The curve of her bottom pressed against him. He could not resist, especially when he knew she shared the sentiment. He sheathed his sword and wrapped his free arm around her waist and then kissed the nape of her neck.

"Shall I give you a private lesson?" He asked, the deep richness of his voice resonating in her ear made her shiver.

"Yes," she replied breathless, wrapping her arms over his. She replied without thinking, surprised by her own excitement. She leaned further into him and nuzzled his neck, inhaling his smell, before kissing it softly. He picked her up quickly throwing her over his shoulder and she cried out with rich laughter that rippled through him seductively as he carried her through the hallway and took her back to her room.

After they entered he stopped her from walking towards the bed, wrapped an arm around her chest as he had in the field and lavished her neck with kisses while he removed her belted scabbard and began untying her shirt. She leaned back into his luxurious touch, and as her shirt fell, with a thud to the floor. She arched her back, her hands on his thighs, breathing in pleasure as he stroked her breasts and decorated her back with kisses and a tantalizing lick down the length of her spine until he gently nibbled her bottom.

She jumped with a giggle from the bite, smiling in a rush of happiness. He looked up to see her dark eyes glowing with spirit.

Quickly he rose and lifted her into his arms, laying her on the bed. He moved back to remove his own belted scabbard and shirt and as he stood before her bare chested Sammie was astonished at his body. She had never seen anyone this sexy before. It was way better than her dream, his muscles were taut and sculpted. Her fingers tingled in anticipation of touching him.

He moved towards her provocatively and with such determination, his body was leaning over hers while he removed her tights slowly. The black leather necklace and pendant of the dream had been tucked beneath his clothing and swung slowly from side to side, emphasizing the beauty of his sun kissed skin. His hazel-green eyes locked on hers as he stared deeply into them, looking at the dark brown sunbursts in them. Her hands caressed his shoulders delicately and her fingers tickled his neck.

"You are beautiful Samira," he said with such honesty.

Her heart ached at his words. He kissed his way down from her neck to her breasts. She gasped as he nipped at them playfully before circling her swollen nipples with his tongue. His mouth enclosed them hungrily, tugging softly in a way that lay fire to her. He kissed further down her body, his hands lingering as he moved.

Samira felt hypnotized as he parted her legs. Her desire overcame her nervousness. No man had ever her wanted her like this, he looked up at her with such intense emotion.

Arkson was overwhelmed by her scent, it took everything to stop himself from kissing her lips.

"I want to pleasure you," he said softly. She opened her mouth to protest but was speechless. His cheek nuzzled her thighs while he lifted her closer to him and kissed there playfully, his lips grazing her skin in simmering motions before devouring her.

Samira grew quietly breathless in pleasure her whole body surrendering to Arkson's delicious appetite. As his tongue tickled her she raked her hands through his hair, and his explorable mouth brought her closer and closer to the peak. He devoured her, his tongue alternating between swirls and strokes. She dizzied as her breasts hardened and body trembled with a powerful surge of ecstasy as she gasped in release. His tongue lapped over her sensitive peak in short delicious strokes until another reverberation erupted through her.

"Oh sweet heaven," she let escape in a whisper closing her eyes and arching into him.

Arkson was delighted by her bliss and wanted more from her, he gently rubbed her folds with his fingers before slipping them into her and stroking her in a come hither motion. His mouth returned to her neck while his fingers played with her core. He stretched her in a rhythmic twist that left her light headed. The warmth from his body casting over hers was overpowering, she grasped at his back, pulling his body closer to hers.

"Arkson..." Samira moaned, melting into him. Her body sizzled with each movement, deepening her feeling until she climaxed harder than she ever had before, her pleasure echoing and lasting for a few minutes before it waned. She still tingled from his touch as he kissed and caressed her body. He savoured her so attentively, he was incredible.

He expected her to rest a bit, as he looked down at her admiring the natural flush to her cheeks. Instead of cuddling closer and laying there, she gently pushed him onto his back straddling his waist. The sight of her naked body above made him quiver with passion. And the feral look of her dark hair hugging her face and falling down to her waist was enough to make him groan. His mouth fell open and lips beguilingly curled with passion. He never had any female do this to him, usually an Akori male took charge in the bedroom. He was a little nervous, despite his desperate want for her.

Samira stared back at Arkson intensely, it was odd to see him a little unsure, she ran her hands slowly from his stomach to his chest and over his arms interlacing her fingers with his as she raised his arms above his head. His body was warmed by her hot touch.

"Keep them there," she commanded seductively. He smiled, which made her melt even more.

Samira certainly did not think herself a sex goddess, in fact most men found her prudish, but something about Arkson made her feel masterful and sensuous. She wanted to pleasure him so desperately and to give him what he had just given her. She rubbed herself against him playfully while they both moaned and lowered herself to him, her hair brushed against his body, tickling him in a way that was rousing. She pulled it all to her left side revealing her full nakedness to Arkson's eyes and he admired her appreciatively.

She leaned in and kissed his earlobe delicately, before gently nibbling at it, her teeth gently grazing against the lobe erotically before trailing kisses down his neck to his chest. His smell was intoxicating as her lips brushed over his flesh with deliberate kisses and she gently licked his nipples tugging at them delicately with her mouth. He sighed in pleasure at her touch, was astonished by her sexual prowess. She could feel him throbbing beneath her waist, making her heart want him.

She unbuttoned his pants and pulled them off of him gracefully. Her eyes devoured him, he was thick and long and throbbing, he looked moist and so delectable that she wanted to taste him. She eagerly climbed up to straddled him again and Arkson yearned to slide into her wet body but resisted.

She kissed his chest gently, trailing down his stomach until she gently stroked him, slowly and rhythmically, her fingers tickled the grooves above his thighs and she kissed them softly. With slightly parted lips at last she licked him in slow circles. He shivered, no Akori had ever done this for him. He suspected in part since they knew he could not be mated to him. He had been alone for so long, and now Samira was offering herself so freely.

She slid her mouth over him hotly her tongue lapping and fingers rubbing while his hands balled into fists from delight. Her movements evoked chills in him emanating from his centre to the tips of his fingers. He could hardly breathe as the minutes passed. He was closer and closer to the brink.

Where had she been all this time? And what had he done without her. She was so determined to please him it burned into his heart. Her teeth grazed against him gently creating more chills before she returned to her playful suction. She feasted upon him so sensuously.

"Samira," he whispered as he reached down and gently caressed her cheek with his finger. She removed her lips from him long enough to gently kiss and then suckle his finger, while her hands still tended to him and then returned to his body. The gesture sent Arkson over the edge and he pulled away from her. He grabbed the towel on the nightstand as he exploded.

"Hey," she whispered softly, and then wrapped her body around his while he sat on the edge of the bed, her hands running over him as he continued to release and she assaulted his shoulder blade with kisses.

"Why did you pull away?" She said after he was done.

"I did not want to... you know..." he replied his voice trailing off.

"You would have just decorated my body is all," she whispered into his shoulder blade, a little naughtily with a mischievous smile.

Arkson was amazed by her openness, he turned and arched a brow and pulled her close to him as they lay wrapped around one another luxuriating in each other's touch. He felt at ease with her, so very peaceful.

He wanted to tell her everything about himself, about his curse, about her role in it, but instead they found themselves conversing about minute things like parts of Akorian tradition that Samira had read or their favourite foods.

Samira chuckled happily in his arms as they discussed some of the differing names for fruits and vegetables. She found that there were a lot of similarities between English and Akorian, as if it were a slight difference in dialect. She smiled when they discovered a shared dislike for tomatoes and green peppers unless they were cooked in a sauce. Arkson seemed so normal to her then.

She wondered if she would ever meet someone like

him on earth. She doubted they would be this interesting to her, this captivating. And she felt warmed and happy until she wanted to lean closer and kiss him, but stopped herself. He sensed her sadness immediately.

"What is wrong Samira?" He asked brushing the hair from her face.

"How do you do that?" She wondered aloud. He always knew how she felt.

He shrugged.

"Arkson..." she said, her eyes narrowing.

He twisted his mouth and then ceded to her, kissing her cheek. "I am empathic, I can always sense your emotions."

Her eyes widened. "Really?" She said sitting up her hand bracing against his chest. She had not read that anywhere in her books. She wondered what else might be missing.

"Yes," he replied pulling her back down to him cuddling closer and spooning her body with his own. "All Akori have gifts such as empathy, telekinesis, energy sourcing, and some others. Some have one gift, the truly special have multiple powers."

"No telepathy?" She asked, afraid her might be able to read her mind as well.

"No, not that gift, regrettably," he said with a sigh nibbling at her neck.

"You must have more than one. What are your gifts?"

"I only have empathy now," he said answering without thinking. He had meant to poke fun at her, asking her if she thought he were special since she assumed he had several.

"What do you mean now?" She asked and suddenly he was not ready to tell her everything. He was afraid she would judge him harshly.

"I used to have others, but not anymore," he said

knowing she would push the matter further.

"Why?" She asked, while her stomach made a rumbling noise.

He placed his hand on her stomach, tickling her. "You sound hungry, we should get you fed," and he left her side in bed getting dressed.

Samira wondered why he held back so much. What was he keeping from her? He was so giving and caring towards her, but she knew so little about him. She supposed he could say the same about her, but she wanted to open up to him, wanted him to open up to her.

"Why won't you tell me?" She asked.

He gave her a look that begged her to be patient with him, "I will Samira, just not now, you need to eat before you faint."

She eyed him, but left it alone. She definitely did not want to drop the matter, but she had learned that with Arkson, if she gave him time, he always proved himself to her.

As they entered the dining hall she realized that there was no one there. They had passed the hour of eating, and Brunelda had told her when she first arrived to make sure she was within the eating timeframe otherwise the staff of the kitchen attended to their other palace duties and she would have to fend for herself. She loved cooking though, so it would be nice to create a meal for a change.

Arkson lead her into the room where all her delicious meals usually came. She was pleased to see that it was incredibly clean, there was a large wooden workspace for preparation, and several large wood stoves. He tossed an apple to her, while he munched one himself.

After she finished her first bite she asked him, "do you know how to cook?"

His mouth curled cutely. "I never have to."

She laughed and looked through the pots and pans

grabbing a cast iron pan so that she could cook for them.

"You know how to cook?" He asked.

She nodded her head.

"Will you teach me?" he asked enthused, "something tells me you would be a good cook."

"Of course," she replied. "I am the best," she teased wriggling her eyebrows.

"You're the best at a lot of things," he said suggestively pulling her into a hug and kissing her forehead softly. He helped her find some vegetables and the necessary tools for their meal.

As she chopped he watched her and listened as she described the recipe. Then mischievously he crept up behind her and wrapped his body around hers, his hands over hers as she sliced vegetables. The cutting became clumsy.

She looked up at him and spoke, "Arkson, how am I supposed to chop with your hands there?"

"I'm feeling the motions," he said to her, kissing the top of her head.

He was adorable.

Veros walked in unexpectedly, and grabbed an apple, Arkson stayed wrapped around her and it made her feel happy to know his affection for her was not being kept a secret.

"Is he impressing you with his passion for cooking?" Veros asked between bites.

She opened her mouth in awe, "You said you did not know how to cook," she accused him.

"No," he said grinning, "I said I never have to."

"Arkson!" She shouted, "you asked me to teach you."

He was still amused.

"Yes, I wanted you to teach me how *you* cook."

She shook her head disapprovingly. He shot a glance at Veros, who promptly left chuckling.

Arkson made her stop chopping and turned her around, tilting her head up so he could look into her eyes.

"Forgive me?" He asked with a wolfish look in his eyes.

"Okay," she said, "I guess you just needed an excuse to spend more time with me." She turned back to her cutting with a sigh.

"I never need an excuse for that," he whispered into her ear planting a kiss at the nape of her neck, sending shivers to her spine with a pang. Sammie wondered, how on earth she had begun feeling so much, for this prince she hardly knew.

Arkson grabbed the plates of food while Samira grabbed the two glasses of red wine he had poured for them. She had made ratatouille and he had sliced up some fresh baked crusty bread for them to eat with it, slathered in butter. It was hearty and delicious, the perfect comfort meal.

They sat at the large dining hall table enjoying their meal when Sammie had remembered Arkson's expression at that very table the first time they ate together.

"What were you thinking when I was sitting across from you at the banquet, on my first day in Zatian?" He smiled at her question.

"You mean when you covered your plate in potatoes?"

She laughed. "Yes, I felt like you were examining me with a magnifying glass"

"I was," he answered, "I was surprised that you said anything at all that night, you seemed so quiet. Well, that was before you blasted me into oblivion."

"I did not blast."

"You blasted Samira."

"Was it that bad?"

"No, I would not have it any other way. You're the only one who speaks to me that way and you're the only one who may. Anyone else I would kill."

"No you wouldn't, you bluff."

His smile faded and he looked serious. His face grew dark, cold. "Yes, I would."

She looked at him wondering if she read him wrong, he seemed incapable of such a shallow action. He valued life, or had she been wrong.

"No, you wouldn't," she said again wanting it to be true.

His face broke into an even larger smile than before and he laughed. "You looked scared for a moment."

"I was Arkson!" She slugged him in the shoulder.

"See, only you." She went to do it again, when he grabbed her hand and kissed it and then nibbled on her fingers.

"You shouldn't abuse me Samira."

"Why?" She asked, taking her hand back and eating the last spoonful of vegetables.

"Because I'll take you to my bed and punish you," he answered her in his matter of fact tone.

She swallowed, but still her mouth went dry, heart thumping, she reached for her wine. "Is that a promise?" She asked him taking a sip.

"Yes, and I'll expect you to make it up to me," he said his voice deep and dark, his look hot and eager.

She stuck her tongue out at him and punched him lightly in the arm again quickly getting up from the table and ready to evade him. He was shocked, but he was much faster and before she had even reached the hall doors he had wrapped his arm around her waist and was carrying her back to the table.

"Truce?" She asked while she laughed. He swept aside some of the centrepieces and laid her across the table, the tall length of his body leaning over her. She tingled excited and reached up to run her fingers through his silky hair.

"No truce," he shook his head, "too late you little

hellcat."

"Are you going to punish me Arkson?" She simpered, her eyes locked on his lips.   "Yes," he said, kissing and nibbling her fingers again, "you've been very bad."

"This isn't your bedroom."

Her chest filling with so much air it pushed her breasts out towards him. His body loomed large above hers and it made her feel feminine. She never considered herself particularly small, in fact she was taller and larger than most of the women she knew, but with him, she felt womanly.

"No, but it is my palace."

He leaned down. His face was so close and his mouth hovered above hers. The rustle of his clothes was a cadence to her senses in the quiet room. He shifted his weight to one of his arms using the other hand to brush back her tresses before cupping her cheek.

"Samira," he said looking serious for a moment, before staring at her lips.

"Yes," she whispered.

This is the moment she thought. He's going to kiss me.

He leaned down so his breath was hot on her lips before he smiled again fully. "I'm going to tickle you silly"

"What?" Before her brain recognized his words, his fingers were all over her gently tickling her neck and underarms, and stomach and even behind her knees. She laughed uncontrollably squirming beneath him.

"No! Arkson, stop, please!"

He looked devilish. "Never!"

Tears ran down her cheeks from laughing so hard. "Please Arkson, have mercy! Mercy!"

He finally stopped letting her catch her breath, she sucked in air quickly. He gazed down at her really wanting to kiss her, but he knew he had to tell her first.

"Samira,"

"Yes?"

"I..."

The loud creak of the wooden doors interrupted his voice and he pulled them off the table, he held her to his side so that she was still nestled into him as Alvaren entered the room. It made her feel good again to know that their displays of affection were not a secret to any of his subjects, his family and guards included.

Alvaren kneeled before them. "Prince Arkson, the nobles and soldiers are gathered in the Hall of Haldero awaiting your instructions on the new terms for the annex."

"Thank you, I'll be there momentarily Alvaren."

He left them then and Arkson leaned down and kissed her forehead. "I should be going."

"Arkson, what did he mean by the terms for the annex?"

He looked at her, his eyes suddenly heavy. He could lie to her, grow cold, and omit the details but not now, not when they had grown so close. He had to tell her, "Zatian was annexed by another kingdom when I was a child."

"What! How?"

"That is a long story, for another time."

He was about to leave when she grabbed his arm. "Is that why you're not a king?"

His looks changed to something darker, pain rumbling beneath the surface of his countenance, "Partially, yes. I'll see you later Samira." He gently lifted her hand to his mouth kissed it and left the dining hall.

So many questions rose to the forefront of Samira's mind. What had happened to Arkson? Who had taken the city from him? Did the annex have something to do with him keeping her in the city? She mentally scoffed at the last question, the two were so unrelated. All the same, she wanted to know more, wanted to be able to help him, somehow.

CHAPTER 18

ARKSON ENTERED THE hall of Haldero. It had been his father's place of strategy, and now it was the same for he and his company. Unthinkingly Arkson had followed in the same tradition. His father was an Akori of fire, a quality so rare among his people. They usually were more earthen or airy in nature, drawing their powers from those elements at the core and building them from their elemental electrical surges.

It was for that reason that most of his group had powers of telekinesis and levitation, it was only Alvaren whose base was water. He could hold his breath for half an hour and in the summer months when the moon was at its strongest he could swim beneath the surface for a few hours. Alvaren had always been his closest friend for that reason, the two of them differing from the rest.

Arkson's powers rooted in the blaze of fire had been stripped of them before he could understand them fully, and although his group were loyal and protected him diligently, he knew that if King Guedan decided to attack his people they would be fearful. How could they be led to victory by a prince without powers?

At first, he had seen Samira as his chance to be the King he had always dreamt he could be, but now things were different, the more time he spent with her, the more he liked her. Possessing her was becoming harder and harder, he did not want to think of her as a belonging. He wanted her to be his queen, his equal. Her intelligence demanded it from him and he knew it was that quality which made him care for her even more.

He had never suspected he would feel this way, in his youth after the curse had drained him and left him sickly, he had swore to Nikelda that he hated the idea of marrying a human. The only human he could stand was Alexandros, and Arkson would never marry him, he was a male!

Even though she was younger than her brother, he was so weak that she stayed with him always to care for him. Nikelda had tried to soothe him, over the months of his recovery, one day telling him that he would someday meet a beautiful human female who would be more than he could ever find in an Akori. She would steal his heart, she warned him, snatch it up and before he knew it he would fall for her. His sister had always been comical like her Uncle Veros. He wished that she were there now to offer him some guidance, there to meet Samira, the one who *was* stealing his heart.

By the look on his guard's face, he knew that the messenger had not brought good news. His second scout Elastor had gone to meet with the northern Batchi who were disbanded from the other tribes and did not partake in the slaving so common with the southern parts. They had weaponry more suitable for fiercer combats because of the harder weather conditions in their lands.

They had agreed to meet with Arkson for a trade and discussion of an alliance, but the meeting was to be held in

Parule, which was days from Zatian. He had to leave Samira behind, it was far too dangerous to bring her with him. Even though the Akorian bore no ill will to other races, he did not know if the Batchi could be trusted in her company. For all he knew, they could have already made an alliance with Guedan.

"What do you say Prince Arkson?" Elastor asked after explaining the news.

Arkson knew he needed to take the chance, if not he could miss out and the opportunity might not rise again for decades.

"We will have to prepare tonight and leave first thing tomorrow. We'll go into the city by the south gate in case Guedan suspects anything and will travel by boat to the port there. We'll have to camouflage ourselves and be stealthy with a night arrival. Alvaren will you arrange the ship?"

He stepped forward. "I will, as soon as possible."

The others looked relieved, he suspected they feared he might not leave Samira, or at least that was what the room seemed to feel.

He would need to make sure she was guarded though, kept safe in the castle while he was abroad. There was no telling what Guedan could be planning. He would have to increase his guards on rotation and ask Alvaren to stay behind with her, no other could be trusted. He knew that word had made it to him of Samira's stay in Zatian, so this trip would need to take as little time as possible.

If he did not need the weapons and potential ally he would not have gone at all. He had met with one of the clan members of the Northern Batchi on his last visit to the Akorian Games. It had been a decade but the friendship still remained. Jav had been a trainer to one of the fighters from the Swati clan of Akori in the north near the Batchi, but sadly that clan had fallen to Guedan shortly after the games too.

They had exchanged several letters over the years and Jav had always kept Arkson well informed on the events of his village as well as his family, which had grown with several children in the past few years. As luck would have it Jav was brother in law to the tribe leader, and although it had taken some time he had been able to convince him of a weapons exchange. Jav had fought for Arkson among the Batchi after knowing first hand how brutal Guedan could be to the colonies.

Arkson had fortune on his side. Hopefully the time it would take to get there and back would also be auspicious.

He went to Samira that night while she slept, brushed the hair from her face. He kneeled against the side of the bed, his chin resting on his crossed arms while he gazed upon her. His eyes were dark with desire and he wished she was laying there naked. She tossed a bit and he felt the urge to lie next to her and comfort her, pull her close. He did not want to wake her.

"Arkson?" She asked sleepily. Feeling the warmth of his breath on her skin.

What a creep, he's watching me sleep. She thought with a smile.

He smiled softly. "Yes Samira."

"Come to bed," she commanded, feeling as though he were her long time boyfriend coming home from a night out with the boys. If only that were true.

He crawled in with her and wrapped his arms around her. She cuddled into him tucking herself between his neck and shoulder. He wished they could stay like that for days, that they could become lost in one another and take the time they needed to share themselves with each other.

"I have to leave," he whispered to her softly.

"Where are you going?"

"To the Batchi city of Parule, near Swati, but I will

return to you in four to five days."

"Why?" She asked him and her brow was furrowed even though her eyes were closed in sleep.

He chuckled, his finger rubbing out the crinkle in her forehead. Even in her sleep she questioned him.

"It is about an important trade between my people and the Northern Batchi," he replied wondering just how much she would absorb of their conversation in her half-asleep state.

"The ones who do not have slaves?" She asked recalling the information she found in the books on Arzule.

"Yes," he replied, "sleep Samira."

"Alright Arkson," she replied with a yawn, "but tell me a story to help."

He began telling her the tale of his sister's sixteenth birthday, his voice so rich in her ear it made her shiver, but then was calming, and coaxing her into a deep lull.

In the morning when she woke, Samira found an envelope by her bedside. Arkson had left her a letter, telling her that he would have guards protecting her while she was gone. She wondered why he worried so much for her safety. What exactly was it that was a danger to her?

THE MORNINGS IN THE NORTH were always much cooler, but being closer to the mountains and deeper in the forests where most of the year there was snow on the ground, had a strangely serene and calming affect on Arkson despite his apprehension.

He waited for Jav on a terrace outside the clan meeting room as he pulled closer his cloak. For this occasion he had worn his father's furs, too opulent to wear on a regular basis in Zatian. His breath puffed out in the air and he used his gloved hands to pull down the sides of his fur hat.

After discovering the spy in his midst, he hoped it

would deter any further advancement from Guedan for the next few weeks. He knew that news of Arkson's plans to attack had reached the King of Alpohalla, but, what he didn't know was whether or not Guedan believed the rumours. So far there was no word of action and that was good since he was too far away from Samira. Time was on his side, the time it took for Guedan or any additional spy would be seven days. He just hoped Guedan hadn't thought to send any in advance.

Caron had given no indication of that, but Arkson knew that Guedan was smart enough to keep the traitor out of the loop. Samira was safe with Alvaren, so at least there was comfort in that. There was no other he would trust with her life. Alvaren knew how important she was to Arkson, understood how much he cared for Samira.

Looking out on the mountains, he knew she would love it in Parule, would love the beauty of the surroundings. She always seemed to appreciate whatever grace unfolded before her eyes. There had been countless times he watched her eyes travel over her surroundings and then with a deep breath she would breathe in life. She was vivacious, but secretive, like himself, and her laugh was the most beautiful thing he had ever heard, it was lush like velvet.

The first few days of travelling passed quickly. When he was away from Samira the minutes seem to be less concrete since he did not try to memorize everything as he did when he was with her. There were many moments when she was in his thoughts and he wondered how long it would be before he could run his fingers through her hair again.

The meeting the previous night with the delegates had involved a lot of negotiation on the price, Arkson had wanted to give them a bonus as thanks but they refused several times before he at last convinced them it would be given regardless. Now that the terms were agreed to and things were finally winding down, he was anxious to return.

He craved affection from Samira, wanted to tell her more than ever about his curse. He never thought he could feel such strong emotions, he had always kept himself objective. The more he thought about how well she had handled everything he had told her so far, the more he wanted to find his horse and ride back to her. He missed her lips, her eyes, the way her skin felt against his, the taste of her flesh.

"Prince Arkson," he heard behind him, turning to see Jav. He greeted him with a smile.

"Hello Jav," he spoke extending his arm to his friend warmly.

"I am glad to see that you were able to make it here quickly prince. I have much news to share with you."

Arkson examined Jav, he was not a tall creature, about Samira's height, but quite stocky and muscular as many of his kind. The Batchi, much like the Akori resembled humans in Arzule with a few distinguishing features to set them apart. For one, Batchi had excellent hearing, often outside the range of the Akori and as a result had extended ears with long flaps similar to that of a rabbit.

Often their ears remained wrapped around their heads folded over and enclosed in caps. In the south it had been a method to trick the human population while the weather in the north was hard on their sensitive ears. A tell tale sign that you were speaking with a Batchi was their long, thin, tail which functioned as a third arm and ended with a tuft of soft fluffy hair.

Jav's messy brown hair was always kept close to his ears peaked out from the cap he wore now. He motioned for Arkson to join him in the room that housed the members of the tribe council, his expressive brown eyes were telling.

They had already loaded the exchange of weapons on the wagon with which the Prince's had arrived, but after realizing he had planned to leave the following morning, Jav had asked a small request that he stay on for another day while they awaited word from one of their Batchi in the south.

Jav's cousin Sebastien stepped forward to shake Arkson's hand. He was the newly appointed leader of the tribe. After Jav's brother in law had served his term, Sebastien had been selected and was one of the most impressive fighters Arkson had ever had the pleasure to witness in action. It must have been a great honour for him to be the new leader of his people and so Arkson congratulated him.

Much like Arkson, Sebastien was driven, calculated with weaponry. He wielded three swords gracefully, one in each hand and a third by tail. Arkson always found it funny that Nikelda spoke of him as though he were one of the most attractive beings she'd ever seen, and even though their relationship was strictly platonic, she ogled him to no end.

He had long blonde hair and green eyes of emerald, his shoulders were the same breadth as the prince but since he was shorter, only a few inches taller than Samira he looked like a massive muscular wall. Despite the colder temperatures of the North he always managed to look sun kissed, in fact all of the Batchi did.

"Welcome Prince Arkson, please join us at our table, we have much to discuss."

Arkson sat in a chair next to Sebastien and nodded towards the males around the table out of respect. It was nice to be warm amongst them, and in the centre of the table was a cast iron fire that vented heat over the feet of each seated Batchi. They were quiet for several minutes passing around a large flask in sharing, a tradition Arkson knew should be respected. He sipped the bittersweet drink, made of fermented yeast and similar to the wine of his city, passing it along to another.

"Guedan is out of control," an elder spoke first, "he must be stopped before the Batchi of the south lose their *Kapal*"

Arkson was surprised, his eyes widened *Kapal* was something rarely discussed in the presence of anyone other than the Batchi. He only knew of it from the books in his library and even that was limited, a mere description. From what he recalled, it was the spirit of the tribe, something which permeated in all of its members and kept them prosperous and happy. Since the Batchi of the north were stronger than the south, he sensed that the *Kapal* was far more resilient, more powerful. What he didn't understand is why it was under threat.

"We must explain," Sebastien spoke, gazing at the elder and then to Arkson.

"*Kapal* is something which keeps us strong, even though it does not need to manifest in physical form, the strongest tribes do have this happen. For our tribe we have this," he gestured to the middle of the table when Arkson saw a large wooden box. Another member opened it and inside was the largest uncut diamond Arkson had ever seen. "Our clan is strong and so our *Kapal* rewards us greatly, but the tribes of the South are polluted from their misdeeds. Slavery has stripped them of their purer energy and if their greed isn't rectified, the *Kapal* may poison them to preserve our way of life."

The elder spoke again before Arkson could answer, "Guedan's been researching into the portals, looking for a way to shift between them without a device. He wants to move through them on electrical impulses only. That combined with his need for raw materials leads us to believe he is planning to decimate our populations for their *Kapal*."

Arkson let it all sink in, "can Guedan use the *Kapal* like a Kaptu to travel?"

"It can be done," Jav answered from the other side of the table, "but it is not easy, only the strongest of minds can show the way, and then it is a burden to them, their bodies usually stripped of much power in the process. If Guedan learns of this there would not be much to stop him from moving on from the southern tribes to us here in the North"

Arkson was honoured. "You trust me with this information?"

"There is a prophecy," a second elder spoke this time, "of one with no power outside of our people, one who has been cursed but who holds the key that would stop the darkness from falling across the lands. There are no others like you," he said with a crooked smile. "We believe it is your destiny Akorian prince."

"For that reason," the first elder continued, "we humbly request your help in fighting this evil, we are a strong people, but not too proud. We know that this could cost the annex Zatian greatly, but this is why we agree to provide you with weapons, not only for protection, but to fight, truly fight against that evil which threatens us all."

The males sat around him quieted, the look on their faces martyred. They wondered if the prince would accept. Guedan was harsh with the colonies and the annex of Zatian was treated far worse that the other Akorian cities since none of Guedan's valued subjects lived there. Even though it had managed to escape regular visits from the beastly king by nature of its distance, he made sure that it paid homage.

They knew that since Arkson's city was the furthest, but since it had been the first that Guedan chose to conquer, he would put up the hardest fight to maintain his hold. Yet, Zatian would be a city situated to all of their advantage, strategically it was a place that could be quickly connect with the other Akorian cities of the northeast. Cities whose leaders were simply waiting to rebel.

Arkson's body nearly hummed with excitement. He had planned to convince them to join him gradually, but here they were offering him what he needed most – an ally.

His mouth broke into the widest smile, one that wanted to find Samira and kiss her silly for the joy that he felt. If his guards had been there to witness it, surely they would have been taken aback by his uncharacteristic show of such clear emotion.

"I would be honoured to accept this alliance. I came here myself in the hope that I could convince you of the same. Zatian will surely fight alongside this tribe."

"We are very pleased," Sebastien spoke standing and extending his arm to Arkson as they embraced, leaning back he looked up at Arkson, "although this may bring us through darker times we must celebrate this opportunity to right the wrong done by our sister clans. Please, let us honour you and your company with a banquet before you depart."

Although Arkson wanted to return to Samira as soon as possible, he could not be rude to the Batchi who had given him so much more hope in the span of a few minutes. He would partake in their meal, eager for the nourishment to bring him home swiftly.

CHAPTER 19

SAMIRA STOOD IN THE training field. She had been so focused in her desire to fight that she had memorized the course and moves that Arkson had showed her. She had spent several hours each previous day training with Alvaren who had picked up where Arkson had left off guiding her swordsmanship and defensive maneuvers.

After she felt she had mastered the moves as well as she could. She had given Alvaren a break and moved onto archery. It was much needed pause since he was harder than her on the Prince, and more than a few times had flipped her onto her bottom. She had been sore in the evenings, but at least she slept more easily.

The bow he had given her to practice with had been Nikelda's in her teen years. Since she had mastered the powers of her energy sourcing, she did not require the skill. It was not of much use since a bow would only hinder the bolts flying from her hands. Or at least that was what Alvaren had explained to her. She had never witnessed any energy sourcing in the palace. Levitation she saw on more than one occasion, a couple of the cooks used their earthy telekinesis, and she knew that the was the constant subject of Arkson and Brunelda's empathy, but she wondered what that skill would look like.

She could tell Alvaren was surprised by how adamant she was to learn. She woke earlier than he had every day, and practiced before she ate. At the present moment, he had fallen back a bit on the field with some of the other Akori. He had still been within viewing distance as he left her alone to deal with the arrow and quiver for half an hour, but returned now and was watching her closely as she pulled the bow and released and hitting her target.

From her practice she improved to the point where most of her arrows landed within the core circle of the target. She had loved archery in high school. It was too bad she never pursued it outside of her gym class. After finishing all of her arrows she looked over to where Alvaren leaned against a tree, he was joined by another Akori, one she had learned the day before was named Elastor.

They were both breathtaking Akori, tall and muscular with golden hair and complexions but they could not compare to Arkson. Not in Sammie's eyes, her prince was so hot he could melt butter in seconds just by looking at it. She knew she was keeping herself busy, but she missed him. If she could get her hands on him when she got back, she might even be tempted to kiss him. The thought made her smile, and gathering her arrows she walked over to where they stood, picking up her satchel and swinging it over her shoulder.

It looked like a heated discussion, and luckily they had not noticed her return so she caught a bit of their conversation as she dropped her quiver and bow.

Alvaren's nostril's flared. "What do you mean there are three Akori awaiting Prince Arkson's return? Did you send the messenger with the details of Caron's assassination?

Elastor spoke quickly, nervously, "the Akori insist they are messengers from the city of Opamut, you know the one with the strongest allegiance to Guedan." He was sarcastic. "They say that they are here by his decree to collect tribute."

Alvaren's voice lowered. "Shit!"

Elastor's shook his head in agreement. "Think they killed Caron?"

Alvaren's eyes widened. "Yes, yes I do. Did you send the—?"

"Yes! I sent the message but Veros said there was no need, Prince Arkson would arrange for providing his family with the proper ceremony despite the betrayal. What will we tell those Akori?"

"Well we can't say he's gone to find weapons to kick Guedan's ass."

"No we cannot."

"Do they know of Samira, these Akori?"

Elastor looked even more nervous, "I don't believe so."

"She's not safe here." Alvaren looked over to Samira realizing she had heard too much. "I have to take her elsewhere."

"Agreed," Elastor said swallowing hard, "Ark will kill us if anything happens to you."

Samira was surprised he spoke directly to her. "Who is Caron? And where are you taking me Al?"

Alvaren sighed. "Must you call me that?" It had been the third time that day she called him Al. Samira was silly and platonic with him. He was unaccustomed to a female treating him in any way other than with sheer awe or desire.

"It's a nickname! It means you're my friend. You know a term of endearment?" She gestured with her hands as if to prove her point.

"Oh," he said, considering her words, "I've never had a female friend," then grabbed her arm, "you must come with me."

Elastor's teal eyes brightened. "I will say he has gone to the Gardens of Pleasure, that will shut them up."

They walked out of the palace courtyard and quickly along a wall leading to the heart of the city, while Elastor walked in the opposite direction.

"What!? What are the Gardens of Pleasure!?" Samira demanded.

Alvaren looked sheepish and shrugged, "you know a place of.." his voice trailed off.

Debauchery?

Her eyebrows narrowed, her cheeks hot with anger. "Does the Prince Arkson go there often?" Maybe she was going to wrap her fingers around Arkson's neck when he got back instead of her lips.

But, Alvaren shook his head without hesitation. "No, he stopped going there years ago."

"Oh." Samira replied, relieved, but then she wondered exactly how many years it had been. It had to be at least two. Alvaren had said years. There was a smidgen amount of comfort in that logic.

He picked up the pace and Samira was suddenly worried. She was walking fast, too fast, Alvaren's long legs covering far more ground than hers. "Wait, slow down please."

"I cannot," he said, his eyes examining everything.

They walked past a merchant and he grabbed a cloak throwing a knowing look at the Akori who said, "we may settle later Alvaren" in a polite bow.

"Put this on," he commanded Samira.

As she fumbled with it she nearly laughed, "won't this make me look more conspicuous."

An unexpected smile dimpled his cheeks. "No, you

already stick out like a sore thumb."

He had a point, everyone did look tall and elegant and elven and Samira was very human. She wrapped it around her and threw the hood up over her face.

"When we get to the gate near the ocean you'll have to stand on your tip toes, hide your hair in the cloak, and lean into me like a lover."

"Arkson won't like that." She said immediately, then wanting to bite her tongue for Arkson's thoughts making their way through her voice.

"Don't worry," he said, "I'll not kiss you, only caress you a little." He wriggled his eyebrows.

"Oh no, buster!" She began, but he interrupted.

"Buster, what is this buster?"

"If Arkson finds out he'll murder you. No matter how long you've been friends," she looked at him with piercing eyes from her cloak.

"Then we must not let him find out, friend." Alvaren emphasized the last word and moved them through a courtyard, "Besides, he'll kiss my feet when he knows I've ensured your safety."

"He will not," she said haughtily.

"Alright so he won't," he said, again with a dimpled smile.

He's so charming. Too bad I can't set him up with one of my single girlfriends, I'd bet he'd be a barrel of fun.

The cobbled city streets disappeared as they reached the gate then and she did as Al had instructed.

"Alvaren!" The guard smiled at him, and then looked at Samira trying to see more of her hidden face so she leaned further into a hard shoulder. "Returning for a little retreat I see."

"Yes," Alvaren said, "much needed," and then grabbed Samira's bum in a squeeze.

"Eep!" she let out before a nervous little laugh she

managed to morph into a giggle.

"We'll be going," Alvaren said cutting the guard off as he opened his mouth to speak again. He continued to walk quickly until they walked through a high dune and she knew they could no longer be seen by the city.

Samira pulled her cloak closer, it was cold but it didn't stop her happiness. She could smell the ocean as she walked further along the trail with Alvaren. Her body tingled with excitement and anticipation to see the waves even though the circumstances seemed peculiar.

She heard a gull and stopped for a second freeing her hand from Alvaren quickly and pulling back her hood as she watched the waves crash on the shore. It was a beautiful beach and she closed her eyes for a moment breathing in the saltiness while a gull croaked overhead. This felt like home.

Alvaren grabbed her. "Come on Samira, don't make me throw you over my shoulder."

"There's no one here!" She protested and looked around, they were on a wooden boardwalk leading into taller grass. In the distance she could see some houses lined up along the shore, she wondered if they were heading there.

"There are eyes everywhere," he said and then rather than taking her out towards the houses on the left they turned right and onto another trail.

"Come on," he said holding a hand out to her. She wrapped her arm around his rather than taking his hand.

He was like an older brother, she liked that about Al. Clearly he was great with the ladies, evident by the lack of surprise in the guard by the gate, but he was very kindhearted, thoughtful. They walked on through another bunch of dunes in what seemed to be a maze, until he stopped.

"You'll want to remove your shoes here. You can warm

them later by the fire." He was already barefoot and walking ahead of her.

"Wait up!" she called out to him and he slowed. The sand was cold on her feet and curved in swirls from the strong breeze coming from the land. She dug her feet in against the grit, enjoying the sensation as they moved along.

They walked for a little while longer until finally in the distance she could see a beautiful beach house.

"Is that place yours?" she asked with eagerness.

"Yes, welcome to my home, Princess." He said with a smirk.

"Princess?" she asked following him up the stairs.

Like as in Arkson's princess?

He sighed again, "a nickname."

"I thought you lived in the palace."

"I do," he said, "but I spend any remaining time here."

"Wowza!" she said admiring the large wooden deck with benches.

The entire wooden structure was quite large and had two levels. It was rustic, the windows opening directly into the rooms, with large panels of heavy cotton behind them. Inside the home everything was beautifully carved wood, stained richly like the palace and there was a elaborate stone fireplace.

"You're home is beautiful, really impressive." She noticed that it did have a lack of anything to soften it's appeal, she continued, "It needs a woman's touch, but the furniture is gorgeous," she added pulling down her hood while he lit the fire.

Alvaren laughed outright, "Prince Arkson made the furniture, I helped though." he watched her face move impressed by that truth. "And no female will ever get her hands on this place."

"Why is that? And why does Arkson make furniture

when he's a Prince?" She asked.

"Well he's got to find something to do with all the extra energy he has..."

She read between the lines. "You mean since he no longer visits the Gardens of Pleasure."

Alvaren was diplomatic. "Perhaps... that bothers you doesn't it?"

Samira shrugged. "Perhaps... how long has it been exactly?"

Alvaren laughed again. "You really weren't meant to hear about the gardens anyway," he sighed in consideration, but answered quickly, "a decade, maybe longer."

Samira whistled. "Wow. Well then, all is forgiven."

"Really?" he asked her, with an arched brow.

"Ummm yeah, that's a bloody long time."

He was quiet for a few moments and then shook his head.

"What?" she asked wondering what the gesture was all about.

"I can see why he likes you, you say what is on your mind."

She blushed.

He likes me?

She did not want to give him anything more to report back to Arkson even though she was dying to ask him for more details. She knew Arkson had wanted her physically but attraction and admiration could be mutually exclusive. Yet Alvaren said that he liked her. She felt a bit giddy.

"You bring ladies here all the time though, surely one of them would want to help you liven the place up."

He laughed again and she admired him. His blonde hair looked adorable, tousled by the wind. His voice was rich but sweet and his honey coloured eyes were gorgeous. If she wasn't so captivated with Arkson, she might find him enticing, he was perfect for her friend Laura though. Warm. Mischievous. Kind of like a certain prince she knew and missed who had a beautiful mouth. One with which he chose to lavish kisses on her naked body. Mmm, how she missed that mouth.

She sat down on a chaise with a heavy sigh. "Do you need help?"

"No," he replied, "hungry?"

"A little." The truth was she was hungry, but every time she went to the dining hall it reminded her that her prince was somewhere far away. She had postponed her meal for the afternoon, but she would never starve herself purposely, not after Uri. She always ate full meals, they were just lonely.

A few minutes later a fire was finally starting to crackle. He grabbed a fishing rod.

"You're going to go fishing now? Will you even catch anything?" She wondered what he would catch. Would he fish right on the beach?

"I'll catch something delicious," he said with a wink.

"Knowing you it would be a mermaid." She replied smartly.

He looked puzzled. "Those don't exist." He left whistling cheerfully.

Samira looked down to her bag, and pulled on the corner of the cloth map that Salha had given her. She had almost forgotten she had tucked it away in the front pocket. It was a beautiful drawing with such careful attention to the details.

She was familiar with some of the places on it, had recalled the landmarks from her journey with Arkson to Uri and back but instead of leading to somewhere western from Zatian, the trail was more northeast.

As she sat there reading and map studying, the details were breathtaking, its almost as if she could see each place visually before her. Each time her fingers crept over another spot along the line of the trail Braedynn had highlighted towards the destination of a place called Brinn. It was as though the line was enchanted and she was in that exact place.

Her fingers moved to the place where Arkson was now, Parule. As they lingered she swore she could see him there, wrapped in furs and looking as handsome as ever, his green eyes strong and focused.

Heated to her bones, she left the comfort of the fire and followed Alvaren to the surf. She watched him cast his line.

"Does he truly like me?" she asked Alvaren suddenly needing his opinion. It was one she knew she could trust. She didn't look at him though, instead she shielded her eyes from the sun and watched the waves rolling up to meet the land. They lapped against the sand with the whoosh of fresh foam, the air smelled salty and invigorating.

"The prince..."

He cocked his head towards her.

"He's mad about you."

Alvaren's eyes glimmered with something in between sincerity and amusement a wide smile on his face.

She smiled in return and left it at that crossing her arms to keep her body heat close in the chilly wind. Thankfully Alvaren was not one to pry and didn't ask her any questions in return.

The night came quickly and after a dinner of fish and potatoes Alvaren showed her to her room where Sammie crept into the large and comfortable bed and drifted off into a blissfully deep sleep.

CHAPTER 20

BRAEDYNN WAS STARING at the guards Thussan had hired for his trip home with Kalawyn and Haloya. They were playing *barukq*, a game that he learned was similar to poker, except it was played with tiles instead of cards. They had planted themselves on the enclosed terrace in the backyard and one of them was losing his temper.

Salha had never seen him like this, Braedynn was so focused in observing them, had already asked her to packed whatever necessary supplies they would need. He had told her when the time was right they would make their move. Only she was terrified, not sure if now that the time was here for them to escape that she could find the courage. Her hands had shaken while she had put supplies into the canvas bag.

"Braedynn, I'm scared."

"I know Salha, it will be fine, just trust me, okay."

She nodded. "I do."

If the guards never left the porch they might be able to make it through the side entrance, but for the last two hours they had sporadically come into the house to check on them. Braedynn was waiting for their current game to end, since he suspected one of them would check on them then, before returning to the candlelit enclosure they were so leisurely enjoying. Braedynn cursed growing impatient.

This is taking too long.

He had a horrible feeling that their time was running short and usually when his gut told him something it was best for him to listen carefully. They had to leave now. He grabbed Salha's hand and pulling on the pack she had gathered for them, they raced down the street.

As they crossed the cobblestone, walking up the sector road and avoiding the street lights as they went, an immediate whirring sound cut through the air. Salha looked back quickly to see a huge wooden log headed towards them. She screamed, and quickly Braedynn pulled her to the ground, shielding her with his body as it tilted in the air from the weight of the throw and met the ground behind them barrelling down the lane.

The dust rolled up from the streets and Braedynn got up quickly, his muscles flexing. He had a few cuts and scrapes but on the whole he looked fine. He was trying to pull Salha up quickly so they could move while they still had the cover of the dust when something let out a loud and fierce growl.

"Oh my god, what was that?" Salha asked him, her legs trying to keep up with his long strides.

"Stop slaves!"

Salha was freaking out. "Braedynn!"

"Don't look back Sal, just keep walking."

Another log came barrelling over their heads. They ducked as it was overshot and rolled down the cobblestone. Between the fog and the dust it was hard to see what was behind them.

"Where the hell do you think you're going?" The voice

called after them.

Salha finally recognized it, "Thussan is here!"

Braedynn let out a curse, stopping and removing the pack on his back. "Take this," he said fitting the pack onto her shoulders and quickly tying the strap over her chest. "He'll be here in a moment Salha."

She mewled. "You see that treeline?" He asked, and she nodded, "run towards it and keep going until your into the woods, I will find you there."

"But Brae...

"Go! Now!" He said with a push. She didn't protest, but looked back to watch Braedynn turn to face the Anuya.

The cloud of dust had settled and even the fog was thinning, but Thussan didn't need his vision to find the human, he could smell him.

"You know human, it was curious to watch you and that bitch slave sneak out from my house. And here I had stopped by on my way back to the Nial Sector to give gifts to those idiot guards. Only to witness your desertion with my own eyes. I might not be able to kill you, but you'll be punished severely for this disobedience."

"That's right Thussan, you can't kill me, and it's not just because you need your own personal slave market."

"Remember you brought this on yourself tal'ak, " Thussan had enough, was about to boil over. He charged forward ready to tackle that idiot to the ground. As he lunged for him Thussan was surprised as he was met with a wall of strength pushing him back and their arms interlocked. Thussan managed to push Braedynn off and he swung at him, but Braedynn had ducked with perfect timing causing the Anuya to stagger forward. Using the force of his weight against him, Braedynn flipped Thussan over his shoulder and to the ground, quickly delivering some stunning blows to the Anuya's face.

"If your smart you'll stay on the ground Thussan."

Thussan's head throbbed. How did this measly human have such powerful hits? His lip was blistered and cracked from the punches and he could hear him walking away. Thussan got up from the ground.

"Don't you dare even try to leave you stupid human." He looked for something to throw at him. His hand moved up to cover his bloody eye while the good one darted around quickly.

"Thussan, this is over. If you keep fighting I'll have to kill you."

Thussan grunted. "No human could kill me," and not seeing anything to throw, he prepared to charge him again, his head lowering, his stance shifting.

Braedynn held his hand out to Thussan's body stopping his movements and locking his legs in place. He released spurts of his powers through slight movements in his finger. Thussan's eyes grew with anger shocked by the power Braedynn held over him, but still fought against him.

Braedynn was annoyed, clearly Thussan would not be giving up any time soon, but he did not want to have to kill him, so instead he summoned a sleep spell and hit him with a small surge of yellow light causing Thussan to curl over and collapse. Salha, who had reached the treeline, but did not want to move ahead any further had turned around to witness the fight between the two of them. She was shocked. She wondered how Braedynn was able to fight so well. What he had done to throw the ball of light?

Braedynn walked quickly towards her, and reaching her side, grabbed the heavy pack from her shoulders.

"How did you do that?" She asked bewildered.

He smiled roguishly.

"Magic."

"Is he dead?" Her eyes were wide.

"No, as tempting as it was to put him out of his misery,

he is still be very much alive, just resting. He'll wake up later with one hell of a headache." His hand grabbed hers and pulled her along into the woods. "Let's get out of here before any one else shows up and sounds the alarms."

Samira awoke to a thud on the roof. It was the early hours of night, the room in which she slept blackened save for the spilling of light leaking through the slatted windows. It was cool, the air in the room bitter on her skin. Her body tensed as she heard the noise again. What the heck was going on? Maybe it was a bird or something, but then most birds couldn't see at night and the moons were waning, there was very little light in the sky. The noise hit again and she shot up from bed, grabbing the sheet with her and peering out the small holes in the window. She was afraid to open them, afraid of what would be on the other side.

Something behind the wooden barrier swooshed down from the roof and hung in front of the window, her eyes still focusing in the dark thought it might be a bat or another nocturnal creature, but then two eyes, cold amber and glowing peered through the hole and she jumped back terrified, realizing someone was hanging from the roof on the other side of her window. She stumbled back as the body kicked the shutters in and rose from the floor gracefully standing in the room a good two feet taller than her. Shrouded in black she could make out no details of the figure.

She wanted to scream and run but her fight senses kicked in and she grabbed a chair throwing it forward. The body not expecting her action cursed and fell back onto the window ledge. She ran forward with a second chair and pummelled him in the stomach, lifting up his off balance foot and with all her force she pushed him out the window and crashing onto the lower roof of the cabin. She ran out the room quickly, she needed to get help.

"Alvaren!!" She screamed out into the cold and quiet house. She was running down the stairs as she heard footsteps meeting her. They thudded into one another, and he quickly pulled her down the remaining stairs.

"There was a creep in my room! A giant with glowing eyes of amber!"

Alvaren snickered lightly and then laughed menacingly.

Wait a minute.

This voice is far too amused. She looked up to see an Akori tall and blond like Alvaren, only his eyes were black as night! She punched him in the chest pushing down with all the force she could muster. Not expecting the move he staggered back. She should have kicked him in the groin.

"Get away from me dirtbag!" She yelled, and just as he recovered and reached for her, an arrow coming from the darkness struck him in the side. Thinking quickly she leapt forward and pushed it in further using her weight so that he tumbled out of her way and getting up, looked up to see Alvaren struggling with a third Akori. He cracked the bow over the Akori's head who stumbled back with a sharp harpy cry.

Samira ran to Alvaren. "What the hell is going on?"

"They're here to kill you! Run Samira! Back to the palace! I'll deal with them." He ducked from a swinging arm.

Kill me?

"But!" She looked back at the wounded Akori grunting as he pulled the arrow from his waist.

"I'll meet you there, go!"

He shoved a copper flashlight into her hand and pushed her out the door, and she turned long enough to see the Akori she had pushed back from the sill, jump from the top of the stairs and dive at Alvaren.

Running as fast as she could she took off. The air was cold and jolted the adrenaline boost she already had pumping. She would need to find her way quickly from the beach back to the boardwalk and through the field. It was no longer than a fifteen minute walk so if she ran she could cut the time in half, but the sand was slowing her down and she was worried about Alvaren. She turned off the flashlight as her eyes had adjusted to the darkness and she didn't want the Akori seeing the direction that she was headed.

At least she found comfort knowing that if the Akorians were in hot pursuit of her they would not be wasting their time torturing him. She had to reach the palace, she thought about hiding, but that would be pointless, they would probably just comb the area looking for her and would have all night to find her.

She needed to split them up. She could handle them individually, but if they all attacked at once she would be a goner. Hopefully the arrow to that one Akori's side had taken him out of the equation, but she could not count on that, she had met some Akorians who could heal themselves.

Reaching the gate to the beach she rolled under the gap in the bottom, squeezing her body through. As she got up her shirt was caught and she tugged hard on it ripping the sleeve. She swore under her breath. Finally, she had reached the cobblestone.

The moonlight was brighter on the stone here, reflecting off the smoother surface. Before her was a wide open space of the market place and without the vendors and booths it was so sparse and haunting. The shop signs around the square were casting spectral shadows on the walls made eerie by the fog drifting in off of the water. Samira wished her bare feet had been socked and purposely tried not to make so much of a scuff against the stone. She ran along the edge of the square not wanting to be a sitting duck in the middle.

She cut up the left alley towards the palace closer to the south entrance by the water. She thought she was making good time until amber eyes jumped down from a rooftop. He pulled her back by her long hair and she stifled her own cry, which would alert the others to her location. She swore under her breath, her hand squeezing a death grip on the flashlight from pain, but also as not to drop it against the stone.

His eyes were glowing in the night as he grabbed her arm and threw her towards the wall. She used her leg to brace against the stone and pushed back quickly landing on him as he was splayed. She elbowed him in the gut to add further injury.

Getting up as fast as she could she cut through a tiny side alley running towards another one of the Akori. It looked like it was the second who took the arrow to his side. He held no weapons and had not spotted her, so she rushed him with her weight, stomping on his foot and using his weight against him she slammed him into a wall, hitting him with the barrel of her light. He towered over her and would recover quickly, so she pushed over a few barrels for collecting water outside the shop entrances hoping they might slow him down.

She wondered why they kept expecting her to shrink in fear, by now the idiots should have known she would fight against them. Cutting up the alley, she came out to the clearing where she had practised her fighting skills that very morning, she ran as fast as she could her sides burning, her chest so filled with air she thought it might burst. She could hear them behind her, amber eyes using his levitation to push up off the ground in jumps and make up for lost time. They were both quickly gaining on her.

She saw a figure ahead of her running into the field

from the sideline of the trees and prayed it was a guard or Alvaren. As it ran toward her she realized in horror it was the third beefcake who was jumping quickly towards her with his levitation. She couldn't stop and so ran wider, frantic now. She was giving herself as much of a berth as she could between herself and the Akori coming towards her, but he could quickly cut off her access to the south gate.

Shit!

She could hear a rumbling from behind the treeline. It sounded like water rushing. The beefcake was parallel to her and pulling ahead. In a matter of seconds she would be a goner. He was too close, would be able to slam into her. Before he could grab her a large wave ripped out from the trees and engulfed him, pulling him back from her. She stopped short shocked by image and the water swirled away from her, but still came roaring out over the trees, and swept up the other two Akori behind her.

Alvaren was perched over the water riding it as though it were a surf board. As it spread out over the land, the water dissipated hitting the ground and soaking the field as Alvaren collapsed. Samira ran towards him turning on the flashlight and waving the light frantically at the guards by the gate who hearing the loud rush of water were looking in their direction. It was not long before they were running full speed towards her.

She cradled Alvaren's head, his breathing was laboured, "Are you all right?" She asked looking to see if he was wounded at all.

"Winded," he managed to say with a quirked smile, catching his breath and sitting up in a sopping mess of wetness. "I swam up the coast and used my powers to push me up here to the south gate. You're a smart woman Samira, I knew you would run here first."

"Thank you," she said sincerely, squeezing his arm.

"You saved my life." She kissed him on the cheek.

"Prince Arkson better kiss my feet now," he said with a laugh, and then collapsed back on the ground comically. Samira nearly collapsed herself.

SINCE THE ATTACK FROM the spies of Guedan, the guards at the palace tripled their watch. Samira had been cordoned off to a particular section of the palace and after the harrowing experience of being chased she actually didn't mind.

Alvaren visited her regularly throughout the day and she was glad it was him who had stayed back to protect her. Brunelda also stayed by her side and they both eagerly awaited the prince's return, which would be later that day. She had questioned both Alvaren and Brunelda extensively on why she had been attacked and who the heck this King Guedan was, but they gave her little information, advising her it would be best to direct her questions to Prince Arkson. It had been two days since the attack and she spent most of her time reading, but found her mind distracting her.

There was something about Arkson that always made her feel comforted. After returning to the palace, he was invading her thoughts. Alvaren had told her Arkson liked her, but that was like telling someone you had a crush on them in grade school. She wondered why he kept her safe? Why he had rescued her from a worse fate? She knew it was in his nature to help others, now she realized more than ever his cold exterior was just that, beneath it all he was such a caring person.

She felt foolish though and doubted his feelings for her. Maybe she was a pet project? And where could what she felt lead? She feared the future more than anything. What was stopping him from finding an Akorian bride? What if she left and joined her sister? Was there a way for them to go back to Halifax? Would Salha even go back now? She doubted it. He still had not answered any of her questions, and she had yet to figure out the answers to her own. As time passed she grew more and more restless.

Close to the hour of Arkson's expected arrival, Veros called a meeting of the guards to greet Arkson with his return. Samira had been included in the welcome party and was glad that he had considered her. Veros was always kind to her, and she always enjoyed their discussions.

The moment that Arkson had returned with his party his eyes searched the crowd for her. When their eyes met, she could feel his happiness even though it was only the look in them that betrayed his feelings. He wore the same expression of nothingness as always, but he still looked so very handsome.

She stared back at him with a closed mouth smile hoping that he would make time for her. She had many questions and this time he had to answer them, but to her dismay the first thing Arkson had done was to call a meeting with his company in the Hall of Haldero. Her heart sank a bit, feeling like she might not see him for a while if he and his group had matters to discuss. To her relief, Veros escorted her to the hall to meet with them all.

She arrived amidst his speech. "Now we have the firepower to protect ourselves from Guedan, our soldiers just need the incentive," he finished saying to the guards. He glanced at her and could see the curiosity on her face.

Sammie wished she knew more about what was going on, she listened to Arkson's conversations whenever he was around, tried to learn things by observing but he was too careful to reveal things around her. Only in his absence had she found out about the spy who he and Alvaren had caught shortly after her arrival. Only then did she realize she posed some threat to this King Guedan who sent spies to kill her. She wished she knew why.

Alvaren stood. "Maybe not that much incentive, they are ready to fight, eager for the chance to prove themselves, especially after the callous attack on Samira."

Elastor added, "I am ready to fight, and I know the infantry are itching to as well. Guedan has been dirty too many times now. It's time we pushed back."

Veros interjected, his arm reaching out to Arkson's shoulder. "It is more than that my son, far more. Your guards are not only eager for your vengeance they are full of pride. They know a worthy leader when they see it, they know that you can bring our Akori to victory."

Arkson almost smiled, feeling elated by the support of his people of his new alliance with the Northern Batchi.

Samira's eyes had wandered over the crowd while Veros spoke with Arkson, she wondered how many Akori were in attendance, until she noticed an Akori who looked nothing like the others, his markings on his neck were red unlike the green of Arkson's Akorian people and the shape of them was more triangular, the exact same as those creep spies who had attacked her days ago.

Her body tensed in fear. Her eyes widened with horror. She could see the hatred in his eyes as he prepared to throw a spear at her. She had read about the weapon in her Akorian history books, recognized the look of it from its distinct plated side of circular pattens, its shorter length much like an arrow. It would kill her.

Arkson suddenly felt a shadow creep into the room from behind him. The emotions in the room suddenly darkened. There was someone heading for Samira. He turned abruptly looking back to an Akori with icy grey eyes. He threw a *triuny*.

What the hell!?

It was soaring straight for Samira's body and was blinding as he jumped in the way of its trajectory, being thrown back as it pierced into the flesh of his shoulder.

He could not see much, his eyes saw shades, and then they were blinded from the light pulses. He could hear some of his soldiers as their bodies ran in the direction of the attacker who escaped out of the window followed by any with levitation.

The pain seared through him and his body grew numb. His chest felt as if it was ripping apart. He could hear the groans of those closest to him.

Where was she? Where was Samira? Was she safe? Please let her be safe.

Samira wanted to run towards Arkson, but Alvaren held her back. She watched terrified as the bright light filled the room in a radiating circular shimmer before it disappeared into the spear. Her heart pounded loudly in her ears as she watched time slow and Arkson's body fell to the floor. The air crackled from the charge of electricity. She watched the other Akori around him crumple in anguish. She pulled away from Alvaren, who was falling to his knees in pain from the pulses, and found herself running towards her prince. No one was moving towards him! She wanted to yell, but would not be heard over the whirring noise of the spear.

Why aren't any of you helping him!!

Terrified by the look on his face, she stared into his eyes. They were growing pale. His face quickly losing colour.

Frantically, she moved to pull the spear from his shoulder.

"This is going to hurt, forgive me."

If she did not remove the tip of the blade he would die in a few minutes.

As she pulled blood trickled and she heard a loud crack. There was a searing pain against her side as a charge of electricity shot her back from him. Akori in the room had fallen to the ground and some of them were shaking as if possessed. Samira was determined to get back to Arkson. She was the only one that could. She crawled forward to him and seeing a red circle on the spear, twisted it until it was green the sensations of pain slowly faded from her hands.

She rolled it away from Arkson's body looking disgusted at the horrible object. She looked at his eyes. They seemed lifeless, his chest did not move from breaths.

She had to resuscitate him. She plugged his nose and leaned forward to breathe air into him, trying to remember the proper way.

As she leaned down to him, she could hear Veros yell to her.

"No Samira!"

He had regained his strength as many of the others around her had and were slowly recovering and moving towards her and the prince languidly. They were drained, but she paid them no attention. Arkson was her concern.

She didn't even look at Veros as she alternated between breaths and pumping beats. She wanted to panic fearing it was too late, but calmed herself to keep on. Her lips were on fire.

"Shit!" She swore. "Get up Arkson!"

Arkson did not move though her hands continued to pump his heart. She had to keep it beating, his pulse was unrecognizable. She breathed into him again, but his chest simply collapsed. Tears began streaming down her face.

"No!" she sobbed. Hushed whispers encircled the room as Arkson laid there, still.

"No!" she repeated, beating her hand against his chest.

Alvaren was behind her, trying to pull her up. It took all her strength, but she found herself standing over Arkson in shock. She wanted to run away from his body in disbelief. He was dead.

She pushed away from Alvaren, wanted to leave the

room, but she was frozen. Her prince was dead. His eyes cold and white rimmed. His skin pale and translucent. The room was so silent, transfixed with horror. All Samira wanted to do was run, but she couldn't. She couldn't leave him.

Then the pain suddenly hit, wracked through her entire body and she fell to her knees. Her body tensed tightly, and she felt a feeling of energy pulling from her arms as it erupted into a fiery tingle against her skin. Her neck and arm burned fiercely. What was happening to her?

She looked at her Prince, her eyes glazed in agony. She had lost him, and closed her eyes as she let the discomfort wash over her in collapse.

Arkson awoke then. His body jerked up with a deep breath of life as he saw Samira crumble further forward in pain. He moved over to catch her in his arms.

She had saved him. He felt a surge of his powers as his mark burned into her flesh and his own neck tingled. Their eyes met for a moment before overwhelmed by pain she lost consciousness. He touched her side gingerly, near where she had been struck, kissing the top of her head fiercely. The room hushed, many of his company were staring at him and Samira in shock.

"Get a healer!" He shouted and one of his guards ran to the infirmary. He sat there cradling Samira in disbelief, she had saved him, breathed life into him again and bound herself to him unknowingly. The curse was broken! Arkson's powers now returned flooding into his lacerated body. He was already starting to heal himself, but he was too weak to extend the same power to his beloved.

Arkson was mated to her. Samira was now his wife.

CHAPTER 21

SAMIRA'S WOUND WAS DEEP and it took the healers an hour to close her side's gaping hole. All the while she lay there unconscious. Arkson worried for her and had her brought to his chamber where she remained over the course of the next few days. He slept on the chaise while she laid in the bed drifting in and out of consciousness.

He conducted all of the mapping and planning for the attack that he expected from Guedan in the meeting room outside his chamber, with his most trusted guards Alvaren and Elastor. Regrettably his other guards had been unable to catch the assassin, but he had more important matters on his mind.

He refused to be separated from Samira in case she took a turn for the worse. He feared her human body might find some way to reject their mating, but his heart knew it was only a matter of time before she awoke.

Daily his powers strengthened and he knew word surely would have made it's way to Guedan that Arkson would assume the position of King of Zatian when he married Samira formally by ceremony. It would mark the start of a war.

Arkson had so much to tell Samira, and he hoped that when she woke she would be lucid enough for him to tell her it all.

The fall weather was starting. Soon the ground would freeze and winter would begin. He knew that if Guedan were to start a war it would have to be before the change in weather. He would be foolish to drag his troops through mounds of snow with over a week of travelling to attack. It would not be an easy victory either, which would cause elongated fighting. He was lost in his thoughts when Samira awoke with a ferocious roar of anger and pain.

She cried out in agony and he rushed to her side. Her arms travelled over her body frantically until she realized she was not bleeding. Arkson knelt beside her. She felt disoriented, it took a few seconds before her eyes completely focused and she realized where she was. She had only seen the room once before. She gazed down at her arm and saw the green markings etched into her skin, she remembered the burning sensation on her neck before she blacked out and touched her neck carefully.

Her mouth felt dry as she spoke, "what happened Arkson? I thought you were dead. You were dead. I cried."

He sat by her, stroked her hair while she looked at him waiting for an answer. He poured her some water from a nearby pitcher and took it to her helping her drink carefully. She coughed from the wetness.

"I was dead," he said, "you brought me back when you breathed life into me."

"How is that possible?" she asked.

"I have a lot to explain to you Samira. I want to tell you it all," he looked at her with sincerity. She lifted the covers on the bed and scooted over so that he could crawl in next to her. After he had lain down, she leaned against him with her open eyes anxiously awaiting his words. He wanted to kiss her so desperately, but could feel she was guarded, knew that he had to speak with her first.

She spoke before he could start. "We are mated, aren't we?" She touched the markings on his forearm.

"Yes," he replied, "when your lips met mine, it was like us kissing, you must have read that when an Akorian mates their Zain markings meld, that happens after they kiss, something about the skin on the lips there brings them together."

"That was why you always hesitated to kiss me," she said to him, and continued, "when Akorians mate, their lives are bound to one another, that was how I brought you back to life."

"Yes," he said to her, "I suspected we were mated, but the melding can be a bit painful, and you had no markings, I did not know how it would happen for you."

"How can you be mated to a human Arkson? Is that why you brought me here?" Samira felt herself becoming angered, so she pulled back, she had to keep objective.

"I will explain Samira," he began, feeling the tension in her body, wanting to reach out and stroke it away.

"A long time ago, my father, King Mactyllo did something he should not have. My mother had died shortly after my sister's birth, and being royalty he had enough power to outlive the sickness which plagues someone after losing their mate. A sister clan's leader was also widowed and following a similar fate. Her name was Arielda, and she desperately wanted my father to marry her so that our clans could unite. She wanted her son Guedan who was older than me to be the rightful heir to the two lands."

"Can an Akori mate more than once?" She asked him, a bit confused by what he mentioned and the differences with what she had read, the books left out many details. She wondered what else had not been written on the pages.

"Yes, if an Akori is strong enough like my father was, his base element was fire, which is rare, then yes we can mate more than once. Arielda was insisting that it was fate, even though sometimes two Akori can kiss but their symbols will not bond. My father had gone to her once before when he was younger and had kissed her with no connection. It was probably because it was something he did not truly desire, and that same feeling remained with him. He did not care for Arielda and had already fallen in love with another."

Samira interjected, "A human?"

Arkson nodded. "Her name was Kae, she was a human, but not from here in Arzule, she was from somewhere else and had used a Kaptu necklace she found in her world to travel here with her son Alexandros. My father had already melded with her, so when Arielda had arrived uninvited she was furious with him and used her powers to kill Kae. It was awful, Alexandros and I had been in the garden with her when Arielda's troops overpowered us all. When Kae died, it left my father to die very slowly without her. He was strong enough to hold on for a little longer after Kae's death, but losing two mates took a toll on him."

"I'm sorry Arkson," Samira said squeezing his arm.

"Don't be Samira, my father always followed his heart, he let the fire rule him and not the other way around." Arkson had been living with the truth for so long, it no longer affected him. He continued, "it was not enough damage to leave Zatian without a King, as he had taken so long to die, Arielda was not satisfied, but because I was his son and rightful heir to the Zatian throne, a city which she felt she had the rights to rule. She believed my father had polluted our way of life by marrying a human. She cursed me, stripping me of my power, and stating that the only way for me to be freed was to mate with a human."

"How old were you?" She wondered how long he had waited.

"I was ten," he replied, "I grew up like my peers but was robbed of the rights of a true King of Akorians. I have been alone all of these years waiting for this to all end. I was waiting for you," he looked at her hopeful, she was deep in thought, processing all that he told her. Her anger still surfaced first, made her wonder if the Kaptu necklace was something that could take her back to her world, although at the moment she did not want to leave him, could not.

Samira softened, she had been falling in love with Arkson. She finally understood why he was so cold, why he took so many things seriously, and why he seemed to need control of things.

"So you could mate with an Akori, now that the curse is lifted?" She asked him wondering if he might want that. He had never considered that before, he realized with her comment that now that he probably could. Yet, he did not want to, would never. Samira had captured his heart with her manner, with her beauty, and with her intelligence. No one else in Zatian could compare.

"No," he replied to her, "I want no one but you."

Her heart rate increased, did he love her? He had said 'want' not 'need'. She felt peace in his choice of words, if he had said need she would have felt trapped, might have pulled further away from him, from the danger of someone needing her. She did not need him, she wanted him, and that was how she felt it should be.

She had been needed by men before, and they smothered her, holding onto her so tightly she could not breathe. It was why no one had appealed to her for so long. It was the need that scared her about Arkson before, and him keeping her there in Zatian, but now she realized why. He wanted the chance to prove himself to her, he wanted to win her love.

She scratched at her bandaged side. He could tell she was still absorbing everything that he had said.

"I understand now," she said to him, and although she was still a bit distant, he felt relieved.

"I should draw you a bath," he said stopping her hands from the itching. He helped her from the bed. Her legs were weakened from the pain of her side as it was still an undercurrent making her body sore. She was thankful he had his own bath tub and as he guided her into the enclosure, she leaned against a table while he turned the water on and the tub began to fill. He came back to her and helped her remove her clothing and the bandages which were protecting the healing scabs on her side. He rubbed an ointment over the wound before helping her into the tub when the water was cooled enough.

She began to relax in the warmth and expected him to leave her alone to bathe, but instead he rolled his sleeves up and kneeled behind her, grabbing the oils for washing hair and poured water carefully over her head. He washed her hair gently massaging her scalp. Her overactive brain began to calm and when he rubbed her tense shoulders and neck, she felt like she might slide beneath the water and sleep.

"Arkson," she began, "what happened to Alexandros?"

His jaw flexed, clearly this was a sore spot with him. "He left about five years after his mother died, wanted to live with other humans, you know, start a family." His face fell.

"What is it?" She asked gently pushing further.

"He died, a few years ago in a slaver raid. I had not seen him for years." He resumed his shielded look. "Nikelda and I mourned him honourably marking the wall of the dead with his name close to his mother's engraving."

"I'm sorry for your loss Arkson." She felt guilty for

asking, placed her hand on his forearm in comfort.

"Thank you my sweet." He kissed her wet forehead, and left her there to relax.

"Call me when you are done," he said.

She nodded her head. She sat there for fifteen minutes wondering what powers had returned to Arkson. Through the lattice window she could see Arkson reading on the bed. She wanted to call him to her, but stopped herself. Instead she watched drops of water trickle off her fingers until she got up to get out of the tub. Even though she felt a little off balance, she wanted to be fine. She wanted to be able to get out on her own. Yet, Arkson appeared before her and had already grabbed a large towel to wrap around her.

She nearly slipped on her way out and he caught her, letting her legs down on a towel he had laid out before leaving her to soak. The beads of water along her neck and the heart of her chest made her beauty more apparent. Each droplets reflected shimmers in her dark eyes. Instead of just handing her the large towel he mildly wiped her dry and then wrapped the towel around her.

He was so very loving as she observed him, the tenderness showed how much he cared for her, tore into her. It was hard for her to be distant from him as he rose from his kneeling, his body casting a shadow over hers. He had dried her feet with another towel and suddenly threw it into a basket in the corner.

She had always taken care of herself. Samira was used to being the caregiver and taking care of others. No one looked into her the way he did. He saw past her exterior, knew how much she needed love.

"You did not call me Samira," he looked at her with a quirked smile.

She did not respond to him and instead made an observation aloud as she admired his broad shoulders. She felt enraptured and captivated with the tall sensuousness of Arkson that stood before her body.

"Your shirt is wet. Let me remove it."

He glanced down at it and then to her. Heat rose over Arkson's body, the coolness from the water faded. His chest heaved with anticipation of her touch and he breathed in the smell of Samira's freshly cleaned skin, which played havoc with his senses. She admired the firm muscles of his chest beneath her fingers. He was quiet, intoxicated with her, his eyes gleaming.

She began to unbutton it slowly, and as each button opened she could see more and more of his beautiful skin, his scars like her own were enticing, he watched entranced by her as she pulled the fabric tucked into the back his pants and pushed it off of his shoulders to the floor. He wanted to tell her he could get another, but she leaned into him, traced his delicious looking lips with her fingers.

"Your lips are soft Arkson."

Samira wondered why he had not kissed her yet, the surprise was over, she knew his secret. What held him back? His self-control was admirable, but she wondered what he would be like unrestrained.

Her eyes were dark and thoughtful as they examined his lips. He kissed her finger and let out a deep growl as she wrapped her hand around his neck and pulled his mouth to hers. Arkson's lips met Samira's with soft and delicate warmth, despite his ferocious want of her. He kissed her firmly, but so very sweetly. Samira leaned further into him and he wrapped his arms around her body. She rubbed her body against him, standing on her tip toes.

Their lips met in fire, consuming one another energetically. Samira's whole body simmered and pulsed with heat as Arkson's hands cupped her face. He was so intimate, so caring with her. Her fingers were caressing his back and chest in a way that made him tingle and ache. She massaged the hard steel of his muscles until he pulled her even closer to him pushing her back against the table and making her sizzle from the force of his mouth against hers. He kissed her breathless, left her legs further weakened. His tongue danced with hers until his passion overflowed and he explored her mouth more aggressively, sucking on her bottom lip before biting it as he had wanted for so long.

"Mmmm you taste so good Samira."

He wanted to love her with all of the passion she evoked from him and Arkson craved her affection. As if reading her mind, Arkson lifted her onto the table, grabbing a towel and placing it underneath her bottom. She sat on the edge of it and pulled him to her wrapping her legs around him and crossing them over his firm buttocks. This woman knew how to make him feel wanted. His heart pounded as her own hands were cupping his face equivalently. Now she was kissing him, her mouth wild and hot on his. She wanted him as much as he wanted her.

He yearned to unfold the towel wrapped around her body and let his hands explore her body. She had no idea what she did to him. He throbbed against her, and all he could think about was slipping himself into Samira's warm and naked body. He wanted her so much he could already feel himself inside her, but he regained control and resisted his primal desire.

Samira let a deep breath escape as Arkson's warm hands moved rawly down her back.

"I want to touch you everywhere," he said raspily.

"Please Arkson..." she pleaded.

Her body arched with a tug of desire as Arkson rubbed himself against her, and she grew ready for him. He could not resist the wicked gesture, wanted to do so much more. She leaned back and bit her lip as Arkson's hands found her breasts and they kneaded them, his lips and tongue hot on her neck.

He shifted to see her eyes, the desire so evident on her face fuelled him and sent him further over the edge. He tugged at the towel wrapped around her he couldn't wait anymore and smiled as it fell to her sides. Arkson looked at her with determination.

Samira feeling the same determination moved her hands from his face and massaged the length of his chest, her fingers stroking his nipples and stomach before she pressed her hands against his pulsing nether beneath his pants.

He leaned into her neck, still massaging her breasts before lapping over them with his hungry mouth. He sucked hard on a taught brown nipple before delivering the same attention to the other, repeating the gesture as he massaged. Samira was spinning.

She was slowly massaging and stroking his glorious length before she wrapped her hands around his thick shaft and moved her hands up and down. The fabric of his pants was hot on her hands. The flicker of desire in his eyes was reflected back to him by her own and they stared into one another intensely until he gasped from the mounting sensations. Arkson pulled her hands off of him and rested them on his chest while his mouth claimed her mouth once again.

Feeling far less inhibited Arkson rubbed his body against Samira's playfully, teasing her with the thin material between them as their bodies continued against one another in constant friction.

He wanted to savour her, his lips left hers and he kissed her neck down to her breasts again where he met them with hunger tugging at her nipples and then sensuously licking the length of the scar beneath her breast, he moved down further to kiss her stomach. A trail of pleasurable sensation whispered over her skin. As he bent down he guided her legs to his shoulders so that he could spread her legs further apart in comfort. He kissed her thighs, swirling his tongue over the surface of them, branding her with his hot breath. Then he stopped and eyed her.

"I want to taste you more Samira."

"Arkson," she said his name with such need, arching her back in anticipation "I want to taste you too." She bit her lip, her heart bouncing around in the cage of her chest.

"Me first."

His tongue slowly licked her folds before, spreading the lips tenderly with his fingers to find her delicious nub. He playfully flicked his tongue over it as she squirmed in glory. He increased the intensity of his flicks until at last he inserted a finger into her channel, stretching the walls in slow rotations.

She moaned. Throwing her head back her fingers tangled in his hair as he added another finger and licked her sensitive tip again. He continued even as her body hitched and tensed in a explosion of pleasure.

"Arkson, let me taste you," she pleaded, while his tongue and fingers continued to torment her highly sensitive flesh. "I don't think I can take much more."

"No Samira," he replied, "I want more. I'm not done with you yet." The look he gave her sent a shiver all over her and he licked and stroked and teased until her body tensed even more than before.

"Arkson!" She panted, her body wracked hard in orgasm again. He kissed his way back up her body nibbling her ear. Her fingers tangled in his hair. Then his lips hot on hers again.

"My turn." Samira voice dry and hoarse, her chest hot and tingly.

"Your pants," she managed to whisper. She wanted him naked. They stopped kissing for a moment as she unbuttoned his pants, pushing them down far enough for him to be freed. He was so gorgeous naked, so tantalizing and muscular.

She nibbled from his ear to his chest, stopping to suckle his nipples and drag her tongue through the grid of his hard abs while crouching. She could lick them all day, in fact, she wished she had some whipped topping. She kissed from each side of his naked hip bone to thigh before her tongue slid across the underside of his penis. She repeated the gesture slowly before swirling around his sensitive tip in circles. He sizzled.

Then she slowly took him in her mouth, all the way down to the base, again and again, careful not to gag from his length. His hand was fisted in her hair urging her on gently, and when she reached the base again and sucked hard over his length until swirling her tongue at the tip. He let out a delicious throaty heave of enjoyment. The repetition made his whole body taut until she couldn't wait anymore.

"Arkson," she said breaking the silence between them as he looked down at her, "I want you to make love with me." Her tongue still slowly teasing. The look in his eyes was bittersweet. He was considering.

"Are you sure Samira?" He wanted her so badly, but he thought they might wait until after an official marriage ceremony until she had recuperated more. Arkson was apprehensive of taking advantage of her at a weakened state. He did not want her to feel like he used her injury to his advantage.

"Yes," she replied, "absolutely certain." Her eyes were clear and focused on him, she had decided. He opened his mouth to protest, but was cut off as she rose to lean against him her lips again kissing him sweetly in short deliberate repetition.

He could not deny her his love, he had promised

himself he would share his whole heart with her when she awoke. He could have lost her. She could be dead this very instant, no longer existing.

He stopped her for a moment, looking her square in the eye before he lifted her back to the table, it would be more comfortable if she was seated, her body already spent and trembling. He kissed her mouth devouring her lips and gently stroking her breasts until his fingers discovered her moist core and he tenderly delved further. His exploration left her cheeks flushed and she fondled him in return.

"Mmmm, I want you now Arkson, please don't make me wait anymore."

Their hands explored one another with the same anticipation, sweetness and craving. Her hands ran up his hard body feverishly, her fingers tracing from the nape of his neck and through his hair and down his cheeks to his jaw line where Samira decorated with successive kisses.

"Samira."

Arkson felt so intoxicated with Samira's passion and presence. His eyes locked on hers as he entered her slowly, their noses and foreheads met while their fiery breath tickled each other's lips. When he had entered her completely she shuddered in satisfaction as he made love with her slowly.

Samira wrapped her arms around Arkson's waist her hands upon his bum guiding him into her while he cupped her face with one hand and held her body close with the other. Her heart thudded in her chest with each deliberate thrust of his body meeting hers.

Samira thought about the way Arkson held her with his strength. Each motion was so calculated but raw, his desire was his undoing, and to see him like this, so open, so unguarded, stole her breath away. He continued to kiss her, fully, honestly, with mounting passion.

Samira had never made love with someone this way.

Every moment that passed was even more powerful than the one before. The burn of fire encompassed her in waves, while Arkson's body so fiercely enjoyed the soft, wetness of her cave.

"You feel so good," he whispered into her ear.

Arkson had never felt closer to anyone, no female evoked such feeling from him, witnessed him unbridled. He felt vulnerable to her, exposed. He had fallen for her, loved her more than he thought himself capable of loving. The look in her eyes had left him undone.

Something within Samira shifted and her entire being glowed with pleasure. She felt intoxicated by Arkson and cried out, holding onto his graceful strength. Their bodies were connected, flames of emotion tearing through him to her.

"Oh my..." she managed to whisper hoarse.

Their love making intensified and quickened. His strokes, deep and hard and gratifying, elated her until her body erupted into ecstasy. As she trembled in his arms she let herself completely open to him. His hands were claiming her body possessively. It was exquisitely stimulating.

Her pleasure soared higher and higher and higher until she cried out and Arkson's mouth quieted her as his own body climaxed with her. He was wrought with pleasure, and the ache in his chest sunk deeply into him from his feelings for her.

They held each other for a few minutes more, noses nuzzling before Veros entered and called out, "Arkson?"

Samira was relieved he could not see them. Arkson had sat her on the table in the corner of the lattice which was covered by cloth on the inside.

Thank goodness.

"I'll be there momentarily Veros." Arkson closed his eyes in disbelief. He did not want to leave Samira now, but it would be important, Veros would only come into his room if it were urgent.

He pulled his pants up and placed several kisses on her lips. "I'll return as soon as possible," he said grabbing his shirt and leaving her there smiling in satisfaction.

Samira's body was exhausted. She wanted to rest, but her head was swimming with thoughts.

Take that Garden of Pleasure!

She recalled all that Arkson was thinking while she slept for days, while they had made love. She had yet to tell him of her new found gift, she was not ready to tell him. His thoughts swam in her head, and she wondered what to do with all this new information. He loved her, he wanted her to be his wife, to be his queen, and he wanted them to marry as soon as possible.

Under normal circumstances she might be excited and incredibly joyous about his desires for their life together, but these were not normal circumstances. She understood now why Arkson was yet to be King, why with all his confidence, intelligence, and skill, he was held back from living a full life. She was his answer but she did not want to be, could not be. If he could not see in himself what she saw in him, he would always need her, think she was the key to his success, and the pressure of that made her chest heavy. She cared for him so much more than she ever thought she could. She knew that now, which made her decision even harder to finalize.

Samira's head hurt. She needed to focus, needed to breath to relieve some of the tension from the voices, from the visions. Things were hitting her a little less intense now. So far she had only seen a few minor premonitions, a sputtering of Arkson's lips melting on hers before it happened. The flashes made their lovemaking more pleasurable, but she had to find a way to direct it more. Right now it was uncontrollable and she was feeling weakened. The energy Arkson gave her was the only thing sustaining her, his love and care comforted her.

As he kissed her before he left she saw a clear image of a messenger entering the throne room with important news from another city. A city that wanted to fight alongside Zatian. The image so concise and clear left her buzzing.

What did this vision mean? How could she sort out yet another thing in her overactive mind?

CHAPTER 22

Arkson entered the throne room with a confident stride. He felt whole, nourished by the love of Samira. Her love had fed into his powers. He almost crackled with an overflowing surge of energy. Veros had led him down the hall, an amused look on his face, but it was as though he were sorry to have interrupted. Clearly the news he had was too important to be kept waiting.

Arkson took his seat and waited while the messengers were brought in. They were from three Akorian cities in the north, their coat of arms ornamented on their cloaks. They bowed before him. The middle of the three spoke first, clearly the leader of this pack.

"My King," he started, "we have journeyed to humbly seek your aid."

Arkson mulled the word over in his mind.

King.

They were Akori from the cities of Boja, Sathan and Piut. The cities were a bit more isolated so they would have no way to know of the events, which had taken place in

Zatian in the last few days. One of his advisors must have informed them of the mating between him and Samira.

King.

Arkson had not anticipated the word to affect him so much.

It was a strange past few days of many visitors to Zatian, all unexpected. He hoped that the bearers of wicked were done though. While Samira rested he had learned from Alvaren that earlier in the week three spies from Opamut had attacked them both ruthlessly.

Alvaren and Samira had defeated them, but not so easily. He had been so thankful to learn that the spies were unsuccessful in their attempts to harm either and had imprisoned them. After intense questioning they had told him all they knew of Guedan's plans, especially of his expansion to the other creatures of Arzule. Guedan wanted his domain to stretch outside of the Akori just as Jav and Sebastian had feared.

These messengers before him now were different than the first and a sign of the good to come. They brought gifts with them as well as news of their people. Their faces were weary, but their spirits were strong.

The messenger who had stepped forward continued, "I am here on behalf of King Arpal of Boja. He has offered the gifts of this ore." The messenger motioned for his accompanying soldiers to open the chest before Arkson's feet, then resumed, "and the blade of his sword alongside yours in the battle against King Guedan."

Arkson motioned for the messenger to come closer and shook his hand nodding in acceptance of the ore and alliance.

The messenger continued speaking, "he also offers you the hand of his daughter the Princess Ziala should you choose to accept. Now that the human in your care has assisted in breaking your curse," Arkson's eyes darkened, but the messenger still spoke, "he thought that perhaps you might prefer a queen of your own kind."

Arkson let his anger seep out slowly, it was not the fault of this unknowing messenger that his king had insulted him. "I have a queen, but please advise your king I will accept the other gifts graciously. I look forward to fighting with the city of Boja in the battle against King Guedan."

The nobles in the hall were heard whispering and though Arkson was tempted to call attention to them in punishment, wanted to yell out "Silence!" into the room, he could not play lecturing father to them in the presence of members of another city.

The other two messengers stepped forward one after the other. They too brought news of their leaders in support of Arkson. From the city of Sathan, King Melosha gave Arkson an ample supply of wood important in the construction of ships and the use of his army, his cavalry notorious for their incredibly swift conquering in any battle.

From the city of Piut, Queen Bradjya offered not only reserves of copper, important for energy sourcing, but also the use of her guardians. The Guardians of Piut were a league of soldiers of varying species from Arzule. It was not known how they came to be united, but their loyalty to their Queen was renowned and was partially the reason, in addition to the rough terrain of Piut, her city had been kept free of Guedan. Now she feared the takeover that all the remaining free cities knew was coming. King Guedan would turn his eyes to her city soon for its copper, if he planned portal shifting.

"I thank you all for offering these gifts to the city of Zatian, please extend my gratitude to your leaders and express my happiness in meeting for arrangements of this union as soon as possible."

The messengers looked pleased and planned to rest for the evening, setting out the following morning to return with word on Arkson's decision.

After they had left Arkson, Brunelda, and Veros retired to the private passage of the throne room.

Veros looked pious. "My prince, you know that your aunt and I have always been here to offer our support to you in your decisions as the future king of our city." His hand wrapped around Brunelda's as he spoke, "We believe you have made an exceptional decision in choosing a queen to lead our people but we ask..."

Brunelda cut him off impatient. "Oh Veros, always so formal, get to the point love. Son..." She had always called Arkson son, she loved him as though Arkson were her own, and it always warmed his heart to hear her say it. "What we were wondering is if you have discussed with Samira whether or not she wants to stay in the kingdom?"

Arkson laughed, his heart warmed by her hope. "I have yet to ask her to stay. I do fear she may want to leave, but the love is clearly there. I can feel it in her heart. I think I just have to coax it to plant some roots here."

Brunelda looked overjoyed and glanced at Veros. "She has not asked anything about being released of the mating mark?"

Arkson shook his head, suddenly worried that perhaps the thought had crossed her mind. "Is that possible?"

Veros shook his head, "We do not believe so, but we feared she may be angered by the circumstances of your union."

"She gave me no inclination." Arkson's heaviness evaporated. "Instead she has accepted every truth."

Brunelda's smile widened, then her brow furrowed. "Oh the gall of that King Arpal, he never knows when to give it a rest. He's lucky you didn't lose your temper like your father would have and cut the poor messengers head off. Seriously, suggesting betrothal to his daughter while Samira is still in the palace." Brunelda tutted and Arkson leaned forward to pat her hand in comfort.

"It is all right Aunt. She cannot be so easily replaced." He looked at the both of them, filled with pride. "I should be returning to my guests now, the sooner I can deal with the gifts and document signing, the sooner I can return to Samira."

BY THE TIME ARKSON returned, the dark night sky had fallen and Samira was fast asleep. He sighed in appreciation of her beauty. She wore one of his black shirts and her hair, left natural, was coiled in waves softening her allure. His *wife*, he thought to himself.

He thought it peculiar that they had reached this point already. He had suspected it would take much longer than it had, and the change, abrupt and unexpected, was well received by Samira. It did not feel jarring. It felt natural to him.

He changed out of his clothing and crawled into bed spooning her body with his own. He wanted to make love to her again, to savour her body slowly with no interruptions, nothing to get in the way of his desire, but did not want to wake her. She needed her rest.

She stirred in his arms, and sleepily yawned.

"I did not mean to wake you Samira," he whispered in her ear before he kissed her cheek.

She turned to him, her eyes opening, "You want to make love," she spoke to him, stating his thoughts factually.

He smiled slowly, sexily. "You're tired Samira, you need your rest."

"I have been resting for three days Arkson." Samira wanted to bask in his affection. Her fingers tickled his naked hipbone.

She enjoyed Arkson like this, when he was elated by their new marriage. He still wanted to have a ceremony, which touched her. Their marriage had no announcement, no romance, it has been a life altering decision made on a whim, but if she had the choice to save his life again, she would do it in a heartbeat. His life was priceless to her. She could no longer deny that she was in love with him.

During the day, Samira had considered what it meant to be his mate now. Their lives were bound by life force. If he died she would as well, but if she died, he might live. With his powers restored, he probably would. She should resent him for not telling her, but she felt no ill will. Instead she wanted to be wrapped up in his arms.

She got up from bed and poured herself some water from the night stand. As she drank he watched her lovingly, she returned to him slowly, with sensuality. He had kneeled on the bed, waiting for her. He held his hand out for her and she took it as he pulled her close. She straddled his knees sitting in his lap.

Arkson brushed Samira's hair out of her face as he pulled her into a deep forceful kiss as though he had longed for her all day. He pulled her closer and she nestled into neck, breathing in his scent and letting her lips gently brush against the hollow.

Her finger gently traced along his collar and deep breaths escaped from him as though she singed him with her hands. Arkson closed his eyes and breathed in Samira's scent as his fingers brushed through her hair.

"Not as guarded now?" He asked, hoping she would not take offence.

"I still have questions," she began, "but I understand you."

"Good," he replied lightly running his finger down the bridge of her nose. She moved forward to kiss him, but he stopped her lips with the same finger, "allow me, Samira," he said appealing to her.

She locked eyes with him and nodded. Tilting her head back his fingers tickled her neck before he kissed all around her lips, teasing her, making her crave him. Instead of satisfying them both with another kiss, he unbuttoned her shirt, staring into her eyes so intensely she thought she might liquefy.

Arkson's eyes hungrily travelled over her naked body he pulled her higher onto his lap running his hands over her thighs and up to her waist, gently leaning her back. Her chest burned in anticipation as he throbbed beneath her. The sensation of his hands firmly pressing over her skin was riveting.

"If the Anuya who caused these scars was not already dead, I would kill him. How dare he mar my love."

"Oh Arkson..." she said softly. She was touched by his concern and his tinge of anger, which quickly made way for his passion.

Samira was surprised by how Arkson trembled with desire as his hands moved further up her body, they moved up to her chest before trailing down discovering her breasts, massaging and cupping them, until at last he could no longer resist and quieted her pleasurable moans with a deep sensuous kiss. He continued kissing her as his fingers stroked her succulent core before exploring her further in deep circles.

She gasped when he lifted her slightly and sank himself deep within her. Their lips met furiously in overlapping kisses as he plunged into her repetitively. His hands firm on her hips and rotating her against him. Samira's dark eyes looked at him ardently. He could feel her quiver in his arms with each thrust.

He felt her heart pounding against him, could see the pleasure on her face, which sent him higher into his own delight. He had wanted to caress and love her so candidly since they had been married but he had waited patiently, completing his daily duties.

She moved her own body to his meeting him stroke for stroke. Her body was so heatedly tight and ready to be sent over the perilous edge. With each mounting swivel he devoured her with kisses as he cupped a hand around her bum and thrust a deeper stroke into her.

She erupted into a leg weakening orgasm from the force of his body which was met with Arkson's throaty climax as he grunted sexily. Falling back onto the bed, he pulled her with him and they lay there together elated and feeling heady, but weightless.

Mmmmm her smell, he thought to himself as his eyes closed in rest and for a few seconds before opening them to memorize the moment he shared with her. He kissed her lips tenderly.

Samira felt such joy and peace. In his arms, as his wife, she felt as though she belonged there, that she should not ever leave him and she let the peace of the moment wash over her.

CHAPTER 23

Arkson was lying in bed, but he was alone. His body was covered in a cold sweat. He stared out into the room, but it was black, no light skimming over the objects he expected to be there. He could see nothing but the posts and curtains on his bed. The bed was large and he looked down at the edge of the mattress leading off into darkness his feet ending somewhere in the middle of its surface.

Where is Samira?

He sat up panicked, unable to move any more. His body felt heavy, stuck in place and suddenly stricken with pain. It was the same pulling sensation of his powers being lost as when he was a child. Long and arduous it had been torture to his small body. Tensed and catatonic, he had lain that way for days before some of the rigidity disappeared. It couldn't be happening again, not now, now that he had Samira.

"Are you all right Ark?" A small voice spoke.

He looked over to see Alexandros appear from the darkness his black hair hanging into his icy blue eyes. He looked the same as he had when he was eleven.

"I.." Arkson's voice began, but he was unable to speak, his hand finding its way to his vocal chords he pushed against them wondering why the words would not come out. The pain was still that ebbing pull of power and he weakened moment by moment. His Zain markings were colder than ice and the bitter withdrawal of energy from them cut through him violently.

No, not again! His mind screamed.

"Ark?" Alexandros asked again.

Arkson pushed the covers off and looked down, his feet were small, child-size, he looked at his hands, and they were the same. He felt his face, looked at his stomach to see it small, scar-less. He was a child. He wanted to jump from the bed, to run away. He closed his eyes from the pain.

"Arkson?"

He heard the voice again but it was different, distant.

Samira hovered above him her hands on his shoulders. She had awakened from his dream, its potency blending into her own and the tormented look of Alexandros's face still burned into her eyes. It was such a familiar face, one she swore she had seen before. Jumping up from the pain and out of the dream Arkson lurched forward; his face bore such martyred heaviness. Samira quickly moved back to give him space. She should have woken him sooner, but her own mind was befuddled by the same emotions he had felt. It was clouded with the same anger.

"Arkson," she said bracing her palm against her head to sort through his racing thoughts, "are you okay?"

He let out a deep sigh lying back down, the fear slowly seeping out from him.

She is still here, with me.

He wrapped an arm around her, pulling her to him. He was so grateful for her presence. Countless times he had awoken from the same dream to a cold and silent room, to loneliness and the darkness of the night. Samira kissed his cheek and got up disappearing into the bath enclosure. He closed his eyes as he listened to her turn on the water. His heart was still thundering, his body still tense from the agony.

She returned to him moments later with a dampened cloth and wiped his chest slowly, then lightly massaged the Zain marking on his arm. She knew that was where he felt the pain the most. It was where the pain still seemed to tingle on her. He laid there silent searching out her eyes in the moonless room. He was stunned by her presence as she soothed him. His pallor looking sickly, she worried he might never speak.

"What were you dreaming?" She asked, wondering if he would answer.

Arkson's mouth had gone completely dry. His wrinkled brow softened as he sat up gently so that Samira was not taken aback. He poured himself some water from the pitcher on the nightstand drinking the liquid slowly.

Clearing his throat, he reached out for Samira, pulling her body into his own. "I dreamt of my curse."

"What was it like?" She asked him, her fingertips running along his muscles.

"It was nothing," he said, "we should go back to sleep."

"Don't lie." She said to him, her eyes meeting his.

His jaw tensed a second before he spoke, "I'm sorry, I should not lie to you."

He kissed her hand.

"It was excruciating," he admitted ruefully.

"I felt it." She confessed. "I awoke because I could see, and hear, and feel your pain."

How can that be? He thought.

"I think your powers unlocked something in me when we mated", she responded to his thinking. "I see things now, before they happen, and I can hear people's thoughts." She paused, "I can hear your thoughts right now."

"What am I thinking now?" he asked, the seriousness making way for play as he pictured them making love, heatedly and erotically slow.

Her cheeks flushed. "Oh I know what you're thinking Arkson." She looked down to his lap, his body already ticking in response.

Arkson laughed richly, and his body now free of tension, pulled Samira closer in tenderness. She clutched his shoulders as their lips met in harmony.

"I am much better now Samira."

"Don't lie to me again Arkson." She looked at him stoically waiting for his answer.

"I take an oath my love," he spoke softly, his hand reaching for hers, his eyes regretful. "I will never lie to you Samira." His words were cut off by his hot breath branding her mouth with kisses.

THAT MORNING AS SAMIRA woke, her thoughts returned to the face of Alexandros in the dream. She lay there pressed against Arkson's body, her lips resting on the skin of his delicious neck. Arkson had been so haunted the night before. Yet what burned in her mind was the image of Alexandros. He was spectral, his skin pale and translucent, his dark hair and icy eyes in contrast. She felt as though she knew the boy. He had been like a brother to Arkson, that much she could tell. It made her think of her own sister. She wondered how Salha was, was instantly riddled with worry for her.

Suddenly a wave of emotion hit her as a vision, dream-like and cloudy, opened up. She saw Salha's face. Images of Braedynn flickered into her, as he led Salha up a mountain path. It kept cutting ahead every few seconds as they neared closer and closer to a beautiful wooden house on the clearing of a cliff. There was a man waiting for them there, with long black hair to his shoulder fluttering in the wind, his back facing them. Samira's breath caught as the vision unfolded further. Suddenly, her sister and Braedynn were before the man and he turned, his pale icy blue eyes coldly examining them.

It was Alexandros! It had to be. He held his hand out to Salha but she was afraid. Alexandros seemingly frustrated with her response to him lifted his hand in the air and spoke something over the surface of his ring. Samira witnessed Braedynn's body dematerialize into a dust and return to the dark haired man's ring. What had happened? Samira's chest burned from the heaviness her sister felt, the irrevocable fear and worry overcoming her too. Was Salha in trouble? How could the man who seemed so eerie, who haunted her husband's dreams be a friend?

She jumped out of bed and grabbed her clothes, looking for where she had left her satchel. Arkson awoke then, and looked at her with eyes so expectantly that she knew this was the moment he had decided to ask her to stay. Her heart was still drowning from the vision. He wanted to convince her they were meant for one another, that she was needed here at his side. No, wait it was not needed, it was that she belonged there.

Shit! Is this what I want? The perfect guy and a crown, plus a kingdom handed to me on a silver platter? What about my sister? You told her you would meet with her. You promised Sammie, and with that vision who knows what will happen to Salha. You need to be there for her Sammie, you have to get your ass in gear and get out there! Pronto! You could tell him Sammie, you could tell him that you will come back. But... if he knows you'll come back to him will he always think he needs you, despite the fact that the words are never on his lips. Will he think you are the reason he has become the Akorian he was meant to be?

"Sammie?" Arkson spoke, using her nickname for the first time. His eyes looked hurt as he watched her dress quickly. "Where are you going?"

She looked away from him. "I have to leave Zatian, Arkson."

"Leave?" He asked getting up and putting on his cotton pants.

"Arkson you don't understand, my sister needs me." Her gestures betrayed her frantic desire to leave the room.

"Then let me come with you." He said his arms firmly planted on her shoulders.

"You'll leave your kingdom behind for me, while you're on the brink of a war?" His face darkened.

"What do you know about that?" He asked.

She sighed and placed her hand upon his cheek. "I can hear your thoughts remember?"

"Then let me send Alvaren with you." He gently stroked her hair, pleaded with her.

"So that he can bring me back?" Her brow furrowed, angered.

"Yes," he said as he held back a smile.

"No, Arkson you need him!" Sammie's cheeks burned. "Arkson, you're not listening to me!" She pushed his hands away from her hair.

"You won't be safe without him Samira!" His eyes grew dark with worry.

"I should be fine Arkson, you taught me well remember. I survived those other spies? Plus, I'm apparently psychic!" She arched a brow at him.

Or just psychotic she thought wryly.

He was silent for a beat.

"You planned this Samira. You never intended to stay did you?"

"I never said anything about staying or going."

"You're my wife!" His voice was ragged, demanding.

"By circumstance, not by choice." Her words made him cringe, "Let's say it wasn't me, let's say it was my sister who was the human you freed that day in Uri what would you have done then, tried to woo her?"

He didn't answer, telling the truth in his silence.

"I was just the necessary human to fill the void for you. Now you're fixed, you don't need me."

His face fell, "I don't need you, but I want you."

His words felt like a dozen knives stabbing into her heart, and she nearly crumbled from it, tears slipped from her eyes. He was— She was— She— needed to leave! She wiped the tears and then straightened.

"You'd want me caged."

"Do you mean that? You feel as though I have trapped you?"

"Yes! No! Sometimes! Look Arkson, Salha may be in trouble and I think it has to do with Alexandros." She broke a little, his confession got to her.

Damn him and his earnest demeanour, damn him and those beautiful emerald eyes shimmering with hurt.

"That cannot be."

"Why not?"

"Because Alexandros is dead."

"How do you know that?"

"Because I looked for him, when the slavers ripped through his village I tried to find him, Nikelda and I searched for him for months to no avail. He is dead Samira."

"I'm not going to stand here and argue, I'm going—"

"Is this because of my dream?"

"No, Arkson I know what I saw, even if you don't believe me."

"Wait Samira...please wait..." He sighed deep in his

chest, he wanted to go with her, but the plans had already been set and the city anticipated the attack from Guedan any day now. He wished she would wait, would wait until this was all over.

He went to the wardrobe near the bed, pulling levers and shifting its mechanisms. The doors sprang open and he pulled something from its depths, returned to her.

"Take this with you," he said, his hand stretched out to her. He handed her a dagger. Its handle was finely carved of ivory in the shape of a horse. "This will protect you. You don't need to be close to your opponent. It ejects a bolt that stuns them when pointed in their direction. Just press the ruby near the blade. Use it sparingly, the energy is not unlimited. And if you run out, you will need to use your sword and the dagger as weapons." He paused with a sigh, "Please, be safe."

"You're letting me go?"

"You haven't given me a choice."

"No, I haven't."

"I would drag you back to the bed tie you there to keep you with me forever, but then you would hate me."

"I would," she spoke softly, her voice cutting into him like knives.

"Come back to me Samira. Find what you are looking for and return to me, the sooner the better."

Samira walked along the same palace wall as she had when she ran from Guedan's scouts. Elastor escorted her. If she was going to leave him, Arkson did not want her sneaking off unprepared. She had packed up what she could and the rest Arkson had packed for her, all the while silent and brooding. He worked quickly knowing that the sooner that she left, the sooner that she would hopefully return to him.

She placed an innocent kiss on his lips as she said her

goodbye not wanting her departure to be so bitter. She thought he might leave it at that, but instead he pulled her into his arms and kissed her senseless, his tongue heedlessly exploring her mouth for all in their presence to see, his hands firm on her waist.

She would have blushed had she not known it was a ploy. She could still taste him, her lips swollen from his. She knew that he planned it that way, wanted her to have his memory imprinted upon her, but what he did not understand was how much it already had been.

The palace was so quiet in the mid-afternoon. There were guards at their posts but there were far more concerned with assailants trying to make their way into the city rather than a woman leaving.

Arkson instructed Elastor to give her his finest horse, Thunder, insisting that she ride the beast of an animal to her destination wherever that may be. He was beautiful, and did take quite a liking to her the last time that she and Arkson had travelled together.

Knowing that she was as ready as she ever would be, she mounted the horse pulling out the map that would guide her as she tried to find her sister. She looked up to the large palace window on the grand terrace where Arkson's throne room was built. She could not see into it from here, but didn't need to, sensing that he was standing behind it and watching her go.

As soon as she had left Arkson had advised Elastor to follow her out of sight until she reached her destination. Arkson instructed him to only interfere in her journey if it was absolutely necessary and only then to protect her should a larger evil try to hurt her. However, when she reached her point of interest he would return to Arkson and the prince would let Samira decide if she wanted to come back to him.

He could not force her to love him. He wanted to make

sure she was safe, wished he had pried further into the details that she would not share. She had already closed him off to her emotionally to protect herself. She blocked his mind from hers and everyone else's for that matter.

Along the first part of the trail out of the kingdom Samira realized that she did not need to look at the map, she knew the way and could sense which direction to follow. What bothered her more was the nagging feeling that she was being followed. She suspected Arkson had arranged for someone to follow her to ensure her safety, but she did not want to assume that this was the person following her now. She was too tired to try and send out her new psychic feelers, and she did not even know how her mind and body might react to them. Whoever they were, they were definitely good at staying far enough behind that they were out of her sight. She hoped they stayed that way.

She rode for as long as she felt Thunder could without rest and then stopped at a rocky brook. Night would fall in another two hours, and she doubted she wanted to be riding along the road then. It seemed a much safer idea to stick to the paths during daylight, this way she could see any danger she might face.

She decided now would be a good time to start setting up camp, especially being so close to a source of water. She walked into the woods a good fifteen minutes from the bank, so as not to be too close should any night travellers make a stopover. She didn't know what type of creatures might travel in the shadows.

Then, she cleared Thunder a patch of the woods, removing anything that might be uncomfortable for him should he decide to lie down and rest. She wanted to make him more comfortable, even though she knew he didn't sleep for very long and often did so standing. She would need to rest longer so she tied him to a nearby trunk and looked at him sternly.

"Now I know you may not understand me Thunder, but I need you to listen really closely. I am going to need some rest, and I really can't have you wandering off, so please take this time to relax, and in the morning I'll make sure we give those long legs of yours a good stretch."

Maybe Samira was really starting to lose it? At this point, in the past five months she had been a slave, been taken to a city far away from her sister, met a powerful prince, somehow found herself mated to him, and then discovered she had telepathic powers. Now she was talking to a horse as though he knew every word she spoke. She wondered if faeries might suddenly appear in the forest.

"You need rest," she said aloud to herself, "quit quibbling and get a move on it, Sammie." Thunder neighed in agreement.

"Great, even the horse thinks you're crazy."

She laid down a blanket for the horse and then followed suit with the same for herself. Tomorrow was going to be a long day, but if she managed to travel in the same fashion as she had that day, she could make it to the town of Brinn well before nightfall, and that was a necessity. She already felt like she had wasted too much time arguing with Arkson.

Her head still throbbed from all of the information, voices, and visions spilling in and out. She didn't even know if the vision she had seen had already taken place or was yet to come. Having powers was proving tricky and she prayed she could find some way to deal with them. She needed to, as soon as possible. Tomorrow she might try to open herself up to them again, but for the time being, she needed to rest.

CHAPTER 24

The Hall of Haldero was filled with warriors from varying parts of Arzule. The leaders of the northern cities of Boja, Piut, and Sathan had arrived in addition to the Batchi of Sebastian's and four other tribes. The room was not large enough to hold them all, but they made space for as many Akori and Batchi as they could. Overnight the walled city of Zatian had been filled with visitors. The leaders sat around the table in counsel, Arkson at the head.

"We know now that King Guedan has prepared for attack, after learning that Prince Arkson's human mate was not successfully killed and the coronation is scheduled for tomorrow, his troops are anxious to litter the roadways. They await deployment, which will be signalled at the end of next week." Sebastian spoke to the table, "Our Batchi spies have advised us that the full disembark for Zatian will be in a week, giving us two weeks to prepare."

"Is that enough time," Queen Bradjya spoke, concerned about the multitude of resources they would have to organize and pool.

"It is more than enough," Arkson spoke, "I have been preparing for this day long before I knew it would come."

She nodded her head to him.

King Arpal spoke, "we must elect a leader to meet with King Guedan on the field before the battle." Some in the room believed that it should be him, seeing as he had the largest number of forces in the fight, was the eldest King, had more battle scars.

Sebastian answered, "we have already elected a leader alongside our people." His eyes fell upon Arkson.

King Arpal countered, "we should place a vote."

Arkson eyed him, even though this was his kingdom, or rather would be in a day King Arpal clearly did not respect him. He knew he would still struggle with this problem in his new alliances, but he had not expected it from such a well reputed Akori.

"Very well," he responded, his eyes asking Sebastian to permit him the liberty. Sebastian nodded, but Arkson could tell he would much prefer to be led by someone he knew and trusted.

The votes were cast Queen Bradjya and Sebastian elected Arkson, while Kings Melosha and Arpal elected Arpal as the chosen leader for the ride out. It was evenly split, and Arkson's vote would be the deciding factor.

Although he was grateful for the support and help of King Arpal, he knew that were he to lead the company, his city may be lost. Arkson had far much more at stake in this fray.

"King Arpal, although I agree you are well suited to this task, it is here in my city that we will make our move against Guedan. For my people I will step forward, because I could not bear to sacrifice their lives heedlessly. I will not be a king for long when we march out to meet our enemy, but I will be a king. I have been fighting this war for far longer than any other Akori. I have been fighting King

Guedan for a lifetime and in due course I will end this."

King Melosha nodded his head in approval, with admiration clearly steeped in his eyes, but King Arpal frowned and clearly wanted to protest.

"I do not belong to this city, but I am Akorian nonetheless, I would do Zatian justice, but as you are meant to be King to these walls, and we are here out of respect of our alliance, I will agree to these terms."

Arkson looked determined. "I appreciate your support. Let us map out the battlefields."

It took close to four hours for the map to be properly laid out. Each ruler had their ideas about which troops should be placed where and what advantages each place would have. They speculated on where the greatest weaknesses would be, what strengths they should play up.

Yet, Arkson knew the land the best. He knew that near the south gate the treeline there needed to be guarded well, it was the area of greatest weakness. He knew that Guedan would come from the west, meeting in the plains of Zatian, but also send troops through the mountains to the north. They of course would take longer to reach Zatian and so would either be sent out early or arrive later as a reserve.

They had decided that King Guedan should not be killed immediately. They were mostly Akorian and believed in the rights of the old code. He would receive a trial, but would be judged harshly for the crimes he had committed. The council would bring him to justice.

After a long day of planning, Arkson retired to his room. The halls of the palace had been decorated in celebration of his kingship. Even on the brink of war his people were eager to celebrate this small victory. Thankfully the passage had been left bare and it gave Arkson's senses a peaceful rest.

Entering the room, it seemed quite bare without Samira's presence. Part of him wished she were there now, while the other half never wanted to see her again. She was a painful reminder of what make him weak – love. How he hated the idea of love so much now. Yet, he knew that in truth *she* was his greatest strength. He longed to pull her close to him, to inhale her scent, and to nibble her lips. Sitting on the chaise he closed his eyes in longing for a few minutes before he snapped himself out of it in disgust.

He had found his own strength now though, would not wait any longer for the coronation. It was as it should have been. She would return to her sister and perhaps find a way back to her world, and he would rule over his. He did not know why he waited for tradition to dictate he was now a suitable king. He had been prepared for years. Even without his powers, he should have fought Guedan years ago, but then, there was no telling if he would have succeeded.

Tomorrow would come quickly, and it would be a ceremony lasting majority of the day. Even though Veros and Brunelda would be there with him, without Samira or Nikelda, he felt like the room would seem empty. For the first time in a little while he would once again be completely alone.

The Zatian Great Hall, abandoned since the death of King Mactyllo, had been bustling with Akori for the past two days. Its walls had been revived with new life and decorated for the coronation. The purple and red velvet carpets rolled out and dusted, every part of the altar polished, and the room lined with the ceremonial candles.

Arkson was in his room, dressed in his plain white shirt and pants. He waited for Veros to enter the passage and advise him of the ceremonial beginning. The great celebration to follow would be thrown in such merriment, but he knew that it would be short lived. War was fast approaching.

It was hard to be in his room and not think of Samira, her scent still lingered on his pillows. Every time he bathed he could only think of the way her skin looked wet and naked. He remembered the soft curve of her flesh against his muscles. It was a gnawing feeling that divided him, but he was trying to let that go, to be made whole by the right of kingship.

Veros had arrived and he knocked lightly on the door.

Arkson opened the door facing his uncle with confidence. Veros was adorned for the ceremony, and would be the officiate to crown Arkson. Honestly, Arkson preferred for no other to complete the task, no other would be more suitable.

"Zatian awaits, King Arkson," he smiled at his nephew.

Arkson walked through the passage following the procession of the Zatian high priestess and the temple bearers. Their long velvet robes were dragging down the corridor. The hall was filled with Akorians, all of the villagers outside of the castle wall had been brought in for refuge. They filled the Great Hall, wearing their very best and eagerly awaiting the prince.

All eyes were on him as Arkson walked the aisle. He stared at the altar awaiting his presence, there were four chairs there, the King's, the Queen's to the right of that and on either side of each chair were two that had been erected for Nikelda and himself. It had been a very long time since he had sat in one of those chairs.

As the procession in front of him reached the pulpit, carrying his royal crown, jewelled sword, gold sceptre, and embroidered cloak they placed the items down gently and moved to their positions awaiting the commencing bell.

As expected, Arkson faced each corner of his kingdom, the north, the south, the east and the west, all of which pledged their allegiance in unison stating, "all Hail Prince Arkson!"

Arkson swore an oath to his people. "From this day as your King, I proudly bear the right of protection, peace, union, and wealth. In doing so I shall provide all corners of the city north, south, east, and west, the passion of life and love, the balance of harmony and peace, the strength of mind and sword, and the wealth of land and king."

Veros stepped forward as Arkson bent. "I proclaim thee, King of Zatian," placing the crown upon his head. "Is this king accepted?" he asked the crowd.

"All hail King Arkson!" The people shouted with merriment.

Veros stepped back to the altar and proceeded with anointing Arkson with the sword, sceptre and cloak.

Arkson rose and bowed before taking his place in his father's throne, while the crowd, jovial shouted, "long live King Arkson!"

Arkson's eyes examined the room proudly, but as they fell upon the empty Queen's throne he couldn't help the twinge of sadness that rolled through him.

CHAPTER 25

NIKELDA OPENED THE door quickly, her mouth poised in a devilish smile. "What are you doing here Eric?"

What am I doing here?

Somewhere between walking up Clifton and across Robie his feet had found his way to Sammie and Salha's apartment, and he knew exactly why, but hadn't been thoughtful enough to make up an excuse upon arrival. He wanted to see her, couldn't stop thinking about her beautiful melodic voice, her haunting smile, or the way her eyes glistened.

"I think I forgot something here the last time I visited Salha." He lied.

"Really?" Nikelda asked. "Or did you just miss me?" She simpered.

"Sure," he said getting a bit stiff.

Act your butt off buddy. Do not give her the impression you like her.

She gave him a slightly injured look and then straightened opening the door. It was times like these that she wished she had empathic capabilities like her brother, instead she had energy sourcing and levitation. Levitation! Like she was ever going to use that! She would never be so foolish to jaunt around. It seemed so useless to her and was so rare for Akorian females.

"What did you forget? I can help look for it." She looked at him, her smile gone. *Then you can leave and I'll go back to being alone.*

"Aah a book, I forgot one of my books, I think."

He faced her square; they were practically eye to eye. He might be an inch taller her if anything but she was used to being around tall males, all female Akorians were.

His eyes quickly moved over her curvaceous frame before he walked over to the bookshelves where he knew Salha kept her books. He scanned over them speedily, hoping that maybe he had left one of them there, but he was out of luck. There was nothing there that was his. He nearly cursed under his breath, but then on a lower shelf his eye caught one of his discs. Bending down he picked it up quickly and kissed the cover.

She had closed the door and watched him closely, her arms crossed, no expression on her face.

"No book here," he said, "but I did find my album."

"What is an album?" She asked staring at the square shaped object in his hand.

He gave her a peculiar look. "You don't know what a CD is?"

She shifted uncomfortably.

"You know it contains songs, plays music when placed in the appropriate electronic device, replaced the cassette of the nineteen eighties..." he continued.

She shrugged. Her green eyes looked innocent.

"What are you in a cult?" His eyebrows pinched in speculation. "Is that what you meant by far, far away? Are Salha and Sammie on some type of new cult exchange program?" He was beginning to ramble.

"No," she said defensive, "I'm Akorian." She had the urge to slap a hand over her mouth to keep any other details about her from spilling out, but that would only make him more suspicious. She had probably said too much already and never should have invited her to return with him to Zatian, but there was just something about this human that made her tell him the truth.

Then, Eric had an idea that was genius.

"Ummm okay, look I'll show you," he said, walking over to Samira's radio. It was his Phil Flowers album so he skipped to the slowest track, "People People". He needed an excuse to dance with her and the beat was slow enough to set the tone. He held his hands out to her.

"Dance?"

Her arms fell to her sides as she walked towards him, "I haven't danced since I was sixteen." She tucked her hair behind her ears before placing one hand on his shoulder, the other awaiting his hand in the air.

"You waltz?" He asked.

"You said you wanted to dance," she said suddenly feeling a little foolish. Perhaps they did not dance the same way in Halifax as they did in Zatian.

He had hoped she would lean against him and wrap her arms around his neck like a teenager. He felt like a teenager. He placed his arm around her waist, his hand resting on the small of her back all too aware of her smell and the heat of her body next to his. They moved slowly, hardly shifting from where they stood.

"You're supposed to lead," she said with a coy look.

"Oh you're a dancing expert," he teased.

"Well I am a prin- pretty good at it I mean." She corrected quickly and looked down to their feet. "I'm afraid I'll step on your toes though," she said.

"They've been through worse," he replied with a smile.

Hopefully he hadn't caught onto what she almost said.

"I've never heard music like this." And she hadn't been this close to a male in a long time. She felt good in his arms, was tempted to lean against his shoulder.

"Do you like it?" He wanted to know more about her, needed another excuse to spend time with her.

"Yes, very much."

She looked over to the radio, her eyes considered it thoughtfully as though she had never seen one of those either.

Playfully he twirled her out into the room before pulling her in closer than before. "There I led for a bit, better?" He asked looking at her lips.

"Yes, you've improved," she replied, suddenly aware of a haze of heat surrounding them.

She thought about Farloom he was so different from Eric who seemed shy, sensitive. Farloom was so confident and determined. He had been aggressive in pursuing her like most male Akori. When he wanted something he went for it and initially she had declined him too annoyed by his persistent declarations that they were meant for each other. Over time though something about him had made way for her, made her realize that he did not want to dominate her. He wanted a relationship like her Uncle Veros and Aunt Brunelda they would be equals.

She wondered what type of relationship Eric would want. Why had Salha ended things with him? Would he consider her his partner? She shook the thought from her head, she shouldn't be so foolish.

Eric couldn't help but stare at Nikelda's perfect pink lips. "I don't know your name," he whispered, his hot breaths sweet on her cheek.

"It's Nikelda," she answered softly.

"Nikelda," he said trying the name on his tongue, "that is a beautiful name, fitting." He looked straight into her eyes, so intoxicating and feminine.

She blushed. No male had ever told her she was beautiful. Her brother and uncle always complimented her demeanour, her intelligence, Farloom had praised her skills, her strength, and here was this man, this human who thought her beautiful.

"You think me beautiful?" She asked unbelieving.

He tucked her hair behind an ear attentively and whispered, "I think you're very beautiful."

"Thank you," she whispered, her eyes catching the beam of admiration from his own.

He leaned in slowly to kiss her, and Nikelda almost did the same until she realized a kiss no matter how small would be life changing.

"The song is done," she chirped.

He pulled back, aware of the change in her demeanour. She was nervous. He hadn't expected that since she acted assured and relaxed about everything. It was cute.

"So it is," he said. They continued to dance, but she leaned in closer, nestled into his shoulder so that his lips had no access to hers.

She prayed that it would not be a long night of cat and mouse. She might be tempted to cave in to her pursuer.

CHAPTER 26

Samira entered the gates of the city of Brinn, it was a small town with a few structures. The guards escorting her had been shocked upon her arrival, they yelled questions at her. How could she be an Akori? What was she doing there? Was she a sorceress and so on. She learned that the land was sheltered for humans alone. With her Zain markings they had assumed she was an Akori and had been prepared for attack until she mentioned her sister Salha and Braedynn escaping from Uri to seek shelter there.

They took her to the village elder. She was the apothecary, a short woman with curly white hair long like Samira's and eyes the yellow of a cat. Her skin was weathered and looked like a wrinkly leather bag, but there was such kindness to her face, Samira knew she could trust her instantly. Her new psychic senses told her she had met an affiliate.

"How may I help you, my dear?" She asked.

"I need to see my sister, Salha."

"I do not know of anyone by that name." The woman's

eyes crinkled with kindness.

"What about Braedynn? Do you know of him? There aren't many people here surely if I describe him you could recall."

"Well, what does he look like?" The woman interjected.

"He's six foot two, has dirty blonde hair, bright blue eyes, and tanned from working in the sun all day. You know a big burly guy." Sammie's arms pushed out like she was squaring for a football tackle.

The woman laughed, "Oh that guy, he's gone now."

"Gone!? Well what about the woman he was with?"

"I didn't get a good look at her. She could be anywhere," the woman replied with a flippant waive.

The guards stepped closer to Samira as though they might pull her away.

"Wait, wait," she said her palm pushing out to stop them, "What about Alexandros?"

Anyone in the near vicinity got quiet.

"What name did you say?" The woman's crinkled smile faded.

"I asked about Alexandros?" Samira was determined.

The old woman looked thoughtful for a moment, her mouth twisting in consideration. "He doesn't go by that name anymore, we call him Chief"

"Chief?" She asked. "Okay, well how do I find him?"

The woman waved over a couple of soldiers, "This woman here is asking for the Chief, take her to him but make sure you blindfold her first," she said wagging a finger at them. Sammie suspected the woman lectured them often. Samira's ears perked up.

"Blindfold!? Is that really necessary?"

"Of course it is, we don't know if we can trust you yet, dearie," she said and patted Sammie on the arm.

Samira wasn't sure if she could trust the guards, they

eyed her suspiciously. As they guided her they asked her a lot of questions. She answered honestly. Especially since she sensed smart mouthed answers would go unappreciated.

"We're here," one said knocking on what sounded like a window pane before a door creaked open and she was shoved up a few steps.

The blindfold was removed and Samira opened her eyes, feeling a bit star-dazed. Her eyes adjusted to the light quickly and she inspected the man in the room with her sister, it took a second for her mind to process the recognition.

It was Alexandros, but his face was far more discernible, older than in the dream and clearer than her visions. His long hair was black as night and fell to just above his shoulders, his eyes a fierce blue were like ice, pale and almost grey, but his face remained the same. He had the same jawline and eyebrows, the same lips and nose and she instantly knew why she recognized him. He was actually quite handsome.

Sammie opened her mouth to make a comment, but she was distracted by the sobs escaping from the sitting slump of her sister at what appeared to be a kitchen table.

"What did you do to her?" she asked Alexandros accusingly.

Salha jumped up recognizing Sammie's voice and ran over to embrace her. She hugged her back and wondered what had happened between them. She stroked Salha's back in comfort, but her crying only escalated into a full blown blubbering bawl.

"Whoa, this is bad if you're doing the ugly cry," Sammie whispered unsettled.

Salha managed to laugh in between sucking back air. She tried to speak, but her tears were pouring down like a waterfall and her throat hitched.

"It's okay sis, just think it, I'll know." Salha's face crinkled oddly in suspicion. "Just do it." Sammie urged and her eyes narrowed on Alexandros as she pulled Salha closer into a hug and stroked her hair.

She was silent, closed her eyes for a few seconds as she witnessed the events of the morning. Then opened her eyes aggravated by what she saw. "You're an ass!" She yelled at Alexandros.

He stood taller, insulted, "Who the hell do you think you are? You can't come into my home unannounced and start throwing insults at me! Especially when I am eating breakfast!"

"Shut up Alexandros!" She spat back, with fire in her eyes.

"Oh so you know who I am, but Salha doesn't." He seemed sarcastic and looked at her examined her Zain markings "You're Samira, Arkson's Queen."

"I'm not his queen," she snapped. "How do you know who I am?"

"I have my sources," he said. He eyed her for a beat. "So you didn't want to marry that worthless bastard? I guess I could see why, he is a miserable jackass."

Samira's brown eyes went black. "From where I'm standing, you're the worthless bastard. Don't you dare talk about Arkson that way," she spoke, her hand moving to her hilt. "Say anything like that again, and I'll slit you from your groin to throat, and not quickly either." She was cold, spoke harshly.

Alexandros simply smiled, a wide, warm one that confused Samira. "You're perfect for him," he said.

"How so?" Samira asked still annoyed despite the kindness in his eyes.

Alexandros shook his head. "No Akorian would defend Arkson's demeanour the way you just did, they might agree he is benevolent, a good prince, but he is a bastard, a sour, bitter, arsehole, has been for over twenty years."

Samira saw red. "Take that back! Do not insult my—"

"He is my brother, you know?" Alexandros interjected, "my little brother, so I can say what I will. He is a part of me, like she is of you."

Salha, who had finally stopped crying, looked up stupefied. "What are you doing here Samira? How did you get here?"

Sammie had more questions for Alexandros, but her sister needed her attention first. "Did you forget that you invited me?"

Salha looked apologetic. "Oh right, no I didn't forget, I am just a little overwhelmed is all."

"Well I had to get here the moment that I saw this one here suck up Braedynn into that ring, especially with your emotions shattering through me like an anvil. You know I would never leave you hanging Sal, I'm your sister, and I'll always be here for you."

Salha smiled, wiping away her tears. "You saw that?" She was still perplexed.

"So what exactly happened with Braedynn?" Sammie asked looking at Alexandros.

He shifted uncomfortably. "He's gone now, he was a servant I summoned but he is no longer of use so I returned him to where he belongs. We'll talk about that later Samira, right now there are more important things that we need to discuss."

He motioned for her to follow him to his study. She looked over at Salha who was starting to regain her calm and was now seated at the table.

"Do you mean about Salha because—"

"No," he said, cutting her off, "that's important too, but you're a seer."

"A what?"

"You know a visionary, you have premonitions."

"Sort of," she answered, not knowing what to think of Alexandros, whether to trust him with the details of her powers.

"Anything else?"

If he was plotting evil, he certainly looked innocent, hopeful almost.

"Telepathy, but I think that is just primarily with Arkson, and I guess Salha too." He left the room and she stopped herself from walking down the corridor after him, her eyes still on her sister.

"You need to see the scroll."

"What scroll?" She asked looking to Salha who gave her a don't ask me look.

"Great, he's nice to you," Salha said to her.

"He's not nice to you?" she asked her, her brows furrowed in worry

"He's fine Sammie, I just don't know what to do." Salha blotted at her puffy eyes with a cloth.

"Come back to Zatian with me?" Sammie half-asked, half-stated.

"What about Braedynn? Even though he wasn't real, what am I going to do about him? I miss him."

"I'm sorry about him Salha, I truly am." She walked over and rubbed Salha's shoulder in comfort. "We'll figure it out Salha, I promise you."

Alexandros returned from his library with a large rolled parchment. "You're going to definitely need this to help that husband of yours."

"We're not married," Samira said.

"You share the Zain."

"Well not officially," she answered. He snickered.

Samira snatched the scroll from him annoyed, but proceeded with unravelling it carefully. The language was unfamiliar, unreadable. "I can't read this, she stated.

"You need to touch the parchment," he directed.

Gingerly she ran her fingertips over the characters, and just as it had been with the map, she understood exactly what each symbol meant.

She looked at Salha who still represented a crumpled mess at the table. "This reading will have to wait, you need to sleep." She pulled Salha up, guiding her towards the room she sensed was hers. "Then you and I are going to have a nice long talk, Alexandros," she said looking back at him.

He shrugged looking boyish.

"Whatever you say Samira." Alexandros was grateful for her presence, she knew him, knew his family and she was here to help with Salha, something he so desperately needed.

She sighed.

Now if only Arkson had been so forthcoming with the truth.

CHAPTER 27

Samira rolled up the parchment. She had finally finished reading the massive scroll. It had taken her any spare time she had in the past thirteen days to read and train according to the scroll, in between caring for her sister of course. Now, having discovered more about her powers, she actually felt energized rather than the draining feeling she usually did after an intense course of study.

There was additional information on the human population in Brinn she had skimmed over in Alexandros's collection of records. He had asked her to make time to interpret these works for him, as he, like so many other humans in Arzule was unfamiliar with that dialect. It would be a lot of work, but it was necessary, the humans in Arzule needed to rebuild. If she could help with that she would and Alex had helped her greatly by giving her the scroll on telepathy. Interpreting the works for him was an easy way to say thank you.

She had discovered in her readings that they were several ways for her to amplify her power and to harness her strength. It seemed that there was a natural progression of her predictive powers as they would shift from tactile to spatial to telepathic. The more control and skill she gained, the greater her strength would be. The script encouraged daily meditation, and hydration was a key factor in heightening her powers. To channel her focus there were teas she could drink to bring a sense of heightened awareness and the village apothecary, who she discovered was name Alyce, showed her the plant leaves that were the best and even taught her how to recognize them growing in the wild and the best time to pick them.

She had met with Alyce daily after that to learn all that she could about the local herbs and their medicinal properties. Even Salha managed to push past her now sullen nature, to meet with Alyce and began to take up the same type of work she had loved when she had lived in Halifax. Her interest in pharmaceuticals easily transferred into an interest in natural medicine. So the two of them, Sammie and Salha, learned as much as they could from Alyce who doted on them like they were her own daughters.

The remaining amount of time Samira spent in the training bays Alexandros had set up for his men. It was a rudimentary set up, not unlike Arkson's in the palace. There was an archery field, and a couple of sparring rings, as well as a few totems for swordplay. Sammie practised daily to make sure that her endurance would build. She ran to and from Alexandros's house anytime she needed to travel the village, leaving Thunder in the village stables where the children smothered him with affection. She had to keep her eye on him though. She did not want Arkson's prize horse getting lazy or restless, so she knew she would have to take him on a good jaunt soon. Maybe later that afternoon they could go for a ride.

She spent a good amount of time jarring with his men

and her strengthened powers helped with anticipating each strike. They were transitioning from tactile to telepathic quite easily. Now that she was done with the scroll and the mid-morning sun was strong, she thought it might be a good time to visit Alyce since this was the usual time she opened her shop. She arrived there before the apothecary, but since she had given Salha and Sammie a key to share she went in early to start setting up for her arrival.

"Good morning Sammie," Alyce said announcing her arrival as she set down the weight of her basket. "I went further into the trails this morning to find some fresh herbs and flowers. Mind helping me unpack them?"

Sammie smiled. "Not at all." She loved rooting through Alyce's fresh supplies. That was best way to get first dibs. She pulled out the contents slowly lining them up on the wooden counter. There were some Calendula, Pineappleweed, Nettle, and Filberts. Then her eye caught the colour of the blue flower, and she froze. It was the flower that triggered something instantly in her. Alyce had brought back Forget-me-not.

Samira hesitated before reaching out, while looking at it, all she could think of was Arkson. It was ironic, the flower reminding her of the one who haunted her dreams, her every day, as if she could forget Arkson. She remembered his smile when they had ridden to Uri, could feel the warmth of his skin while her hands were wrapped around him. She picked up the bunch gingerly, closing her eyes in a rush of her senses while she felt overwhelmed with his smell and sudden heat that touched the pit of her stomach.

Her skin was searing in fire as she opened her eyes to the battlefields of Zatian. She was on the mound near the palace overlooking the army of King Guedan. There were soldiers lined the length of the field, legions deep and they all looked fearful, afraid of the Akori who's mind she was melded with so closely.

She could feel Arkson's heartbeat in her chest, could taste the metallic tang of the fight pulsing within him. In that moment she was one with him, was him, felt the blood rushing, her body charged with overflowing energy and a ferocious power of life. She was ready to fight, ready to be the leader of the Akorian people, but there was one resonating cry in her soul. It was the need to defeat King Guedan and set things right. For a few seconds, that rush of enlightenment was all that she could feel, and she knew that she would. She had the command of a King, and looked back to her troops.

There were Akorians lined to match King Guedan, and allies, Batchi and the like ready to balance the menacing evil before them. She was confident, felt ascendance, until there was a potent ache of longing deep in the heart of her chest, a longing that hid in a dark shadow of this mind. When she tilted her sight there to that pain, and lifted the veil, her eyes seeing into the depth of that corner realized it was filled with love, overwhelming love that was meant only for her.

She mounted Arkson's horse with him, riding out to meet King Guedan in the field. If he could stop this before the bloodshed took its toll he would. He had to protect his people, protect so many innocent lives. His thoughts merged with hers.

Stopping metres before Guedan's horse, he dismounted, walking slowly over the grassy plain. Flashing instantly, she could see what Arkson could not, rather than meet honourably Guedan had a trick up his sleeve, standing a few metres from each other, neither moved in to agree on the terms of the battle. Her body left Arkson's, was projected astrally even though their bodies were connected, in tune.

Instead, Guedan pulled his powers from the earth,

huge bricks of earth surged forward slugging Arkson in the chest and smattering into dirt. It didn't stop him though he walked forward biting back the pain, until he let a thunderous yell rip from his chest and his whole body burst into flames, spreading it out onto the grass and encircling the evil King. He hit him with jolts of fire.

Samira could feel the raw edge of the flames, but she knew it was not enough, Guedan had brought a *triuny*, pulling it from his quiver she watched him twisting the knob on the spear behind his back. He threw it swiftly. She watched it in the air, crackling and starting to pull the fire from Arkson's body forward. She felt horrified, angered, and helpless. It was the same menacing swirl of motion as it had been the last time she saw one, and again it had been used dishonourably.

Arkson realized all too late what was happening, there was no way to stop it and even with throwing his fire, it did little to harm the enchanted weapon.

"Samira, I'm sorry." Arkson spoke aloud on the field, but she wasn't there with him, not physically. She felt the biting pain when the spear hit him, and he stood there shocked for several minutes before he collapsed to his knees. The blood trickled from his chest and down his side. It coated his hands, dripping off fingertips and Samira wanted desperately to be there with him, to pull the evil weapon from his body and save him once again.

Even though it had yet to happen, she was overwhelmed with the feeling of loss. She couldn't stand the thought of Arkson dying. She couldn't lose him again. She could feel his life force fade, feel his glowing essence dissipate. The light on his armour faded to a cold tinny gold as the swirling energy ceased and when she reached to touch it, she was jolted back out of the vision.

It hadn't happened yet, but it would. She had no idea when, but she wasn't about to wait for Guedan to kill them.

She had to go back, had to go to Zatian to help Arkson, or he would die, and she would too. Losing her life without being anywhere near him hurt her too much, she had to save her prince.

"Samira?" Sammie fell to her knees and Alyce rushed to her side. "What did you see?"

"I saw my life end." When she spoke the words she thought of Arkson, him there on the field, his eyes whitened, dying.

"Someone attacked you?" Alyce asked, concerned.

"No." She shook her head. "Arkson, the Prince of Zatian. King Guedan killed him."

Alyce looked at her determined. "Well then I guess we better get you prepared to fight that from happening. You know the visions aren't always right? You're never resigned to a fate you don't want Sammie."

Sammie nodded. "Yes. This vision I am going to fight! Give me what you've got Alyce. I'm leaving for Zatian in an hour."

A smile wrinkled Alyce's eyes. "He's a lucky prince, I tell you, finding a fighter of a wife like you. Not many like you in all of Arzule." Alyce helped Sammie to her feet and then walked away, humming as she gathered things that Samira might need in Zatian.

SAMIRA PLEADED WITH Alexandros, "Arkson is your family, you said so yourself, why not rid him and the others of their grief, Alex? He believes you to be dead, surely you must know that. What point is there in causing him pain?"

"Perhaps it is better for him to think that I'm gone," he answered her brusquely.

Samira did not have time for this. "You're an idiot, you know that? He would ask nothing of you other than to be a part of your life, to be a friend to you when it you need it. He would be there for you. He is your brother."

"I know, but...." he paused trying to think of an excuse, but found none.

"But what? You have no choice Alexandros. I'm not giving you one. You want Salha off your hands you're going to have to bring her to me."

He scowled, "I never said that was what I wanted"

"Well, what you said doesn't matter. I don't have time to argue this out. Will you help me or not, brother?" Sammie emphasized the last word intently.

He looked at her harsh for a few seconds until he softened, "Arkson better be good to you. I'll do as you ask."

"Good," she said, "now I need to find that sister of mine." She found Salha in the garden and explained that she was leaving all the while moving in a brisk walk towards the town stables.

Salha followed her, whining in complaint. "Why do you have to go right this minute?"

"Salha, I have to go, I love him." Her sister looked pained but Sammie continued. "In my vision his whole body was afire. I felt him die." Sammie held back tears as the gravity of her words struck home. "He can't die."

"Please don't leave me with him," Salha protested.

"Salha, Alex really isn't that bad and he's already promised me he will bring you with him when he returns to Zatian in a few days."

Now that Samira knew the truth she realized what a good person Alexandros was, he was just like Arkson, beneath his dark exterior his soul was pure.

"Why can't I go with you now?"

"Salha, you'll slow me down. You're safe with Alexandros and he'll bring you to me." She finished buckling her saddle on Arkson's beautiful beast, patting him in comfort.

"Don't worry, we'll be back with the prince soon Thunder," she whispered into the horse's ear. Thunder neighed in agreement.

"What if he doesn't bring me to you? What if he keeps me here captive?" Salha's hands jerked out into the air for emphasis.

"Salha, you've been ranting daily that you think he'd gladly be rid of you, *by any means*, but now you think he'll keep you here against your will?" Salha frowned knowing that Samira was right and crossed her arms.

"He has to finish building that house in lower Brinn before he brings you to Zatian, but he gave me his word and I believe him when he says that he'll help. He's honest and his word means something."

"He's such a grouch." Salha complained

"You're a grouch. You should give him a chance," Sammie chuckled.

"This isn't fair." Salha spoke with one last rebuttal.

Sammie shook her head again. "So stubborn."

Her sister scoffed, but then Alexandros appeared, walking over from the field, his hands darkened from working with the earth. Salha looked at him funny, and Sammie swore she saw that same look Salha had on her face every time she was near a man she had a crush on.

Alexandros extended his arm in support as she mounted Thunder.

"Kick some ass Sammie," he said to her with pride on his brow looking up at her. He wrapped an arm around Salha's shoulder.

Salha glared at him.

"I will," Sammie said smiling, before she urged Thunder to ride out.

The morning rose softly, slowly, piercing through the quiet dark, and it hung heavy on Arkson's soul. The purple streaked sky was warmed by pinks and oranges. He had not slept for long, only a few hours in the early part of the night. He didn't need the rest though. The fire was coursing through him and made him restless.

Arkson could tell that King Guedan's soldiers had bloodlust, on the way to Zatian, they had slaughtered more than fifteen settlements in an effort to warn him what was coming. News spread to Arkson quickly, but rather than demoralizing his soldiers, it fuelled them.

The past few days had been invigorating, the people of Zatian were showing their strengths, all in support of their leader. Guedan was hurting himself by raiding the wayside villages. Word was travelling of the brutality, in turn causing more western cities to defect. He was thankful that Elastor had advised him Samira went to the city of Brinn. At least this way she would be safe, the ground there anchored with magic from any outside harm.

He was angry with her, livid. She had been gone for longer than he had expected. In fact, he doubted now whether she would ever return. His sorrow had washed over him so fiercely after the coronation that he had to tuck it away. Instead he let the fire out from within him, let it feed and guide him. He had mastered his powers in a short time frame with daily practice. Since his discipline and focus were his strongest traits, it had made it easy to regain the skills, but now he had to unleash it from within. If he went to far with it he could lose himself to the fire.

Arkson had stationed his personal guards at the northern gate. Since that was the most difficult terrain and they were most familiar with it, it suited to have them there. The Guardians of Piut were stationed at the south gate, there were a few in the group with their powers linked to water and so it was of advantage for them to be near the coast. The eastern entrance to Zatian was guarded naturally by the mountain range and Cliffs of the Douns. They were large crags which were nearly impassable since the ground was hotter than hell and overrun with Baels, large reptilian creatures who ate anything in sight.

Brunelda helped Arkson with his armour, it had been a while since he had worn it, not since Samira's arrival. The enamelled surface, now connected to his returned powers, swirled from the electricity in his being. The blue, purple, and red were in constant movement against the golden setting.

"Be careful son," Brunelda spoke solemnly her hand resting on Arkson's shoulder.

"I will be." He embraced her in comfort. "Make sure the cook has a nice pot roast waiting for me." He smiled and Brunelda chuckled as she wiped back tears.

Alvaren and Veros would ride out with him to the front of the western plain, but he would be the only one to meet King Guedan.

"My King," Alvaren addressed him entering the room with Veros, "the soldiers await your presence."

Arkson tied a band around his hand for better gripping his sword. He had additionally dusted his hands with the earth of Zatian, to prevent his inner fire from heating the hilt of the sword to the point of melting.

"Let us not keep them waiting," he answered as he sheathed his sword.

Veros nodded, his eyes turned to Brunelda. He walked towards her, stopping to memorize every feature of her face before planting a soft kiss on her lips and turning back to Arkson. They left the throne room.

Suited and ready for the moment he had long awaited, Arkson rode out to the battlefields of Zatian. He reached the mound near his troops on the western flank, overlooking the army of King Guedan and dismounted. There were enemies lined the length of the field legions deep, some of them wore snarled expressions, others fearful.

Arkson looked up at the sky, the light slowly seeping in

was still overcast by clouds of grey. He walked forward to meet with Sebastian and King Arpal, King Melosha had volunteered to join the guards in the north, while Queen Bradjya was with her Guardians of Piut in the south.

"We are ready for you King Arkson," Sebastian spoke with pride, his emerald eyes emitting the eagerness of a young warrior.

King Arpal stepped forward as well. "I trust you are prepared King Arkson."

"Yes," Arkson replied. "Raise the flag for the terms." Arkson called to the bearer.

In that instant it was as if time slowed, he could taste the bittersweet metallic tang of the fight pulsing within him. His blood was coursing, charged with overflowing energy and a ferocious power of life. He soul was strengthened by the one resonating cry within him to set things right.

Arkson looked back to his infantry. There were Akorians and Batchi lined to match King Guedan, ready to carve a balance into the menacing evil before them. The flag of meeting rose and Arkson mounted his horse riding out to meet King Guedan in the centre. If he could stop this before the bloodshed took its toll, he would. He had to protect his people, protect so many innocent lives. The wind whipped at him cooly as the horse galloped, and a fragment of something tore through him as though Samira was there with him, riding out by his side to meet Guedan. He dismounted, walking slowly over the grassy plain.

Samira, already on her way back to Zatian, could feel Arkson's power surge. She was not far from the fields, but she worried that it might be a bad sign her time was running short.

"We need to go faster Thunder, as hard as you can ride." She said aloud to him tapping into whatever powers she could to speak to the graceful animal. Instantly his legs picked up speed, his body hammering forward with all his might. Sammie would definitely be giving him a few extra buckets of oats and some apples for this and she tucked her body lower so they made less resistance in the wind that had picked up.

Arkson moved forward to meet in good will, a handshake usually marking the beginning of the exchange the terms of the battle. Yet, Guedan stood still his cold grey eyes waiting.

"Stay there you little maggot," he yelled at Arkson.

"Too afraid to stand face to face Guedan?"

"How dare you speak of fear to me!"

Arkson never understood how someone so childish and impertinent could be a king. "Well do you agree to the terms of battle or not?"

"I do not you worthless shit! I rue the day you were born Akorian. How you stand before me now as a King is blasphemous!"

Guedan pulled his powers from the earth, huge bricks of earth surged forward slugging Arkson in the chest and smattering into dirt.

Arkson had no time to resurrect a shield, and although the blows were hard it didn't stop him. He walked forward biting back the pain and using his sword carved a symbol into the land which began pulling up a shield of protection for those behind him. If he fell, was injured, or killed, it would give his Akori time.

Guedan continued with his assault until Arkson knowing the shield was fully activated let a thunderous yell rip from his chest and his whole body burst into flames, spreading it out onto the grass and encircling the evil King. Guedan stopped his hits shocked by the sight of the fire. Arkson acted quickly hurling forward a jolt ablaze. Guedan managed to stop it with earth, the flames charring the soil black.

Sammie was so close to the field she knew it was only a matter of minutes before she reached Zatian. She prayed she would make it on time, Arkson's life depended on it, her life too.

Thunder charged ahead quick and fast. There were infantry in her way and although she thought they might not move Thunder gave them no option breaking through the lines of the Zatian flanks. As she rode out into the field, she could hear voices shouting after her.

One of the soldiers had drawn an arrow through his bow ready to fire, but Alvaren acted quickly and knocked him to the ground.

"She is to be the Queen of Zatian, you fool!" Alvaren smacked him over the head for further emphasis. He had grown fond of Samira and the last thing he wanted to see was her lampooned by an arrow.

Samira channelled her vision forward, centred it completely on Arkson, she fed into him all that she could. His body on fire looked frightening and Guedan throwing the blocks of earth, looked like a fool, yet she knew they were just a diversion. She watched the blocks burst apart and when Arkson leaned back a bit from the continuous onslaught Guedan's shoulders arched back. She knew he was ready to throw the *triuny*.

The buzzing whirr of it pierced the air as it cut through the sky towards her husband.

Just before it lanced Arkson's chest, she cried out.
"No!"

Pushing it back with all the power that she could muster, her strength flooded through him, giving him a larger boost of light and fire struck out at the spear flowing over it and stripping it of its power. It fell to the ground deactivated and useless, charred to the bone of the staff. Thunder was still riding hard to meet with his master and Samira still connected to Arkson, though tired, pulled lightening from the sky to smash into the spear.

It shatter into millions of fragments, but blocked by the field of protection that Arkson had summoned, any pieces travelling towards her hit the shield and slid down the wall. Arkson was still aflame, and Guedan stunned by the turn of events had let his guard down.

Hit him now Arkson!

Samira spoke to him knowing the precise moment of weakness. Quickly Arkson threw a bolt of fire and Guedan's body was battered by the blow thrown back halfway through his side of the field. His body, now singed, lay unconscious on the ground that he had so callously uprooted.

Arkson's flames rescinded and he turned to see Samira calming Thunder several metres behind him. His guards were riding out to meet them. Hooting and hollering things he could not quite make out. It was over. The battle with Guedan was finally over.

Arkson stared into Samira's eyes, wondering what had brought her back to him; he had been so sure she had left. Had found his strength despite her departure, was now, a king, the leader he always had been, but had yet to realize. She dismounted from Thunder.

He walked to meet the warrior he saw before him. Her long dark hair was braided neatly behind her, a long feather hanging down from one stray strand. The hairs near her face were windswept, hugging her honey coloured cheeks and sweeping to the side over her eyes. She was still beautiful, breathtaking. The woman he wanted as his wife.

"You saved my life," he said, "again," he added as if he were annoyed by that fact. "Thank you Samira."

"It was my life too," she reminded him, and he straightened thinking that perhaps she had not planned to stay again, maybe she had only come to prevent her death.

"I thought you returned home," he said to her serious,

stern as though it was not his wish to see her, even though he lied to himself by speaking to her this way.

She looked at him a moment, wondering if he might betray his feelings. She tilted her head examining him, a light flickering in her eyes as she recognized his stance shift.

"Would you want me to leave?"

He said nothing at first, deliberating about his response.

"I would not want to keep you from where you feel you belong Samira."

He would never lie to her again, but he feigned indifference, looked to see his soldiers bridging the gap between them. Alvaren and Elastor were riding out to Guedan. The soldiers on the greedy King's side of the field were already beginning to defect or turn themselves over.

Her warrior stance softened and she knelt before him as she had the first time she sought his audience. This time though her eyes met his when she held her palm open to him awaiting his acceptance.

"I am home, Arkson. I belong here, with you."

Samira's heart pounded. She knew she had hurt him, wished she could take back any of the pain she had caused him. She loved her prince, more than anything, and she had missed him dearly. She would do anything for him to accept her love again, for him to hold her.

Arkson wanted to fall to his knees with relief and wrap his arms around her, but he was a King now. He could not do that, not here on this battlefield. His heart wanted to punish and love her all at the same time. His chest grew heavy.

It was the look in her eyes that gave him strength, she did not flinch, did not waver in her looking at him and only him. Not even when his nearby soldiers shifted closer did her eyes move from him. He knew his heart loved her more than his mind was angry with her and it was love that compelled him as he grabbed her hand pulling her up to him and hugging her by the waist. Arkson lifted her off the ground, still hugging her with his arms.

"Then I guess I will have to keep you," he responded at last, a smile breaking on his lips.

She laughed softly decorating his face with quick kisses on his eyelids, cheeks, and lips before he pulled her mouth to his own in a possessive and emotional kiss. Tears slipped from her eyes and he wiped them away.

"Are you here to stay?" He asked her, placing her feet back on the ground.

"Yes," she said softly, smiling before adding, "forever and ever."

"Forever?" He asked with a grin.

"You go it babe," she replied.

Arkson smiled from ear to ear, and Sammie melted even more. He looked at Veros. "Uncle, it looks like we must arrange a wedding."

CHAPTER 28

THE REMAINING TWO weeks of Nikelda's stay in Halifax had gone by quickly. She knew part of that was because of Eric's company. He really was quite the charmer. She was eager to go home though, ready to return to Zatian, and her brother, aunt, and uncle. Her time in Halifax was at the end.

She finished tidying up the apartment, leaving it as close as she could to what it had looked like on her arrival. In case one of them was coming back, Nikelda did not want to be leaving the place in a mess. She prayed that both of them would not be returning.

"Alright," she said excitedly, "I am done. Ready to go Eric?"

He looked at her amused. For the past couple of days he had indulged her with the idea of this trip, in fact he felt as though they were trying on some interesting role play where she was looking to get out of town.

She had put on weird looking necklace around her neck, fastening her bag around her body. Her fingers tightened around the object it's intricate clockwork design was breathtaking.

"You'll have to stand next to me, and it might be best if we hug," she said to him.

"Is that an excuse to get closer to me?" He asked her, putting the knapsack she had made him pack on his shoulders and tightening the straps.

"Maybe," she says her eyebrows wiggling.

Eric stood next to her, his arm wrapped around her waist. She smelled so good to him so he leaned down and kissed her neck. He was waiting for her to walk out the door.

"Stop distracting me," she said, her eyes focused on the large clock-like pendant. She opened the back half of the medallion; apparently it was some type of bizarre and rather large locket. Her fingers pinched together and pulled out a small spider-like filament.

"Well are you going to open the door so we can get going?" He asked, his nose nuzzling her neck. He wanted to decorate that neck with more kisses, but refrained.

"We can't get to Zatian that way Eric." She looked at him in mock annoyance.

Her fingers placed the filament in the middle of the clocks twisting it slowly as she closed her eyes.

"Are you ready?" She asked him.

"Uh yeah?" He said wondering what was going on.

"Zatian," she said forcefully.

The light spilling in from the windows darkened, and lightening cracked into the room, thunder roared in Eric's ears and he jumped, was about to pull away when Nikelda held onto him, pulled him closer and then they were shrouded in pitch black. The only light was emitted from her pendant in a purple hue.

Eric's heart was pumping as a blast of light shot up from beneath their feet and everything seemed to blur.

When his eyes opened he was kneeling on the ground on a grassy knoll outside a large slate wall, voices off in the distance.

Nikelda looked down at him and smiled as she patted him on the shoulder, "You did well." Her hand shot up into the sky and pulled a huge bolt of lightening its glow resonating to mark her homecoming, the thunder a deep crackling rumble afterwards.

"What the hell was that?" He asked jumping up again.

"That was my 'I have returned' warning." She smiled and grabbed his hand pulling him up and walking briskly towards and then through the south gate.

Eric was in shock, there were men dressed in suits something like a medieval festival, and as they rounded the corner, there was a bustling market with people everywhere, all of them with the same tattoos as Nikelda.

"This is Zatian," she said to him, his eyes glazing over in disbelief.

What the hell?

She pulled him through the crowds of people, male and female Akorians speaking quickly over the low murmur of the hoard. She stopped in front of a large palace, nodding to the guards there before they allowed her to pass.

Eric thought he was about to collapse and Nikelda noticing he had gotten groggy gave him a light pinch on the arm. "Wake up mister, or you'll miss it!" She stopped walking for a few seconds, letting him catch his breath and adjust.

He looked at her peculiar until something else caught his eyes. It was a group of men, or at least something that looked something like a men. They were stocky creatures, with hats and long wispy tails poking out from their dust coats. One of them removed his hat and Eric gawked at his long rabbit ears.

"Whoa, what is..." He said aloud.

Nikelda elbowed him lightly since his words had attracted the attention of the Batchi. "It's not nice to stare, come on." She spoke with a smile pulling him along again.

"Am I dreaming?" He asked her.

"Nope," she replied walking straight for the large room at the heart of the palace. She walked quickly, still dragging Eric along, until at last she burst through the wooden doors.

"Hello Auntie Brunie!" Nikelda announced as walked into the throne room kissing her aunt's cheek, and hugging her. "Oh and Uncle Veros," she said spotting him and threw her arms around him in a hug. "How I missed you all so much!"

Brunelda laughed. "You always did have perfect timing, you're just in time for the wedding tomorrow."

"Wedding? Whose wedding?" Eric asked, standing in the background and suddenly afraid that Nikelda was the one betrothed.

Brunelda and Veros sniffed the air and then covered their noses politely for a few seconds. Their eyes met for a moment before they broke into smiles and turned to greet Eric.

"This is Eric," Nikelda spoke introducing him to them.

Eric wondering why they looked so uncomfortable stepped forward and confidently offered a hand to shake with Veros.

"Is it me?" He asked suddenly, "Do I smell funny or something?" Eric pulled his shirt up to his nose smelling it and was tempted to stick his nose in his armpit, but thought it too crass.

Nikelda laughed. "I have a couple of things to explain to you."

Brunelda interrupted, "don't worry Eric, it wore off Samira after a few weeks." She placed a finger on her chin in contemplation, "then again by then she was mated to Arkson...hmmp." She turned back to her niece and shrugged. "Oh, Nikelda the wedding is going to be so beautiful! Did you ever think this day would come?"

"Samira's getting married?" Eric asked shocked.

"Yes I am, tomorrow," she said appearing from the shadows in a traditional gold engagement gown. Her long black hair had been tied up off of her face and waves cascading down her back. "You must be the Princess Nikelda," she said with the proper curtsy.

"You're a princess!?" Eric asked shocked.

"Shh!" Nikelda hushed him. Her eyes moistened and hands extended to Samira.

"I was hoping it would be you," Nikelda said with a smile, "I should be bowing before you, and thanking you" Nikelda helped Sammie up and began to get teary as they embraced. Sammie, who knew she needed to call her prince, sent out a mental call to him. Her voice was a pleasant whisper in his mind.

Arkson, you have a present waiting for you in the throne room.

"I am so glad you'll be here for the party," Sammie said with a smile, "and the wedding ceremony tomorrow of course. I would really love for you and Salha to stand with me."

"Salha?" Eric whispered in the background, but was ignored.

Nikelda gushed happily, wiping back her tears. "Really?"

"Of course," Samira said, "We're sisters now." She squeezed Nikelda in another hug.

"Well, well, look who it is."

Nikelda turned quickly to the sound of Arkson's voice.

She ran to him embracing him wholeheartedly. They laughed happily and he tousled her shorter blonde hair with his hand, followed by an approving nod of his head. She grabbed his crown inspecting it with awe before placing it on her head.

"I really think this would look better on me, Ark."

He chuckled and admitted, "yeah, maybe." His eyes locked on Samira and his heart nearly skipped a beat, she looked amazing. Her dark eyes were smiling at him.

"You can have that one, I'll have another made by the goldsmith," he said his eyes finally returning to Nikelda, "consider it thanks for the gift you've given me."

She smiled. "I knew it would work."

"So you arranged this didn't you, little sis? You couldn't tell me what you planned? Had to leave me worrying about you? And how exactly did you manage to bring my queen to me?" The questions spilled out all at once, and Nikelda laughed at him.

"Well, I had a little help of magic, of course," she began. "Let's just say that the last time I went to a seer to try and find out information on your future, I was told that in order to restore peace to the kingdom I had to go to a land afar with a Kaptu necklace to guide me."

"That is ludicrous Nikki, you just decided to go world travelling on a whim? And it does not explain how Samira and Salha managed to be transported here." Arkson crossed his arms awaiting an explanation.

"Alright Ark fine, I went to the seer Marathi in the borders and she told me that in my future she saw a place called Halifax. She convinced me that I needed to go to Halifax in order to bring about your success, our happiness and restore our family honour and so on..."

"Okay," he replied, "that I believe, but when? You haven't been there since..."

Farloom, she thought finishing his statement in her mind.

"Well, I had to wait for the right time, two days after

your thirty-fourth birthday. Even though there were times I felt like giving up on waiting for so long. She also told me that once I got to this place I had to stay for five months. Then, when portal shifting, I also needed to surge the transportation with a few electrical impulses to trigger the return of another being in the process."

"So you charged it with a bolt?" He asked, amazed that she hadn't killed herself, as well as Samira and Salha.

"Yes well..." she said looking a bit guilty as her fingers twisted together, "the lightening being more powerful than an energy ball ended up transporting both of the sisters in my place. But it worked!" Her finger shot up in protest.

He couldn't stay mad at Nikelda. "Yes it did little sis, thank you." Now was the time for everyone to come together. In Arkson's eyes this was all that mattered now.

CHAPTER 29

Arkson waited for Samira's entrance, their engagement celebration the evening before had been full of laughter and excitement. Even the guests from the other Akorian cities and the Batchi, who had been invited to attend, were enchanted by Samira's confidence and intelligence. It was a large, but simple wedding, all in the kingdom were invited to witness their king join with their new queen.

Some were still disgruntled that their king was marrying a human, others were grateful the curse had at last been broken. Arkson cared about none of their opinions. He knew he had found his love. As the large wooden doors opened he held his breath, awaiting Samira's arrival. In a few minutes they would marry, she would at last be his queen, forevermore.

Samira was excitedly nervous. It was the moment she had anticipated all her life but never quite believed would arrive. This was their wedding day –she and Arkson were beginning a life together. Salha and Nikelda, both dressed in beautiful mauve *skiori*, walked forward down the aisle and stood opposite Alvaren and Alexandros on the altar.

Arkson smiled as Samira appeared in the door. She wore a beautiful ivory lace *skiori* embroidered with gold and beaded with pearls and diamonds. Her face was hidden by a long, sheer, lace veil which draped down to her mid-back. She had been given bridal jewellery from Arkson as an early wedding gift. It was some of the most incredible jewellery she had ever seen and had been saved by the prince from his mother's collection. He had set it aside in hiding for when he found his queen since much of the remainder was paid as tribute to Guedan.

Each piece was made of gold, pearls, and diamonds, much like her dress. The pearls and diamonds had been hand set into the earrings, necklace and bracelet that she wore and each piece cascaded down to a dagger swirled tip similar to a flame. It had been blessed by a fire magus so that the wearer was filled with energy, although Samira felt she had plenty to spare naturally, especially today.

Samira had requested a bouquet of purple, orange, and white lilies, something unheard of in Zatian, but the same arrangement as her mother had chosen when she married. Even though her parents could not be there, she felt as though this small thing was a reminder of their ever present love.

As she stood before him, he smiled and mouthed to her, "you are beautiful."

She smiled back at him even wider, walking in tune to the harp that played while she approached. As she reached the last step of the altar, Brunelda stepped forward from Veros's side and unveiled Samira to Arkson, guiding her to stand directly in front of them. She took the bouquet for Samira and held it to her heart.

Veros stood before them acting as officiate, a small square podium between him and Samira and Arkson.

Samira wanted to squeal with delight, her giddiness overtaking her nerves. In five minutes she would have her prince. She knew he loved her dearly. He had not needed to even say the words because she had felt them in his heart. She would never be lonely again, and he was everything that she had wanted. She looked deep into his beautiful green eyes and he was mesmerized by the dark beauty of hers. Slowly they both turned towards the podium.

Arkson placed his right hand out before Veros and Samira placed her left hand next to his, their fingertips overlapping slightly.

Veros spoke to them and to the witnesses in the room. "In this way you two will be bound," he said as he wrapped a gold chain over their wrists, the weight of it carried by the both of them.

"By metal to keep the strength of your marriage," he continued and sprinkled a bit of dirt over the chain.

"By dust of earth to keep you both grounded, in reason and in truth." Next he lit the candle, which glowed below their hovering hands.

"By fire to ignite a passion of purity and honesty." And lastly, he sprinkled water over their hands.

"By water to cleanse the past and mark the path of new." He smiled motioning for them to turn to one another. Arkson twisted towards Samira and her to him, each cupping one another's face as was customary.

"Finally, by breath in the mark of life, in the kiss to seal the bond of Zain, giving you to one another for all your days ahead. You may claim your right to one another."

Before he bent to kiss her Arkson had yet to tell her all that he felt, and though moment was not private, in the Great Hall, with all the city present, it felt as if there was no one else but the two of them. This moment was for them alone.

"I love you Samira. You are the best in me, and for that

I have to thank you. You are wise, and kind, and beautiful. Your gracious heart knows more of mine than any has ever known, and ever will. I am so very grateful to have you, and from this day forward I promise to honour, protect, and cherish you and all that you have given me. You are the woman, the wife, I have always wanted."

Samira could see no one but Arkson, everyone else, every noise faded away. When Arkson bent forward and kissed Samira, it was a kiss of joy, his lips firmly pressed against hers in love. It was a soul searing commitment that bound them together in fire. When at last Samira could catch a breath she laughed elated and responded.

"Arkson, I love you. I love you now, and forever, and I thank you for this gift of love you return. I thank you for the life that you have given me. I thank you for all that you are. I am blessed to have a husband so thoughtful and honest, you are my strength," he smiled, then she added, "plus your bum is awfully cute."

She wiggled her eyebrows while nuzzling his nose and giving him a light kiss. As the guests cheered loudly, she suddenly remembered that the moment was not really just for the two of them.

Oops maybe I should have left the bum part out.

Arkson didn't seem to mind. The pair turned to the crowd and Samira looked at her new people proudly. She was where she belonged. The Akorians rejoiced and Samira was touched by their show of support.

"Well my husband, my King, let's rebuild our kingdom, our home."

Arkson turned to his people, then back to Samira, a mischievous grin on his face.

"They can wait, the next three days we're not leaving our bedroom and tonight, I'm making love to you until dawn," Arkson gathered her into his arms and carried his queen to their chamber, where he fulfilled that very promise.

EPILOGUE

Guedan sat up in his cell. The small room had only one barred window in the door, and he could feel a presence on the other side of its bulky frame.

"What took you so long Iramet?"

The Batchi's grey eyes peered through the opening.

"Perhaps you did not hear Guedan, there is a wedding taking place in the palace. No Batchi could resist enjoying the festivities of a celebration."

Guedan scowled. Iramet always found ways to test his patience, the sharp witted Batchi was one of the few brave enough to speak so freely with Guedan. The electrical charge in the room had frazzled his powers and the holding chamber was stifling, Guedan had never been this close to being defeated.

"Get me out of here you idiot!"

"There was also the matter of the guards. Mystifying does take some time Guedan, or do you forget?"

"I want out now Iramet!" Guedan was petulant.

The Batchi sighed and reached a brown limb through

the iron bars. "You're ever so patient milord."

Guedan stepped forward and grabbed his hand. The room went blacker than it was before and light spilled up from the floor, it was yellow and eerie as the room blurred.

As things settled, Guedan composed himself and stretched in the comfort of his throne room, in Alpohalla. The Batchi was lying in a heap on the floor and looked sickly. His fingers curled like that of a haggard old man. Guedan leaned over him.

"Well done Iramet, you have proved yourself. You may go." He waved over a guard who picked the stocky man up.

Iramet was clutching his stomach. "What of my family Guedan?"

The king did not respond, taking a seat in his throne.

"What of my family!?" He heard the voice call from down the hall.

"My King?" His advisor stepped forward as if asking on behalf of the Batchi.

Guedan grimaced, "were they killed yet advisor?"

"Only the son Pram survived the torture, my king."

"Then release him to his father," he said with a wave of his hand, "and make sure they leave the city."

About the Author

Zara Steen has her sister to thank for her newest obsession with paranormal and fantasy romance. When she's not reading as many Romance books as possible, she keeps busy working on several different book series. At the moment she's plotting several books on shifters, vampires, and one new young adult series about mermaids.

Zara is looking to connect with other romance writers and lovers of paranormal writing.

Drop her a line at zarasteen@gmail.com
Check out her blog and forthcoming books at http://www.zarasteen.com

Made in the USA
Charleston, SC
25 September 2013